The Lois Meade Mysteries by Ann Purser

MURDER ON MONDAY
TERROR ON TUESDAY
WEEPING ON WEDNESDAY
THEFT ON THURSDAY

THEFT ON THURSDAY

✧

ANN PURSER

BERKLEY PRIME CRIME, NEW YORK

THE BERKLEY PUBLISHING GROUP
Published by the Penguin Group
Penguin Group (USA) Inc.
375 Hudson Street, New York, New York 10014, USA
Penguin Group (Canada), 90 Eglinton Avenue East, Suite 700, Toronto, Ontario M4P 2Y3, Canada
(a division of Pearson Penguin Canada Inc.)
Penguin Books Ltd., 80 Strand, London WC2R 0RL, England
Penguin Group Ireland, 25 St. Stephen's Green, Dublin 2, Ireland (a division of Penguin Books Ltd.)
Penguin Group (Australia), 250 Camberwell Road, Camberwell, Victoria 3124, Australia
(a division of Pearson Australia Group Pty. Ltd.)
Penguin Books India Pvt. Ltd., 11 Community Centre, Panchsheel Park, New Delhi—110 017, India
Penguin Group (NZ), Cnr. Airborne and Rosedale Roads, Albany, Auckland 1310, New Zealand
(a division of Pearson New Zealand Ltd.)
Penguin Books (South Africa) (Pty.) Ltd., 24 Sturdee Avenue, Rosebank, Johannesburg 2196,
South Africa

Penguin Books Ltd., Registered Offices: 80 Strand, London WC2R 0RL, England

THEFT ON THURSDAY

A Berkley Prime Crime Book / published by arrangement with Severn House

PRINTING HISTORY
Severn House hardcover edition / 2004
Berkley Prime Crime mass-market edition / February 2006

ISBN: 0-425-20747-1

BERKLEY® PRIME CRIME
Berkley Prime Crime Books are published by The Berkley Publishing Group,
a division of Penguin Group (USA) Inc.,
375 Hudson Street, New York, New York 10014.
The name BERKLEY PRIME CRIME and the BERKLEY PRIME CRIME design are trademarks belonging to Penguin Group (USA) Inc.

PRINTED IN THE UNITED STATES OF AMERICA

10 9 8 7 6 5 4 3 2 1

*Grateful thanks to
my friend Lis,
who researched the legend.*

ONE

❧

"SHE DONE 'IM IN," THE OLD MAN SAID WITH RELISH. "Poisoned 'im . . . Then she opened 'im up with a bread knife and took his heart. Sewed 'im up agin. Very neat job, they said. Pickled it in incohol. Look, you can see the pair of 'em, there, look."

Lois Meade leaned forward. "I can't see much, Cyril," she said. They were peering at a gravestone in Long Farnden churchyard. Most of it had sunk into the mossy grass, but on what remained above ground, Lois could just make out two figures, sitting either side of a shadowy table. The inscription was all but erased, but a rough outline of a heart between two names was just discernible.

"Is it a man and woman?" she asked.

"Yep," said the verger, "man and wife."

"So are they both in the grave, then? Reunited in death?"

"Not likely! It's only 'im, Willy Mellish. They wouldn't've buried Sophia in a churchyard. She were a murderer, and got dragged on a pallet be'ind 'orses to Tresham. She were tried, found guilty as 'ell, and burned at the stake. Last one to be burned at the stake in the county, they say."

"Charming," said Lois, with a shiver. "Why'd she do it, then?"

"Money," said the old man flatly. "She thought he 'ad a lot, and she set out to get it. Everything'd be 'ers, see, if 'e snuffed it."

"But they found her out before she got it?" Lois glanced at her watch. She should be back home by now, not being waylaid by Cyril. Unwilling to hurt his feelings, though, she'd stayed to listen to this tale of murder and deception with growing fascination. But now Derek would be coming home for his tea, and Jamie and Gran would be waiting.

"Weren't nuthin' to get." Cyril shook his head. He spoke as if it was only last week. "'E didn't 'ave much, after all. Mostly debts. She were so angry, she gave 'erself away by sayin' it were a waste of what she'd spent on mercury to do 'im in. Baked it in a special loaf, kept only for 'im. So they got 'er. She were barmy, I reckon. 'Ow could she've got away with it, with 'im 'avin' all that needlework on 'is chest? When they got 'er, they said she boasted she still had his most valu'ble possession . . . 'is 'eart . . ."

"Ugh!" said Lois, turning away.

But Cyril hadn't finished. "Old Willy was a silly sod," he added. "'E might-a known she were up to somethink, she bein' years younger than 'im, and not a bad looker! Still, Mrs. Meade, there's no fool like an old fool."

"Very true," said Lois firmly, and set off back down the little hill that led to the lychgate of the churchyard.

LONG FARNDEN WAS A SMALL VILLAGE IN THE MIDDLE of England, of no great distinction except for its eighteenth-century poisoner and twenty-first-century female sleuth. Lois Meade, proprietor of cleaning service New Brooms, had attempted some years ago, when her children were small and free time was negligible, to become a special constable. As a troublesome teenager she'd had one or two brushes with the law, and fancied trying to put things straight. To her great irritation she'd been turned down, and decided to go it alone. With a taste for detection, she was well aware that as solo house cleaner, going from house to house, cleaning every room and overhearing conversations not meant for her ears, she had a unique position when a crime was committed and investigations began. Her usefulness as a source of information had been spotted by Detective Inspector Hunter Cowgill, who had found her reluctant and prickly, with no great love now for the police. But he was determined—and attracted—and had won. Lois's own victory was that she never accepted payment.

It was several years now since she'd helped him, and though she sometimes thought longingly of the buzz she felt when pieces of a jigsaw began to show a clear picture, her husband had no such yearnings. Derek, a competent and hard-working electrician, a good father and loving husband, who admitted that he did not always understand his wife, was unreservedly glad that Hunter Cowgill no longer haunted his life.

"How did you get on with the new vicar?" Derek said, as his wife came into the kitchen. Following the long interregnum, when they'd had a different preacher each week, a middle-aged single man had finally been appointed. He had moved to the cramped, modern vicarage and raised his hands in horror at the idea of fitting all his books and papers into such a small space. An efficient system was what was needed, and Lois had approached swiftly with details of New Brooms' excellent service. This afternoon she had clinched the contract.

"A doddle," she said now, sitting down at the tea table to be served by Gran, her long-suffering mother, who had lived with them for some years and was an invaluable fixture. "He's a real innocent. First parish of his own. God knows what mincemeat those church people will make of him."

"Well, he's come late to the cloth, apparently," said Gran, "so I expect he'll be keen. Anyway, the PCC chose him, so they must know what they're getting." Gran was the only churchgoing member of the family, and reckoned she spoke with authority. She'd been invited to join the Parochial Church Council, but told Lois they were in her view a collection of the least Christian members of the community. "Holier-than-thou lot o' nobs, mostly," she said.

"I came back through the churchyard," Lois continued, "and got caught by old Cyril. He spun me a long tale about some woman in the old days who poisoned her husband, and then stole his heart. There's this grim gravestone he showed me. Never noticed it before, have you, Mum?"

Gran shook her head. "He's an old liar, anyway," she said comfortably. "Still, what's the story?"

"Mellish, their name was. She was after his money, Cyril reckons. Bad luck for her he didn't have none. So she stole his heart. Anyway, she got caught, and they roasted her on a bonfire like a witch. Nice little story for a summer's day . . ."

Derek was not fooled. "Caught your fancy, didn't it, me duck," he said with a smile. "Lucky for us it happened so long ago, else you'd have been off on the trail, hand in hand with Hunter the cop, bringin' the woman to justice."

Lois sighed. "Not me," she said sadly. "Haven't heard from Cowgill for years, have I?"

"You were sharp with him once too often, Lois," said Gran. "And a good thing too. We've been a much happier family without all that malarkey. Now, eat up, and I'll get the sweet."

Derek looked at his lovely wife. Dark hair that shone like deep water in the sun. Beautiful long legs. They had attracted him straightaway when he'd spotted her working in Woolworths, a rebellious school-leaver, and attracted him still, thank God. She don't look a day over twenty-five, he thought fondly. Nobody'd think she had a daughter of twenty, and nearly grown-up sons. Jamie, the youngest, had finished his A-levels, and would be off to college soon, and then there'd be just the three of them, he realized, him and Lois and Gran. Still, Douglas from university, and Josie from her shared flat in Tresham, still kept in touch, and Lois and he were the first to hear if they had worries.

He looked at Lois's long face, and said lightly, "Never mind, me duck, somebody local's bound to get bumped off sooner or later, and then you'll be happy."

In due course, he had reason to wish he'd not tempted Fate.

Two

❧

LONG FARNDEN WAS NAMED FOR ITS ONE LONG, NAR-
row street with old stone houses either side. More mellow in colour than the neighbouring Cotswolds, the houses
shone dark gold in the evening sun, and Gran walked
slowly down the road towards the church, counting her
blessings. If she and Lois hadn't agreed, she could still be
living in an old folks' bungalow on a rundown housing estate in Tresham. She was early for choir practice, and
stopped to look back down the street. Maybe someone else
would be on the way. She didn't want to be first.

"Evenin', missus," said a cracked voice from behind an
unruly hedge.

"Ah, Cyril, how are you?" said Gran, looking at her
watch. Early or not, she didn't have time for a garrulous
old man.

"All the better for seein' you, Mrs. Weedon," grinned
Cyril, emerging into sight. He looked at the trim figure in
front of him, and wished he had somebody like that in the
house behind him, cleaning up, maybe, and doing some

home cooking. He sighed. "Off to choir singing?" he asked.

Gran nodded. She supposed he wasn't such a bad old bloke. "The new vicar's coming along," she said. "Got an announcement to make, he said. We're all a bit worried. The old parson used to let us get on with it."

"That Gladys still taking practices?" said Cyril, stepping forward in an attempt to prevent Gran from moving on. "She were the reason vicars don't stay long in Farnden, if y'ask me."

"She's threatening to resign," Gran said with a smile. "Been doing the job for thirty years, she says. Reckon she don't take to the new chap. Still, from what I hear, did she ever?" Gran neatly side-stepped the old man, and carried on her way.

When she walked into the church and up to the choir stalls, she could see trouble was afoot. The half-dozen who formed the choir were in a huddle, whispering. When they saw her, they broke apart and drew her in.

"She's given up," they said.

"Thought she would," said Gran, unsurprised. "Been in charge too long. It'll be better for the new man. Easier than tryin' to please old Gladys."

The others had been surprised. They had all been prepared to defend Gladys and her right to hold the post of organist and choirmistress unchallenged. For as long as they could remember, Gladys had sat at the organ and played very slowly the most mournful hymns she could find. Easter was her favourite time—that is, the part of Easter before the joyfulness of the resurrection. Good Friday brought an extra enthusiasm to her playing of "Throned upon the awful Tree, King of grief, I watch with thee."

Now she had upstaged them all by pinning a brief note to the old wooden music stand in the vestry. *"I hereby resign,"* it announced formally. *"You'll find somebody else, no doubt, and I wish them joy of it. Gladys Mary Smith."*

Gran read the note and put her membership of the choir in jeopardy by laughing heartily. "Good old Gladys," she said. "Still, she's right. We'll find somebody else, I'm sure. What about you, Mrs. Tollervey-Jones?"

Thin-faced, aquiline-nosed Mrs. T-J, as she was universally known, shook her head modestly. "Well, actually, I'm much too busy," she said. "Though, of course, should it be absolutely . . ." Her voice tailed away as she waited for someone to insist, but their attention was diverted by quick footsteps coming up the flagstones of the church path.

"Good evening, everyone!" The tall, rangy figure of the new vicar strode into the chancel and approached the group.

"Good evening, Vicar," said Mrs. T-J, taking the lead as always. "You are very welcome to our little group. We have not started our practice, since this note has rather taken us by surprise." She handed him Gladys's resignation, and all eyes watched for his reaction.

"Ah, what a pity," he said. "But extraordinarily enough," he continued with a bright smile that hardly seemed appropriate, "I have this very morning heard from the son of an old friend. My godson. The young man is moving to our village, intending to commute into Tresham, where he will be working as an estate agent. But his hobby is music, and he is a trained singer. Now, isn't that a wonderful coincidence?"

Six blank faces stared at him. Then Gran spoke. "You mean he might take us on?" she said. "Always supposing he's a churchy person."

"Oh, yes, certainly one of us," said the vicar. "I believe he will be a terrific asset. New broom, and all that!"

"We got one of those already," said Gran. "My daughter runs a cleaning—"

"Of course!" interrupted the vicar. "She kindly came to see me. Charming person. Most helpful. Well, there you are then, that confirms it. Clearly God meant us to have young Sandy among us."

Vicars have a direct line, of course, said Gran to herself. Ah well, should bring a bit of spice to choir practices, and God knows they'd been dreary enough before.

"By the way, Vicar," she said. "What *is* your proper name? I've heard Robertson, Robinson, Roberson . . . ?"

"Brian Oswald Rollinson," said the vicar. "But we can forget the Oswald! We'll all get to know each other so well that surnames won't matter. And yours is . . . ?" he asked Gran, smiling disarmingly at her.

"Mrs. Weedon," said Gran firmly, with not a sniff of a Christian name. "Now, we'd better get on with the hymns. We've all got homes to go to and work to do. Nice to meet you, Reverend Rollinson," she added politely, and the discomfited man retreated, feeling he had not handled his first foray into church duties all that well.

Mrs. T-J stepped forward and said that under the circumstances, for one practice only, she should perhaps take charge.

THREE

ॐ

B Y MONDAY, WHEN LOIS HAD HER WEEKLY MIDDAY meeting with the cleaning team, gossip had spread the news that Gladys had been supplanted by a young music teacher, new to the village, friend of the new vicar, with new plans for the choir. "New" had become a dirty word by the time Sheila and Bridie, Hazel, Enid and Bill assembled in Lois's office for their meeting.

"He'll be lucky to have any choir left, with all his new ideas," said Hazel with a grin. "All them old tabs'll be off like a shot."

Hazel, daughter of Bridie Reading, pregnant and married to a young farmer, lived in a farm cottage on the Tollervey-Jones estate. Up the road, in Cathanger Mill, Enid Abraham lived alone, coming to terms with a period of relentless family tragedy. Enid had worked hard to smarten up the old mill house, now a listed building, and happily took in bed and breakfast visitors who appreciated the tranquillity of the shady spot, with the old mill wheel and Enid's chickens clucking about in the yard.

Neither Hazel nor Enid had any real need to work for New Brooms, but the team had cemented over the years into a tight little group. There had been initial doubts about their one male cleaner. "That Bill Stockbridge won't last for more than six months, him being a farmer's son from Yorkshire," Gran had said when Bill joined the team. But he had proved her wrong. Now he divided his time between cleaning for Lois, and helping out at Charrington's veterinary practice, where his gentle hands and quiet manner were as useful calving cows as when dusting delicate porcelain in the Tollervey-Joneses' drawing room.

"OK, Mum," said Lois, coming into her office, where Gran had been enjoying a good chewing over the Gladys affair with Bridie and Sheila. Sheila Stratford was one of the original members of the team. Solidly rooted in the area by generations of forebears, she thrived on the circulation of local news. She knew Gladys, of course, and could not conceal her delight that the old bag had had something of a come-uppance at last. "She's bin in the job far too long," she said. "I know people who'd rather worship in Waltonby than put up with her dirges on the organ," she pronounced.

"Right, Mum," repeated Lois, sitting down at her desk. "Did you get that message for you to ring Oxfam in Tresham? I expect they want you to do extra hours. Better go and ring them."

"I'm going," said Gran. "And I was anyway, seeing as you're here now to start the meeting." There was more than a suggestion of flounce as she left the room.

"Morning, everybody," Lois said, looking round at expectant faces. "Now, this new vicar." They brightened. "No, I don't want any more gossip about Gladys, or new young choir blokes. Just the cleaning schedules, if you don't mind. I went to see the vicar, and we've agreed one afternoon a week."

"I've got Wednesday afternoons free, now Mrs. Brown's

gone from Fletching," said Hazel. She didn't really fancy the new vicar job for itself, but it could be interesting with all the ructions there were bound to be in the village.

"Yep, I'd got you down to do it, Hazel." Lois sifted through her papers. "And Bill, could you do a couple more hours this week at Farnden Hall. Mrs. T-J is having a party to introduce Rev. Rollinson to the nobs, and wants extra help."

"Fine," said Bill. He didn't mention that he and Rebecca, his long-time partner, had received an invitation. Rebecca taught in nearby Waltonby village school, and was known to be a favourite with Mrs. T-J, who was, of course, on the board of governors of the Church of England school. Some disapproval had been expressed by conservative board members when it became clear that there was no prospect of marriage in the offing for Rebecca and Bill. Acknowledging the fact that many young people lived together before getting wed, they had appointed Rebecca straight from college, certain that all would be regularized shortly. But it wasn't, and one or two had said she was setting a bad example to the children.

Bill had said he was more than ready to take Rebecca to the altar, but she had dug in her toes. "The more I'm shoved, the more I stick," she'd said succinctly. And so, because she was an excellent teacher, the situation had been accepted and no more was said.

The sun shone temptingly through the window of Lois's office, and Enid Abraham shifted in her seat. "Excuse me, Mrs. M," she said, this being the title for Lois tacitly agreed by the team, "there was something I would like to mention, if we have finished our business."

Lois looked at the small, insignificant figure, sitting so neatly on her chair, scarcely disturbing the air around her. She might look like a mouse, she reflected, but she'd proved to have the guts of a terrier. "Go on, then, Enid," she said. "Don't keep us in suspense."

Enid smiled. "Oh, I don't think it's that exciting . . . it's to do with the choir."

"Ah," said Sheila with satisfaction. "Somethin' to do with that new young chap?"

"Well, yes . . . um, you know I sing with them . . . not very well, of course, but . . . anyway . . . Mr. Mackerras, our new choirmaster, hopes to enlarge the choir, and we're asked to spread the word. It's all going to be much more fun . . . he says . . . jollier music and . . ." Her voice tailed away as always, and she looked tentatively round the room. Her appeal was met with total silence at first. Sheila, at least, had been hoping for something a bit juicier.

Then Bill cleared his throat. "I could ask Rebecca," he said. "She's always warbling about the place. And—maybe I shouldn't admit this—I was a boy chorister in our church at home. Up North, that is. Suppose I could give it a go."

Enid's face lit up. "That would be marvellous," she said. "Thank you, Bill."

But he'd not finished, and with a sly grin turned to Lois. "How about you, Mrs. M? A little bird told me you used to sing with a band in Tresham in your misspent youth."

"Me?" said Lois in astonishment. "I sing like a cracked kettle. You ask Derek!"

But Lois's traitorous husband Derek, when he met Bill in the pub that evening, said that Lois could sing very nicely when she tried. The difficulty would be getting her to have a try, they agreed, and had another pint to give themselves the strength to persuade her.

Four

֍

Chief Detective Inspector Hunter Cowgill sat at his desk, eyes closed, apparently asleep.

"Your usual, sir?" said the tea lady, coming in with a rattle of crockery.

Cowgill opened his eyes and stared at her as if he'd never seen her before. "Sorry? What did you say?" he said. He had been dozing in another, alarming world, where crime had been eradicated, and all around were good, law-abiding citizens.

"Coffee and shortbread?" said the tea lady indulgently. Inspector Cowgill was one of her favourites. Always the gentleman, she told her friends. Her days were numbered, her job to be taken over by an anonymous machine in the corridor, and she'd miss Cowgill especially.

"So sorry," he apologized. "Miles away . . . er, no, no shortbread this morning, thanks. Too much flab, my wife tells me. She's given me orders to avoid all sweet things."

He looked so sad that the woman tried a joke. "Right," she said, "you'd better give me a wide berth, with or without me trolley." He smiled dutifully, and took his coffee, waving a denying hand at the sugar.

After she'd gone, he stood up and went to the window, where he looked down at the busy Tresham High Street, thoughtfully sipping his coffee. Perhaps he should start thinking about early retirement. His wife reminded him repeatedly that it was time they did more things together, went on more holidays, had a social life like other people. But the truth was that he hated holidays, disliked his neighbours and was only really happy when on the trail of a wrongdoer, the more slippery and potentially evil the better.

The market day crowds thinned out for a moment, and his attention was caught by a tall, immediately noticeable young woman, her dark hair swinging as she walked. Was it . . . ? Then she turned and glanced up at his window, quite obviously seeking it out from the forbidding stone face of the police station. Then she grinned, and waved. Yes, it was Lois Meade. His pulse quickened, and he did not notice the coffee dribbling over on to the floor. Lois. He waved and smiled his chilly smile, then turned away and returned to his chair, setting down his coffee mug with shaking hands.

Well, that's the first time I've seen her since . . . He tried to clear his mind, but the image of her walking out of sight along the High Street would not go away. He groaned. No fool like an old fool, he told himself, unconsciously echoing old Cyril in Farnden graveyard, though the circumstances could not have been more different.

LOIS WALKED ON AROUND THE CORNER INTO THE MARket Place, thinking how much she missed her old dingdongs with Cowgill. He'd valued her help, but could never drop his official approach, finding it difficult to appreciate that she pursued her amateur detection like a serious hobby, wanting no reward but appreciation of her part in tracking down the guilty. Sometimes the hobby had turned into a crusade, like the case where drugs had been involved, and young people she knew had almost had lives wrecked by uncaring dealers.

One such young person had been her own team member, Hazel. Also recruited by Cowgill, she had had her own experience of addiction and a difficult retreat from certain death. This had given her ammunition to help the police in their never-ending battle, though with impending motherhood, she'd given up all of that.

"Two pounds of tomatoes," Lois said, refusing to have anything to do with kilos, and handing over the exact money to the market trader. She walked on, buying Derek's favourite matured cheddar from the cheese stall, and a bunch of sweet williams for Gran. Errands done, she realized that she still had Cowgill's coolly smiling face in front of her inner eye, and sighed.

"Mrs. M?" It was Rebecca, trailing a small group of six-year-olds behind her. Lois greeted her with pleasure, and they fell into happy conversation about school and the fortunate approach of the end of term. "We're doing some practical arithmetic, going shopping," said Rebecca. "At least, that's the intention. Most of this lot think we're on an outing, and just want ice-creams and the toilet. Everything OK with you, Mrs. M?"

Watching the effortlessly capable Rebecca manoeuvre the children like sheep through the market crowds, Lois thought how lucky Bill was, and what a pity they didn't settle down and start a family of their own. Hunter Cowgill was forgotten, for the moment.

On the way home, Lois thought again about Enid's appeal for new choir members. After the team meeting, Derek had said again that she should join. "You don't do nothing much for pleasure. Just for you." He'd gone on about how hard she worked, looking after a family and running a business. They'd both ignored Gran's muttered comments that Lois would have to work a lot harder if she wasn't there, cooking and cleaning, washing and ironing, being there when needed. All three knew that the arrangement suited them well. Lois was able to concentrate on New Brooms, and when the kids had all been at school, she'd had no worries about them coming back to an empty house. For Gran, it was a home. Once her husband had died, the bungalow had been no home at all, and she'd been relieved and grateful to be part of her daughter's lively lot. And for Derek, anything that made life easier for Lois, and therefore for him, was a bonus.

Approaching the entrance to the vicarage Lois stopped the car. She would just drop in to confirm a few points about Hazel starting work there. She was about to knock on the door, when she hesitated. Voices were in heated conversation, and she drew back. Then a face appeared at the window, and it was too late to retreat. The tall figure of the vicar appeared at the door, smiling in welcome, and asked her in.

"Have you met Sandy?" he said, waving a hand towards a young man with curly, reddish hair. "Mrs. Meade—Lois, if I may?—this is Sandy Mackerras, who is our new choirmaster. He's staying here with me until he can find a suitable place to live in the village. I am delighted, of course, to have his company. We were just discussing hymns for Sunday, weren't we, Sandy?"

Sandy seemed to be having trouble smiling, but eventually made it, and put out a hand to Lois. "Hello, Lois," he said. "Pleased to meet you. Are you one of our singing ladies?"

Silly sod, thought Lois, who knew only too well when she was being patronized. "No, nor likely to be," she said. "Croaking frogs sound better than me," she added.

"Not at all!" said Brian Rollinson, "Sandy here believes everyone can sing in tune, given a little help."

"Mostly a boost in confidence," said Sandy. "People are nervous about singing in public, and then their voices don't function. Particularly elderly people."

"Rules me out, then," said Lois, guessing that the knowledgeable Sandy was about twenty-five at the most.

The Rev. Rollinson touched her arm lightly—Oh God, thought Lois, a touchy-feely vicar—and said they'd give her time to think about it, but she would be most welcome to come along and try it out. "No obligation," he said, laughing an unexpectedly booming guffaw. "Now, when is the lovely Hazel going to start cleaning me up?"

Well, reflected Lois, on returning to her car, the lovely Hazel is just the one to sort out that duo. Until the baby comes, anyway.

"What do you think, Mum, of our Sandy?" Lois said at lunchtime.

Gran shrugged, and began to clear away plates. "No, sit down, Derek," she said, as he had pushed his chair back in a half-hearted attempt to help her. "There's a choice of puddings," she added. "Apple crumble or stewed apricots and custard."

"Young Sandy, Mum?" repeated Lois patiently. "What d'you reckon? Will the old ducks stage a walk-out?"

"Doubt it," said Gran. "He's a bit of a change from old Gladys, but that's a good thing. He made a good start. Mrs. T-J was eating out of his hand, and the others were warming towards him slowly. You know Farnden, Lois. Usually takes half a lifetime to be accepted here. Still, he's got a nice way with him. Brings out the motherly in some of 'em. Then, o'course, we've only got one young woman— that squint-eyed Sharon from the shop—but he'd got her offering to sing solos, play the organ while he conducted, take on the treasurer's job—a doddle, that, since we ain't got no money—and more besides. Reckon she'd have offered to let him wipe his muddy boots on her if we hadn't started at a gallop on 'Praise my Soul'."

"What'd *you* think of him, Lois?" said Derek. He was still hoping to persuade Lois to join the choir, knowing that there was a small gap in her life, and preferring it to be filled by singing rather than sleuthing for Cowgill.

"Patronizing little git," Lois said flatly.

"Lois!" said her mother. "That's not a nice way to talk."

"Derek asked," Lois said defensively. "That was my first impression, and I'm willing to be proved wrong."

A swift glance of disbelief passed between Gran and Derek, and he smiled. "Well, anyway," he said placatingly, "the new vicar's a reliable client for New Brooms, and no doubt we'll be hearing more about Brian and Sandy."

"Blimey," said Gran. "When you say it like that . . ."

FIVE

❧

JAMIE MEADE SLOPED ALONG WITH A LONG STRIDE from the bus stop towards his house. He'd finished his A-levels, and had an offer of a place at York University. All summer he had taken temporary jobs, but had begun to think he might take a year off before going to York, if they'd hold his place. It would be nice to forget studying for a while, get out into the real world and earn some money. Live it up a bit. But music was his life as well as his subject and he would be looking for something connected to that.

Derek had offered to take him around on jobs and teach him some of the electrician's trade, but Jamie had refused, reasonably politely, saying it would be a waste of Dad's time, since he had no intention of following in his footsteps.

He found Gran in the kitchen, ironing shirts and grumbling gently. "Some men iron their own shirts," she said, looking at him fondly as he folded himself into a chair. He'd been such a charmer at eleven years old, but teenagehood had moulded him into a lanky, casual young man. Cool, they called it, Gran knew, but it was all an act with Jamie. He was still her same sweet-natured boy at heart, and still passionate about his music. She remembered when he'd been encouraged to play the piano by Enid Abraham, one of Lois's team and no mean pianist herself, and—contrary to his parents' expectations—he had stuck to it, taking exam after exam and doing very well in them all. Now Gran approved of his intention to make his career in the musical world.

He grinned at her. "I don't mind havin' a go at ironing," he said, "but I don't see that as a proper job. I have got a possible, though."

"Good," nodded Gran approvingly. "That new bloke," Jamie continued, "Sandy something, him what's taken on the church biddies, he works in an estate agent's in Tresham and goes in every day by car. He might give me a lift."

Transport was a problem in Long Farnden. Two buses a week went through the village, picking up shoppers who wanted a couple of hours in Tresham before returning home. The workmen's bus had long since been discontinued, and young village people without cars or motorbikes found it impossible to live at home and work in town.

"Mm," said Gran, with an apparent lack of enthusiasm for the Sandy plan. "You could bike, if you got up early enough."

"Oh, fine," said Jamie. "And what about when it rains?"

"You won't dissolve," said Gran, punishing a linen tea towel with a hot, steaming iron.

"Well, anyway," Jamie said, "I've said I'll go round and see him. Livin' at the vicarage at present, but means to get his own place. What's for tea, Gran?" he added, and she let the subject drop. No doubt he would talk about it to Lois and Derek later.

AT THE VICARAGE, THE ROW THAT LOIS INTERRUPTED had continued on and off all day. "I wish I hadn't taken time off," said Sandy sulkily. "They were nice about it when I explained I'd still got my stuff to sort out, but made it clear I'd have to make up the hours. And now all I've done is argue with you."

"And all about nothing," said the vicar miserably.

"It's not nothing! You know what people will say . . . two blokes living together—sure to be gay. And you being old and me young looks even worse. So there's no point you making all kinds of arrangements here for me. I'm not stopping any longer than necessary."

Brian Rollinson sighed. "Very well, Sandy," he said. "I must say I think you're wrong. I've made it clear you are my godson, the son of an old friend."

"That was a long time ago," said Sandy dismissively.

Brian said mildly, "The fact that he died so young doesn't mean I have forgotten our friendship, Sandy."

"Oh, yeah, yeah," said Sandy, sitting down heavily on a protesting chair. "I've got my own life to get on with, and the sooner I find a place of my own the better. It'd be much more convenient living in Tresham, dump though it is."

"I'm sure something will come up in Farnden," said Brian Rollinson quickly. "I did promise your mother I'd keep an eye . . ."

"Oh, for God's sake! I don't need a minder!" Sandy saw Rollinson wince, and for a second felt ashamed. "Sorry," he said, more quietly. "Yeah, I know you mean it for the best. But this is all far from satisfactory, so I'll be off as soon as poss."

"And the church choir?" Rollinson's voice was low.

"Oh, I'll carry on with that, whatever. Looks like being

a real laugh, and once I get a few extras—hopefully girls, and hopefully under ninety years old—we'll make your church a legend in the county."

"Yes, well . . . be careful, Sandy." Rollinson walked towards the door, lightly touching the top of Sandy's head as he passed. "You may end up with no choir at all. Village people are very conservative, you know. Just bear that in mind."

"Yes, Brian," said Sandy in a mock-weary voice. "Whatever you say, Brian. Ah," he added, looking out of the window and brightening, "there's that lad I met in the shop. Jamie Meade, I think he said. Son of the excellent Lois, d'you reckon? He's finding a job in town, and needs a daily lift, so I said I'd oblige. Will you open the door, or shall I?"

"WELL, I DON'T SEE NOTHIN' WRONG WITH THAT, LOIS," Derek said that evening. "Good idea, I reckon. All Jamie's got to do now is find a job." Jamie sighed with relief. His mother, like Gran, had not been keen on the daily lift with Sandy Mackerras, and had hinted they might help with a motorbike. Anyway, now Dad had backed him up, it was safe to make his proposal.

"I've already found something," he said. "You know that music shop in Church Lane, off the High Street? Well, they need some help, they say. Lots of kids with nothing to do get in there and spend hours driftin' round. They got instruments as well as CDs and sheet music an' that . . . Need somebody to keep an eye open, an' help advise and sell."

"Advise?" said Lois. "Advise on what?"

"Music, Mum," said Jamie. He was resigned to a certain lack of understanding in his parents. "It's what I know most about."

"O'course he does," said Derek. "You just go ahead,

boy," he added. "And some of your wages goes to Mum towards your keep. When I was your age . . ."

Laughter drowned out the rest of his sentence, and broke the tension. "Not that old thing!" said Lois. "Well, you can only give it a try. Now, can we please have the telly on? We're missing Mum's favourite rubbish."

Six

❧

BILL STOCKBRIDGE TOOK OUT HIS KEYS AND PREPARED to unlock the front door of the cottage. To his surprise, the door swung open before he could turn the key in the lock. Rebecca must be home, though he could have sworn she'd said there would be a staff meeting after school.

"Rebecca?" He walked through to the kitchen, and saw her cutting bread, making sandwiches.

"Hi," she said, and kissed him with buttery lips. "Got home earlier than expected. Just as well, though. I've decided to have a go at the choir—first practice tonight. You coming?"

He had forgotten. It had certainly never loomed large in his thoughts, and he was surprised that Rebecca seemed so keen. They were not churchgoers, and he was astute enough to see that the new vicar had seen expansion of the choir as a way of increasing his tiny congregation.

"Oh, well . . . I thought we'd have a talk about it first. Haven't really discussed it, have we?"

Rebecca looked at him. Stolid, square and handsome in

his outdoor, reliable way, she wished sometimes he would surprise her, make a decision on the spot, take a controversial line on something. But that wasn't fair. Hadn't he done the most controversial thing the farming community could have imagined? Gone cleaning, like a skivvy . . . like a woman! He'd put up with constant ribbing in the pub from the lads, but had stuck to it, until even they had got used to the idea, and accepted him as one of them.

"No, we haven't," she said sweetly, smiling at him. "But I reckoned when you said you'd been a choirboy meant you'd decided . . . hadn't you?"

He hugged her, unfortunately with a slice of greasy bread between them, and agreed to go with her and give it a try.

"You'll need to change now, then!" she said, pulling away from him gently. "You've just got time before I finish these, and then we can eat."

THE CHURCH WAS GLOOMY, EVEN THOUGH THE EVENING sun still lit up the village outside. "Just putting some lights on," a voice came from the bell tower, and then Sandy emerged. He squinted at the two of them silhouetted against the low sunlight.

"Hi there!" he said. "Not sure we've met, but come on in and let's introduce ourselves. I'm Sandy . . . and I'm sort of in charge."

"I'm Rebecca and he's Bill." Smiles were exchanged, and the three walked with clattering steps along the red-tiled aisle into the chancel, the noise softened there by a warmly patterned carpet.

"We're early," said Rebecca. "I expect the others'll be along soon?"

"Oh yes, there's a core of old faithfuls, and I'm hoping for one or two more like yourselves. We've been spreading the word. Brian—er, Rev. Rollinson—gave out a notice about it on Sunday. Fingers crossed!" He looked down the empty aisle, and his face brightened as he heard voices approaching from the churchyard.

Mrs. T-J was first in, of course. She led a small company of elderly ladies, plus the squint-eyed girl from the shop, and, trailing behind, Jamie Meade, looking embarrassed and tentative.

"Hi!" said Sandy loudly. "Good evening, Mrs. Tollervey-Jones, and welcome to Jamie, our new and very much needed tenor." Steady Sandy, he said to himself. Don't frighten the lad away.

A few minutes later, Brian Rollinson appeared at the door. "Coming to sing?" said Sandy, and his tone was not welcoming.

"No, no," Rollinson said quickly. "Just checking the church was open, lights on and all that. Got everything you need, Sandy? Good, good. Have a great practice, then— see you later."

Sandy frowned. Why couldn't Brian keep out of it and leave it to him? The less they were seen as a pair, the better he'd like it. He turned to his little flock, rearranged them in the choir stalls, diplomatically leaving soprano Mrs. T-J at the front where she could be seen as self-appointed leader, and moved across to the organ.

"Um, excuse me, Sandy," said the squint-eyed girl. "I think I'm better at playin' than singin', and I wondered if you'd like me to do that always now, so's you could conduct? We got plenty of sopranos, now Rebecca's here, and . . . ?"

"Great idea!" said Sandy vigorously. "Many thanks, dear. What was your name again?" She blushed, and said, "Sharon, Sharon Miller."

"Of course," said Sandy, bestowing his sunlit smile on her that caused her to blush ever more deeply. "Now, everybody, I've a nice surprise for you! Mrs. T-J, would you hand around these books?"

Nobody had ever called her that to her face, and she blanched, swallowed, and then managed a small smile, as Sandy held out a pile of slim, gold-coloured books. "I think I'd rather stick to my full name," she said icily.

Sandy replied innocently, "Oh, so sorry! You'll probably have to remind me again, Mrs. T-J . . . oh, oops . . . anyway, these books . . ." He continued that an anonymous donor had paid for them, hoping that the modern tunes and words would jolly up the Sunday services.

"Jolly up?" echoed Mrs. T-J, holding each book between thumb and forefinger as if contaminated by revolutionary ideas.

The choir dutifully opened the books, titled optimistically *Sing with all my Soul*, at number six, "Bind us together, Lord," while Sharon Miller played through the tune with a pleasing fluency. Jamie, sitting behind the altos and next to the only other tenor, a reedy renegade from Waltonby, was surprised to hear such skill from a girl who'd weighed out potatoes for Gran only hours ago.

"She's good, isn't she?" he muttered to his neighbour, who didn't reply, being busy with wavering over notes under his breath, ready to start singing.

"OK, ready everyone?" Sandy began to beat time, and his eyes rested on the shining face of Rebecca, singing with all her soul. My God, she was a bit special! Sandy licked his lips involuntarily, and held up his hand. The choir tailed off, with Mrs. T-J holding on to her note much longer than anyone else. "Let's just try that bit again," he said. "Bar ten, we hold 'there' for a full three quavers. Once more, then."

Some of the older members of the choir had no idea what he was talking about. Bar ten? Quavers? Weren't they some sort of potato crisp? They'd always ignored the music as being an irrelevant collection of black dots. Tunes were what mattered, and the old tunes were in their blood.

"Excuse me!" said a particularly forthright alto. "Who's

idea was these books? None of *us* was consulted." She sniffed. "We've managed perfectly well with *A & M* up to now. And what's more," she added, warming to the attack, "the congregation knows the old tunes. How are they goin' to sing this stuff? Sounds more like one of them gospel choirs on the telly than our village church."

Sandy took a deep breath. Brian had warned him, and he was prepared. With a glance constantly returning to check on the smiling Rebecca, he explained that he hoped the choir would perform anthems occasionally, singing by themselves on special days in the church calendar. "And this is not a new idea, Mrs. er . . ."

"*Miss* Brown, if you don't mind," retorted the alto.

"Yes, well, as I was saying, choir anthems are as old as this church. Nothing new there . . . as traditional as you could wish. Now, if we could just try that again?"

The jolly, lilting tune was mastered, with the help of Mrs. T-J's piercing soprano, and they went on to more familiar hymn tunes. The hour went quickly for Rebecca, who had forgotten how much she loved to sing. And in the quiet church, with its wonderful acoustics, even this scratch group of people produced a shivery, good sound. Between hymns, while Sandy searched for an alternative tune in *A & M*, and everyone was quiet, a blackbird suddenly began to sing its liquid, remarkable song outside the open church door. Rebecca felt tears come into her eyes. It was like a blessing, showing the way for this oddly assorted bunch. She looked over at Bill in the basses, but he was looking up at a monument in the chancel. Then Sandy caught her eye, and she felt a flash of understanding between them. He'd heard, and felt, just like she had.

LATER, WHEN REBECCA AND BILL SAT IN FRONT OF THE telly, watching the news, Rebecca said, "It was good, wasn't it? Singing, I mean."

"Mm, it was OK. Do you think that Sandy's a bit of a . . . well, you know . . . ? Still, best to give him a chance. Means well, I dare say."

"Bit of a what?" said Rebecca sharply.

"Well, you know . . ."

Rebecca, who'd received all the right signals from the young choirmaster, shrugged. "Fully paid up," she said. "No doubt about that."

Bill did not reply, but switched from gloomy news to a game show that took idiocy to supreme heights. He watched without concentrating, and wondered why he could not shake off an uncomfortable feeling of apprehension.

SEVEN

"YOU ARE INVITED TOO, SANDY," SAID BRIAN Rollinson. "Mrs. Tollervey-Jones was most particular in mentioning it."

"Very broad-minded of her, considering," said Sandy knowingly.

The Rev. Rollinson frowned. "What do you mean?" he said.

"Well, considering I persistently called her Mrs. T-J at choir rehearsal, and her just having told me off for doing so." He was grinning now, happy at getting one up on Brian.

"I see. Well, don't rely too much on your undoubted charm, young Sandy," replied the vicar mildly, turning over sizzling bacon in the pan. "She can be a vicious old bird, so the locals say. And has influence spreading far and wide in the county. Husband was Lord Lieutenant, and all that."

"Wow!" said Sandy. "Am I supposed to be impressed?"

Brian Rollinson sighed. His promise to Sandy's mother

to see him settled down happily in his new job was going to be difficult to fulfil. She had more or less blackmailed him into giving Sandy a lodging until he could find his own flat. "He's never lived away from home before," she'd said, and when Brian had raised his eyebrows, had continued, "and since his father died such a long time ago . . . well, you know all about that . . ." Her pause had been pregnant. ". . . Well, I suppose I'd persuaded him to stay at home to keep me company for a while."

So Brian had promised, convincing himself that it was a duty for him to do so, and not admitting to himself that the presence of the personable young man in his house was anything more than that. But Sandy was a prickly lodger, quick to take offence. Brian constantly reminded himself to tread carefully, and though in some ways he dreaded the thought of his lively young companion moving out, he knew life would be more peaceful without him.

"I might as well come to the party, anyway," said Sandy. "Should be good for a laugh, and there's not much else to do in this godforsaken place."

"Surbiston was different, was it?" said Brian, losing patience. "A dead-and-alive former steel town, distinguished by its derelict factories and preponderance of drunks on the streets at night? That was your idea of a lively place to live?"

Sandy did not reply. He pushed his chair back from the breakfast table, and stalked out of the room. "What about this bacon?" shouted Brian. Sandy's reply was fortunately inaudible.

BILL HAD DONE A GOOD JOB. WHEN BRIAN AND SANDY stepped in through the open front door, the elegant black-and-white tiled entrance hall sparkled. Surfaces had been polished and scrubbed, the spindly legged chairs and console tables shone silkily under silver salvers and small vases of exquisitely arranged flowers.

"D'you reckon the sturdy Bill did the flowers too?" whispered Sandy to Brian. He had been doing some research on Rebecca, and had discovered that her live-in boyfriend Bill worked for New Brooms. A cleaning boy! Shouldn't be too difficult to muscle in there, then, he'd thought.

"Of course not," said Brian crossly. "For goodness sake, behave yourself, Sandy. This party has been very kindly organized for me to meet local people. Please do not let me down."

Sandy laughed. "Don't worry, dearie," he said, and, leaving Brian to a group of equestrian women who bore a remarkable resemblance to their mounts, he went off in pursuit of Rebecca.

Halfway across the room, he was waylaid by a small, plain girl in a frilly, unsuitable dress, carrying a tray of glasses that rattled against each other perilously as the tray tipped. "Glass of champagne, Mr . . . er . . . Sandy?" It was the squinty girl from the shop, his willing choir dogsbody and very competent organist.

He put out a hand to steady the tray, and said kindly, "Lovely, thanks very much, Sharon."

"Oh!" she said, blushing again. "You remembered this time!"

"How could I ever forget," he said smoothly, touching her bare arm. "Now, mind how you go with that precious load! See you, Sharon . . ." And he was off through the crowded hall towards the seats under the long windows, where he had spotted Rebecca, sitting for a moment on her own.

"Can I get you a drink?" he said, standing smiling in front of her.

She shook her head. "Thanks, no. Bill's just gone to get

one. I hate champagne, so he's gone out to the kitchen for water. Knows his way around here, luckily."

"Ah yes, one of his cleaning jobs?" Sandy managed to convey a certain amount of contempt into the innocent question, and Rebecca was not slow to pick it up.

"It is," she said shortly. "And his expertise is much appreciated. And, as it happens, he'll be off shortly to calve a cow up at the farm. Ever helped a cow deliver her calf, Sandy? No? Well, I thought not. Now, if you'll excuse me, I'd better go and see where he is."

Sandy smiled sadly. Oops! he said to himself. Cocked up that one. Never mind, there'll be lots of other chances. He gave himself a little shake, and moved away to survey other possible talent.

Brian, meanwhile, was getting along splendidly. He towered over most of the guests, and as he bent his head down to listen to tales of county intrigue and village scandal, the general impression whispered from group to group was that they'd got a good man. A good man at last. One who would listen to them, and appreciate how things had always been done. A good man, who would recognize those who had influence and power, and conduct the business of God's elect accordingly. A very pleasant atmosphere prevailed over the party, and when they began to drift away, effusive in their thanks to Mrs. Tollervey-Jones, the good folk of the parishes felt satisfied and looked forward to a period of calm and uncontroversial churchgoing.

IN THE CHURCHYARD, WATCHING THE BIG CARS LEAVING Farnden Hall and winding their way through darkening lanes, old Cyril sat on the rickety wooden seat by the line of yew trees and chuckled. Poor chap! Full o'new ideas, no doubt. But they'd soon drum 'em out of 'im. Mrs. T-J and 'er lot'd soon lick 'im into shape.

Cyril turned in his seat and stared up at the church

tower. There it was, same as every year. The date and time were exactly right. As he watched, a solitary brick, mysteriously included in the ironstone tower, glowed as if lit from within. There were no rays left from the dying sun, and no reason why a single brick should shine out into the night. Except that, as Cyril knew better than anyone, it was the anniversary of poor old Willy Mellish's untimely death. Every year Cyril kept vigil, and now, as the glow slowly faded, he got to his feet and stumped off down the path. "Silly old fool," he muttered to himself, as he passed the ancient gravestone with its ill-fated couple either side of their table. But there was a touch of sympathy in his voice. Women could be a terrible nuisance. Maybe he was better off without.

EIGHT

❧

LOIS HEARD THE TELEPHONE RINGING AS SHE CAME into the kitchen, and half-ran through to her office at the front of the house. "Hello? Oh, Derek, it's you."

"Yep, it's me," Derek said. "Are you sitting comfortably?"

"What d'you mean? What are you on about?"

"Well, I just don't want you falling down in a dead faint. The thing is, me duck, I just saw our Jamie walking hand in hand down the High Street in Tresham with a very attractive girl."

"So? Wouldn't be the first girl he's taken out, for goodness sake. He is eighteen, after all!"

"Ah, but this one is different. She's the granddaughter of that old boiler up at the Hall, Mrs. Tollervey-Jones. I seen her up there when I went to do a rewiring job in the stables. Annabelle, they call her, and she's not more'n seventeen."

"Oh, blimey," said Lois, sitting down. "He's kept that under his hat, close little devil."

"I bet he's told Gran," Derek said.

"Right. Well, if he has and she's not said anything . . ."

Lois's voice was vengeful, so Derek said quickly, "Better go careful, me duck. We are living in the twenty-first century, y'know."

"Not in Long Farnden we aren't," replied Lois, and put down the phone. She marched off towards the kitchen, where she found Gran peacefully cleaning brass candlesticks and listening to a play on the radio.

"Cuppa tea, Mum?" said Lois, deciding that a softly-softly approach was best.

Gran looked up at her. "So what d'you want, Lois?" she said.

"To know if you'd like a cup of tea," said Lois defensively, filling the kettle. "A perfectly innocent question."

"Mmm, well, thanks. Yes, I would. And what else?"

"Oh, all right," said Lois, laughing. "Do you know anything about Jamie and Mrs. T-J's granddaughter? Derek saw them holding hands in Tresham."

"Annabelle, d'you mean?" said Gran. "Yes, of course I know her. Very nice little thing. She's been here once or twice—probably when you've been working—and seems very pleasant. No side at all, unlike her grandma."

Lois was speechless. "Why?" continued Gran. "Is something wrong? Have they quarrelled? Both very young, of course. She's seventeen, though. Not all that young, nowadays."

"I should've been told," said Lois.

Gran bridled. "What do you mean, Lois? Aren't you being a bit ridiculous? It's not as if she was a royal princess . . ."

"Thought Jamie'd have more sense," said Lois without thinking.

Gran put down the bottle of metal polish with a bang. "That's enough," she said. "Can we change the conversation? Your son Jamie, a very nice lad, has got a very nice girlfriend, and nobody's complaining except you."

"And Derek," said Lois. "Well," she added, aware that she was not being quite fair, "not complaining exactly, but he obviously thought it was a bit dodgy."

"Mum!" Jamie's voice shouted from outside the kitchen window. "Door's locked! Let us in!" He was grinning at her, and she understood, really understood, for the first time that he was a young man, and a very attractive one. But that doesn't mean I can't have my say, she reassured herself, and went to let him in.

"Thanks," he said, and looked across at where Gran had resumed her cleaning. "What's up, Gran?" he asked.

"Nothing," she said.

"Come on," he said. "I know that face. What's Mum bin saying?"

Lois decided the time was ripe. "We were talking," she said, "about your new girlfriend. Annabelle Tollervey-Jones."

"Right," said Jamie, a soft look on his face that jolted Lois. "Did she ring? We were in Tresham, shopping. Did she forget something?"

"Um," hesitated Lois. "No," she said quickly. "No, she didn't ring. Gran was just telling me what a nice girl she is. You must introduce me."

"Blimey, that's a bit formal!" said Jamie. "We're not engaged, or anything! You'll meet her, Mum. She's been here once or twice, but I expect you were out. Anyway," he added, "how's about a cup of tea? I'm thirsty." He looked at Gran, but she waved a hand at Lois.

"She's doing it," she said flatly. "Make the most of the offer, Jamie. And don't make it too strong," she added to Lois.

"Don't listen to her, Mum. Gnat's pee, that's Gran's tea," said Jamie cheerfully, and turfed a snarling Melvyn off the chair in order to sit down.

• • •

IN THE LONG DRAWING ROOM AT THE HALL, MRS. Tollervey-Jones looked around her with pleasure at the muted colours of her interior décor. It had been newly designed by the friend of a friend, and though she had been rather shocked at the invoice, tasteful as it was on thick paper with a gold heading, the total was twice what the girl had estimated. Still, she was a sort of friend, and Mrs. T-J had swallowed hard and paid up.

Widowed relatively young, she ran the Hall and its estates in a very efficient, businesslike manner. From her farm manager down, all her employees respected and admired, but did not love her. She had always regarded Long Farnden as *her* village, and filled the positions of President of the WI, Chair (as she hated to be called) of the Parochial Church Council, Parish Council, and school Board of Governors, with what she saw as firmness and tolerance. That was not how her reign was seen by other members of these organizations, but on the whole they went along with it, having little ambition to replace her.

She was not a fool, however, and was well aware that she was probably the last representative of a dying breed. Incomers with new ideas were beginning to challenge the old guard, one or two turned up at Parish Council meetings, unheard of in the old days, and were anxious to have their say. And now this new vicar, though Mrs. T-J had approved his appointment and could not fault him at his first outing at her party, he had an air of reserve, of holding something back.

She walked across to the grand piano, and adjusted a wedding photograph. It was of her own wedding, and she looked at the smiling, fresh young faces with a sigh.

"Annabelle looks so like me," she said smugly. And was reminded of something unpleasant. A word had been dropped in her ear that her granddaughter had been seen in

Tresham, lovingly entwined with Jamie Meade, son of that cleaning woman in the village.

The door opened, and the old gardener in his socks advanced a couple of paces. "The vicar, Mrs. Tollervey-Jones, is here to see you, to thank you for a lovely party, he says. An' I've just brought some veg in—they're in the scullery."

The vicar could surely just have telephoned, thought Mrs. T-J, that would have been quite adequate. Still, he was new. She must give him a chance. "Right, wheel him in," she said, and put on her welcoming face.

"It was such a lovely occasion, and so kind of you," said Brian, overstepping all the boundaries by planting a firm kiss on both of Mrs. T-J's cool cheeks. "Now," he added, "I would really appreciate your advice on an idea I have for getting some of the young mums and babies to come along to church. A pram service, I thought. Once a month to begin with, and on an early weekday afternoon, so they can go on and meet other children from school with no trouble. Keep it light, bit of fun. What do you think?"

Mrs. T-J was saved from having to say what she thought by the precipitate entrance of her granddaughter, Annabelle. "Hi, vicar!" she said happily. "Gran, can Jamie have a go on our piano? He's really good. Have you heard him?" she said, turning to Brian with a smile.

"Um, no, but I think he has joined Sandy's choir, and sings very nicely," he answered, uncomfortably aware of a distinct chill coming from Mrs. T-J's direction.

"I think not, Annabelle," she said. "It has just been tuned, darling," she added. "Now, Reverend Rollinson and I have business to discuss, so perhaps you could be an angel and bring us some tea. And darling, I'm not awfully keen on being called Gran. Grandmother is so much more ... well ..."

"Acceptable?" said Annabelle acidly, and left the room without another word.

NINE

BRIAN ROLLINSON GOT UP NEXT MORNING FEELING pleased with himself. His first venture—well, second, if you counted setting up Sandy as choirmaster—had received guarded approval from Mrs. T-J, and enthusiastic encouragement from Lois Meade, whom he had met in the shop on the way home. Shop, pub, school, all these were places where he intended to be seen frequently, getting on with the people of the village, gradually erasing that centuries-long barrier between vicarage and community. Doctors, schoolmasters and vicars had all been put on pedestals in the past, but no longer. He was going to be best mates with the coalman, the paper boys—um, well, yes—and the district nurse. Coming late to the job, he considered, was an advantage, in that he had been one of them, an accountant in a busy practice, and knew the ways of the world.

"Sandy?" he called, as he looked at the clock. Time he was up. His answer was a long groan, coming from upstairs. "Sandy? Anything wrong?"

"Sick!" Sandy's voice was feeble, and then Brian heard

the unmistakable sound of someone throwing up. He rushed up the stairs and into Sandy's bedroom. "Good heavens, boy!" he said. "What on earth have you been eating?"

"Dunno," managed Sandy, and added, "I think I've been poisoned . . ."

"Rubbish!" said Brian. "Probably drank too much last night. You were very late back from the pub."

Sandy began to say something, but was overcome by another bout of nausea. Brian stared down at the white, sweaty face, and wondered if something was really wrong. Better get the doctor, just in case. Sandy's mother would never forgive him . . . again.

As he was dialling, there was a knock at the kitchen door. He hastily made his request for the doctor to visit Sandy, and shouted, "Come in!" He walked through and saw an attractive young woman, carrying a box full of what even he recognized as cleaning materials.

"New Brooms," she said, "Hazel Thornbull . . . was Reading . . ." She smiled confidently at him, then glanced around the kitchen. "I can see you need our services," she said. "Shall I start upstairs and work my way down? That's what we usually do, if it's convenient."

"Well, no," said Brian, holding out his hand and receiving a firm shake from Hazel. "I'm afraid Sandy is still in bed, and far from well. He's been sick, very sick, and I was just sending for the doc. Oh," he added quickly, "you'd perhaps rather not stay this morning, with you being . . . ?" He glanced at her distinct bulge. "I don't know what's wrong, but it may be infectious."

Hazel shook her head. "Tough as old boots, me," she said. "I'll not go in his room, though. Leave him in peace." She pulled on an overall, sorted out what she would need, and went off in the direction of the stairs. Brian rushed after her. "I am so sorry," he said. "Haven't made the bed yet! Quite forgot you were coming . . . shall I . . . ?"

"No, don't worry," she answered cheerfully. "We meet all sorts of stuff. An unmade bed is nothing. Just ignore me, and I'll get on. Coffee around eleven, if that's OK with you."

Sandy had stopped groaning, and Brian tiptoed upstairs behind Hazel. He peeped into the half-open door and looked at Sandy's humped figure under the duvet. "Sandy," he whispered. No reply. Oh my God, supposing . . . Then he saw movement, and was reassured. Perhaps the lad was asleep. That would do nothing but good . . . unless it was a coma? Oh, Lord, please send the doctor to us first on his rounds. Just this once.

Hazel, who was adept at gathering information without appearing to do so, noticed everything. The anxious figure of the vicar peering into Sandy's bedroom, the unmade bed and its elaborate satin headboard, the neatness and cleanliness of everything else in the house. Someone was a good housewife, and Hazel was certain it wasn't that bouncy little twit who worked at the estate agent's. She began to hum under her breath. It was going to be an interesting one, this.

THE DOCTOR CAME TO THE VICARAGE, NOT FIRST ON HIS rounds, but soon after lunch. He examined Sandy carefully, and frowned. "Not sure," he said honestly. "Could be a flu thing . . . his temperature's up. Did he eat the same as you? Are you OK?"

Brian said they had both had the same supper, but that Sandy had gone down to the pub afterwards and stayed until late. "I've no idea if he had more to eat," he said. "He certainly had plenty to drink, judging by the noise he made when he came in." He smiled at the doctor, wanting to give the impression of being an unflappable, responsible man, who nevertheless knew what these young people got up to. But his hands were shaking as he helped pull the bedcovers back over the comatose Sandy.

"Mmm," said the doctor, still staring at his patient. "Probably flu. But it could be something he's eaten. Better do some tests. Get as much fluid into him as possible. Don't take no for an answer. He'll keep it down best just after he's vomited. Keep him warm," he added.

The vicar accompanied the doctor to his car, and thanked him. "Not in danger, is he?" he said, as the car door shut. But the doctor did not hear, and drove off with a wave. His mind was already on his next patient.

"Afternoon, vicar." Brian wheeled round to see old Cyril, propped up against the vicarage wall, idly swiping at a clump of nettles with his stick. "Lovely weather," he added, wondering if the vicar had heard him. Mind somewhere else. That was the doctor, wasn't it, so there was sickness in the house.

"Nobody ill, I 'ope," Cyril prompted.

"Nothing serious," said Brian, pulling himself together. "Young Sandy has a stomach upset. Soon be right as rain."

"Ah," said Cyril, nodding his head wisely. "Needs some o'my pills. You tell 'im. Troublesome things, stomicks. Did I ever tell you about old Willy Mellish, 'im that's in the churchyard?"

"Yes, indeed, several times," said Brian hurriedly. "Now, Cyril, you must excuse me. Got things to see to. Good morning!" The last thing he wanted to hear was the grisly tale of Willy Mellish and his poisoning wife Sophia.

Ten

❧

Sharon Miller, now twenty-two, and still stubbornly refusing to have her eye straightened, was the daughter of the Millers at the garage, which occupied the old Baptist Chapel in the High Street. Don Miller had, of course, built on to the old chapel, needing workshops, an inspection pit, somewhere to park vehicles. The site had been for sale, and he and his family had moved in with high hopes. These had been somewhat dashed when his first planning application was rejected out of hand. "A conservation village with a *garage* in the High Street!" Mrs. T-J had been almost apoplectic. But for once she was overruled. A major redrawing of the plans, hiding all the nasty new buildings behind the chapel and out of sight, pleased the planners, and the whole project fitted in well with the current government proposals for encouraging light industry into rural areas.

"I'll be bringing job opportunities," promised Don Miller, and he had been true to his word. Two of his original apprentices had stayed with him, and local car-owners were quick to recognize that his prices were reasonable and the care he gave to their cars painstaking and personal. "Yes, yes," he said to Mrs. T-J, when she finally brought the old Daimler for his attention. "We'll get it all tickety-boo for you. Lovely job, these were," he added, running his hand lovingly over the bonnet.

The Millers were good parents, if over-protective. Sharon found ways of covering up her bids for liberty, but so far had had few serious transgressions to conceal. She resisted treatment for her eye, saying Mr. Right, when he came along, would love her for herself. It would be a good test. Her parents had given up trying to persuade her, although they wondered if she was giving herself the best chance of a husband and children. This was all-important to them, and up until now, lads were not particularly attracted to their Sharon, seeing no further than the eye and the glasses. Sharon's Mr. Right, who would notice her soft hair, her peachy skin and ripe curves, had not yet turned up.

Now she worked in the village shop, efficient and relied upon totally by the ageing shopkeepers, Mr. and Mrs. Carr. They were childless, and had taken to Sharon straight away. "Like a child to us, she is," they said to their friends. "Heaven-sent, under the circumstances."

Sharon was uninterested in the concerns of her peers. She didn't much like the taste of alcohol, resisted with ease the temptation of drugs, and found clubbing disappointingly noisy and boring. But she did have an addiction. This was innocent enough, on the surface, and merely made her mother and father smile. Romantic fiction filled her leisure hours. She borrowed four such novels at a time from the Tresham Library, and read compulsively. "Just wait until she has a boyfriend of her own," said her mother, "and then she won't need those. Meantime, they'll do her no harm."

Which, of course, they did not. It was the other books she had to conceal in her library bag. Richly written tales of sex and violent crime lurked at the bottom of her wardrobe, well concealed behind her shoes. The latest, an account—satisfactorily dramatized—of Madeleine Smith, the Victorian Glasgow girl who poisoned her treacherous lover by anointing herself with arsenic-laden cream and then encouraging him to lick it off, had caused her one or two tumultuous dreams. The wily Scottish girl had somehow escaped punishment, and Sharon's imagination filled in the gaps left by the writer's decorum. But she'd nearly finished that one, and this afternoon was off on the Tresham bus to find more stories to feed her habit.

"Will you manage all right?" she asked her elderly boss.

"O'course we will. Don't miss the bus, now," he said.

Mrs. Carr added with a chuckle, "You run along, Sharon. Don't do anything I wouldn't do!" As if Sharon would! Their little guardian angel, they described her to themselves. They dreaded the day when some man would recognize her worth and carry her away from them. But for the moment, they were grateful for their good luck. They had been the village shopkeepers for nearly forty years, and could not manage without her.

On her way to the bus stop, a car passed her slowly, and then pulled up by the path. When she drew level, the window was wound down, and Sandy's cheerful face looked up at her. "Need a lift, Sharon?" he said. "I'm on my way to Tresham."

"Goodness, that's kind of you!" said Sharon, her face scarlet.

"Hop in, then," said Sandy.

"You've been poorly, I hear," Sharon said, when she had settled herself. Her skirt was shortish, and she tugged it down, but it would not go far enough to conceal a very appealing pair of knees.

Sandy shifted his eyes away from them, and said, "Oh, it was nothing much. Something I ate, I reckon."

"Her up at the Hall?" said Sharon with a smile. "That

party? Them tiddly bits were a bit off, I expect. She puts
'em in the freezer if they're left over, then out they come
again next time round! That'd be it. The tiddly bits."

She laughed now, and Sandy glanced across at her. Her
profile was very pretty, he realized. Pity about the eye.
"Next time up at the Hall I'll know to abstain," he said, and
they both laughed. The sun blinded Sandy momentarily,
and he reached across Sharon to pick up his sunglasses.
"Oops!" he said, as they dropped into her lap. She handed
them to him, and he fumbled with her hand, his eyes on the
road. "Sorry!" he said, and finally got hold of them.

"Now we're fine," he said, speeding up.

Sharon stared straight ahead, and wished the journey
could go on for ever.

IN HER OFFICE OVERLOOKING THE ROAD, LOIS STOOD AT
the window, thinking about Jamie and his posh girlfriend,
and Derek and Gran, and what would be the best way of
sorting it out. She had decided that doing nothing at all
would be the best policy, when her eye was caught by
Sandy Mackerras's car, picking up speed on its way to Tresham. Somebody was in the car with him . . . was it Sharon
Miller? Well, that would be a turn-up! A reversal, really.
Jamie and Annabelle . . . Sandy and Sharon . . . Wouldn't
it have been better for Jamie and Sharon to . . .

"Lois!" It was Gran, and sounded urgent. As Lois went
through to the kitchen, she saw her mother sitting in a
chair, doubled over and moaning. "Mum! What on earth's
the matter?"

"Sick," was all Gran could manage before getting up
and rushing away to the lavatory. When she returned, her
face was pale and drawn.

"Mum! Better go and lie down. I'll bring you a hottie—
come on, I'll help you up." They just made it to the top of

the stairs, when Gran had to rush into the bathroom to throw up again.

"Right," said Lois, who had heard from Hazel about the Sandy Mackerras episode, "I'm ringing the doctor right now." She settled her mother in bed, and went down to telephone. "She's not a young person," she said firmly to the receptionist, who, as usual, said couldn't Mrs. Weedon manage to come into the surgery? "There's no way I'm bringing her down," Lois added. "And it's urgent. I'll expect the doctor shortly."

The surgery was a client of New Brooms and they all knew Lois Meade. A message was sent through to the doctor out on his rounds, and within an hour of Lois's call, he was there. "What nonsense!" Gran said. "No need to send for you at all. Just eaten something, I expect." But the doctor told Lois not to let her mother get up for at least twenty-four hours, and gave her a number of other instructions out of Gran's hearing.

"Is it a bug going round?" Lois asked. The doctor shrugged. "Well, there was that Sandy Mackerras," Lois continued. "He was throwing up all night, the vicar said."

"Yes, well," said the doctor, uncommunicative as ever. "Goodbye, Mrs. Meade. I'll look in again tomorrow." He strode off down the path, and Lois shrugged. All right, then, she said to herself, don't break the Official Secrets Act. She went back into the house, and rushed upstairs as she heard Gran heaving again.

SANDY MACKERRAS PULLED UP OUTSIDE THE LIBRARY in Tresham, and Sharon struggled to let herself out. He leaned over her, rather longer than necessary, and opened the door. He caught a whiff of a flowery scent, and then she was out on the pavement, leaning down to thank him profusely for the lift. "A pleasure, Sharon," he said, "always a pleasure to give a lovely girl a lift!" She blushed again, and dropped a library book. Confused and burning, she finally reached the library door and disappeared. Was real life catching up with her fictional world at last? She handed in her books with a flourish, and ignored the librarian's raised eyebrows as he noticed the titles of some of them.

The estate agent's office was busy with potential house-buyers when Sandy walked through to his desk. A housing boom had been a godsend to the proliferation of agents in Tresham. This particular one was known to be pushy. Sandy fitted in very well, and had quickly developed the agent-speak which had just worked its magic on Sharon. Flattery, hand-in-hand with exaggeration, was his stock-in-trade, and he loved it.

"Morning, everyone," he said bouncily, and turned his charming smile on to the first customer.

AT THE VICARAGE, BRIAN ROLLINSON LOOKED THROUGH the door into Sandy's room and saw chaos. He sighed. It wouldn't do for Hazel Thornbull to see this mess. He began to clear the clothes and magazines, and sort them into tidy piles. Everything you would expect to find in a young man's room, he thought. No surprises. He picked up a photograph from the table by the bed. It was Sandy's mother and father in earlier years, smiling at the camera in the first flush of a new marriage. Gerald had been such a handsome fellow. That smile. The pain he had almost forgotten stabbed Brian once more, and he put down the photograph quickly. Glancing round the room and approving it as presentable for Hazel, he left and went downstairs to his study to immerse himself in Sunday's sermon.

But his mind kept returning to Sandy and his parents. When had he first met them? Must have been after college, while he was studying accountancy. He put down his pen and stared out of the window. The Tate Gallery, that was it. He'd dropped in to pass away an hour or so, waiting to meet a friend from college, and he had stood in front of a painting next to a young man who was muttering to himself. "Excuse me?" Brian had said, thinking maybe he was being addressed. "Oh, sorry," Gerald had replied. "Just talking to myself. Trying to explain it! Bit weird, isn't it?"

After that, they'd walked on together, and then had a cup of tea in the café. Instant rapport, it had been, and they'd kept in touch. Brian had been best man at the wedding, and now he remembered his mixed feelings as he saw his friend become a twosome, more or less out of his reach.

His telephone rang, and he sighed again. "Hello?" he said.

"Sandy here. Forgot to tell you . . . I'll be out to supper tonight. OK? See you later. Bye!"

Disappointment drove Brian out to the kitchen, where he cut a thick slice of bread, spread it lavishly with butter and honey, and ate it quickly, despising himself.

ELEVEN

❧

"B<small>ILL</small>?"

"Hello, Mrs. M."

"New customer—Trimbles, estate agent's in Tresham." Lois had cornered the market in local estate agents some years ago, and this lot had sprung up recently with the explosion of house prices. "Not where Sandy works, you'll be pleased to hear," she added, and thought she heard an answering grunt. "I've signed them up for regular cleaning. Just the job for you, I thought. Starting after the office closes, but still a couple of long-haired blondes floating about. I'm going over this afternoon. Like you to come with me for a preliminary tour around their extensive premises."

"Extensive? You mean that two-roomed job in Cross Street? That's Trimbles, isn't it? Is that what they said?"

"Yes, well, they *are* estate agents, Bill. You know, desirable property, spacious reception rooms, sweeping lawns, etc., etc.?"

"Ha ha," said Bill, who was very fond of his boss.

"Right. See you there, or will you pick me up? I'll be finished at old Madam's around four."

"I'll collect you from home about half-past. See you then."

When Lois arrived at Bill's cottage, it was Rebecca who opened the door. "Hello, Mrs. M, Bill's just on his way. The client kept him cleaning the silver. Family arriving tomorrow, or something. But he rang and said he was just leaving." She stood aside, and Lois went into the cottage, noticing as always the pleasant smell of cleanliness. "No thanks, no time," she said, refusing Rebecca's offer of tea.

"Right . . ." There was a pause. The two of them had little in common, though friendly enough, and conversation flagged for a moment. Then Rebecca said, "Are you coming to sing in the choir with us? Bill's joined, and he's got a really nice voice."

Lois shook her head. "Not me, Rebecca," she said. "Voice like a foghorn. And anyway, I've not got the time."

"Bill says he's heard you singing, when you didn't know anyone was around, and it was good. It's only an hour a week."

"And church on Sundays. I reckon the bells'd crash to the ground if they saw me comin' in. No, our Jamie's going, and he likes it. But then he's musical all round, so no wonder. Says that Sandy is OK. What d'you think of him?"

To her surprise, Rebecca turned away, her colour rising. "Oh, he's all right," she said. Then she added with obvious relief, "There's Bill! Now you won't have to wait . . ."

Spinning along to Tresham in the white van with New Brooms in gold lettering on the sides, and "We sweep cleaner!" emblazoned across the rear doors, Lois wondered about Rebecca's obvious unease. Something to do with Sandy Mackerras? Probably fancied him. He was quite attractive in a freckled, dodgy-quick kind of way.

Bill'd better watch out. Rebecca was quite a catch. Well dug-in at Waltonby school, own cottage, independent.

"Penny for 'em," said Bill, glancing across at Lois.

"I was just thinking you'd better watch that Sandy bloke. He's after all the girls, I hear," said Lois, who was not one for the subtle approach. The vehemence of Bill's reply startled her.

"Him! Oily little sod, with his 'teeny bit louder' and 'lovely tone, Mrs. T-J,' and his eyes undressing my Rebecca every time he looks in her direction! Don't talk to me about darling Sandy!"

Lois laughed as they turned into the car park in Cross Street. "So you like him! But you sing in the choir too, don't you? Rebecca said . . ."

"Got to keep an eye on the bugger, haven't I," growled Bill.

"Well," said Lois, opening the van door, "you could learn a lot about estate agents from this job. Come on . . ."

"Lead on," said Bill, and followed her out of the car park and into the street.

GRAN SAT BY THE FIRE, HOPING LOIS WOULD BE HOME soon. She had claimed she was feeling a great deal better, and had insisted on getting up and coming down to make a cake. But when she stood in the kitchen with ingredients lined up on the table in front of her, her legs felt weak, and she had to sit down for a while. She abandoned cake-making, and sat and dozed in front of a television programme with the sound turned down. The moving, smiling figures were company. She felt a little scared. Never ill, she couldn't remember when she had felt so bad. How could she have picked up a bug? Apart from that Sandy, there was no one else sick in the village. The shop was the clearing house for all such news, and old Mrs. Carr had not mentioned a bug going round.

Indigestion, she told herself. Something I've always had, on and off. Just a bit worse, this time. Maybe get some new stuff from the chemist's when she went in to Tresham.

"Mum?" Lois was back, and Gran surfaced, making a big effort to smile as her daughter peered at her anxiously. "Shouldn't you still be in bed?"

"I'm fine," said Gran. "Shall I make a cup of tea?"

"You stay right there. I'm making tea for a day or two. An' supper and breakfast. Here, I'll turn the telly up. It's your favourite rubbish."

Gran did not smile, and because she didn't have a smart retort, Lois worried that her mother was far from well.

TWELVE

❧

JAMIE MEADE WALKED ALONG THE ROAD TOWARDS THE Hall, whistling. He'd arranged to pick up Annabelle to go for a walk around the fields. She was the best thing that had happened to him for a long time, he thought. Didn't seem to mind that he had no wheels, no money and none of the lifestyle to which she must be accustomed.

He'd first met her last summer, when the village fete had been up at the Hall as usual. Some daft newcomers had decided to have sideshows like in the old days. Or olde dayes. "Bowling for a pig," one of them had proposed. With a sly grin, the local pig farmer—John Thornbull, married to cleaner Hazel—had said he'd donate a young pig if they'd come up and catch it. John'd got some of his friends round to watch the spectacle, and they'd watched for a satisfying hour as the newcomer and his son had slipped and slithered round the pen. Then they'd taken pity on them, and had it tethered in a couple of minutes. "Reckon they wished they'd never heard of the 'olde dayes' by the time we'd caught the bugger," John had chuckled to Hazel over tea.

Jamie smiled now, in recollection. Still, the best thing about that fete had been meeting Annabelle. He'd been doing well at a darts game when he'd seen her, standing watching, all by herself. She had smiled straight at him, and clapped vigorously when he'd won. A blustery wind had taken Jamie's baseball cap and deposited it at Annabelle's feet, and that was that.

The gates of the Hall were open, and Jamie turned in and walked swiftly up the drive. In spite of the pleasurable anticipation of seeing Annabelle, he had the customary sinking feeling at approaching the stately mansion. God, I hope Mrs. T-J is out, he thought. But she never was, not when he was expected, anyway. What did she think? That he was goin' to drag her precious granddaughter upstairs to one of the four-posters and have his wicked way with her? Well, maybe. But it certainly wouldn't be without Annabelle's enthusiastic encouragement.

"Hi!" he shouted as he saw his love's fair head leaning out of an upstairs window. "Let down your hair, Rapunzel! I'm comin' up!"

"What?" she yelled. "You stupid, or something?" She disappeared, and he walked round to the back of the house, by which time she had emerged, pink and fresh as a daisy. "Love you," she said, kissing him softly.

"Annabelle!" The voice was harsh, and came from inside the kitchen.

"Oh God, it's Gran," said Jamie.

"No, it's Grandmother," said Annabelle, and they both disappeared swiftly up the path and into the woods behind the house before Mrs. T-J could catch up with them. As a result, she was in a bad mood by the time the vicar arrived to talk to her about his ideas for a Requiem Mass to be sung by the church choir on All Souls Day. This was such a ludicrous ambition, that she wondered about his judge-

ment. Perhaps it was not his idea at all, but that of his . . .
his . . . his what? Not his son, or nephew, apparently. His
godson, she knew. She planned to inform the vicar in no
uncertain terms what she thought of the Requiem proposal.

By the time Brian Rollinson arrived, she was restored
to her usual battling form. She led the attack, already extremely displeased by young Mackerras's lack of respect at
his first appearance before *her* choir. "So what's all this
nonsense?" she continued. "Do you really expect a few
squeaking women and a couple of growlers to put on a performance of the Faure *Requiem*? I cannot think you are
serious."

Brian shifted uncomfortably in his seat. She had deliberately motioned him to take a spindly legged ladies' chair,
hopelessly inadequate for his attenuated frame.

The Requiem had not, of course, been his idea. He
couldn't tell the difference between Faure and Andrew
Lloyd Webber. But Sandy had been so keen to have a go,
planning to recruit new choir members and even possibly
inviting one of the Tresham church choirs to supplement
the eventual performance. Brian himself had doubts. Though
he had very little musical talent or appreciation, he was
nevertheless aware of the choir's limitations. But Sandy
was difficult to resist.

"Well, yes, I am, actually, Mrs. Tollervey-Jones. Well,
that is, serious in examining the possibility of such a plan.
Naturally, it would be in the hands of Sandy. Who, if I may
say so," he added, warming up, "is quite capable of working a musical miracle!"

Mrs. T-J frowned. "That is very nearly blasphemy,
Brian," she said acidly.

"Forgive me," Brian said quickly. "But what I meant
was—"

"I'm well aware of what you meant. You asked if you
could come and discuss the matter with me, and I have allowed half an hour of my very busy day to consider it with

you. As far as I am concerned, the proposal is a foolish, unrealistic one, and I would certainly not give it my support. But then," she added with serpent-like agility, "it is really not for me to say. You are the vicar. Sandy Mackerras is the choir master, and the decision is yours and his. However," she added, getting up from her chair dismissively, "I would remind you that choir members are there voluntarily. Most cannot read music, some have little voice, but all are there because they love their church, the old familiar hymn tunes, the association with a village tradition which some remember spoken of by their grandparents. And finally," she concluded, walking towards the door, "they are free to leave whenever they choose, and will not hesitate to do so."

Brian followed her to the door, his face burning like a naughty schoolboy. "You can find your way out, can't you," she said, and he fled.

"SANDY, IT LOOKS LIKE THE REQUIEM IS A NON-STARTER." They were in the dreary sitting room of the modern vicarage. Brian had done what he could with paintings on the walls, a few pieces of good furniture. But it was still a skimped, four-square room with metal-framed windows and a characterless beige-tiled fireplace. What a pity he was too late for the old vicarage. He would have felt at home in its lofty rooms and spacious gardens.

"What d'you mean? It's up to me, isn't it?" Sandy sat up straight and frowned.

"Well, we have to tread carefully at first, you know. I had a word with Mrs. Tollervey-Jones . . ."

"That old trout! What's it got to do with her?"

"Perhaps more than you think. She says it is beyond the choir's capability, and they'll just pack up and leave. They like doing what they've always done, and anything new will have to be added gradually. You've made a start with the new books, so perhaps you'd better leave it at that for a bit."

"For God's sake!" Sandy stood up, red-faced with anger. "Well, thanks a lot for your support, Brian," he snapped. "I'm off down the pub. Maybe I'll find some better company, or even the lovely Rebecca might be there without her flat-footed boyfriend." He knew this would annoy Brian, with his strict moral code. Huh! He went upstairs, banging doors and cursing. Then he was back, pulling on his jacket.

"Just go, Sandy," Brian said quietly. "I've had enough. And I've a sermon to write. Do try not to make a noise when you come in."

Thirteen

❧

Sharon Miller stood at the door to the store-room of the shop. She looked around at the high shelves, dusty and unused for as long as she had been working there. Half-empty boxes, jars and bottles were difficult to distinguish in the light dimly shining on them from a low-wattage bulb hanging crookedly from the ceiling. She turned around to Mrs. Carr, and said, "We should have a go at getting this room turned out and sorted. I could do it, if you want."

"No, I don't think so, Sharon." The elderly woman shook her head. "Couldn't afford the extra hours. In fact . . . come back in here, dear . . . we have been thinking that we shall have to cut down on your working hours."

Sharon's face fell. She loved working in the shop, with people coming in and out, telling her their news and troubles. Working in an office would drive her mad, with the same faces day in, day out.

"We're really sorry, Sharon. You know how we rely on you. You're like a daughter to us." Mrs. Carr's chin wobbled, and Sharon impulsively put her arm around Mrs. Carr's stooped shoulders. "The only way we can carry on is by doing more ourselves," she continued. "Jack says he can help more, and I shall do my best. A couple more years, and we'll have saved enough to retire in the way we've always planned."

"Don't you worry," said Sharon, her romantic heart touched by all this. "I shall easily find some other work. Don't you worry about me." As she said it, she remembered the paper pinned to the shop noticeboard. Lois Meade had brought it in a couple of days ago. New Brooms was looking for extra staff. Part-time, local work. Could be just what she needed.

Mrs. Carr followed her eyes, and nodded. "Mrs. Meade's a very nice woman," she said. "Tough employer, but we can give you a good reference. I'm sure she'll take you on."

Sharon had a sudden picture of herself in rubber gloves and overalls, and wasn't sure what Sandy would think of that. But then she thought again. Those cleaners of Mrs. Meade's were a nice bunch, and had made a real profession of the job. And then there'd be the fun of going to different houses, meeting new people. They'd tell her things, and she would listen sympathetically. Yep, just up her street.

"I'll call in on the way home," she said. "Now don't you think any more about it," she added, patting Mrs. Carr reassuringly. "We'll still have our get-togethers when I come to do a few hours. And I'll always be around if you need any extra help. See you after lunch."

Lois saw Sharon coming up the drive to the back door, and knew immediately why she had come. Gran had heard through her busy and reliable grapevine that the Carrs were struggling at the shop. They had probably cut down on Sharon's hours, and here she was, applying for a job.

"Hi, Sharon," Lois said, opening the back door. "Come on in. Come through to my office, where we can talk."

Sharon, who had passed all her formative years in the village, did not think to question how Lois seemed to know at once the purpose of her visit. Of course she would know. That's how it is in villages.

"Any experience of cleaning other people's houses?" Lois said, picking up a pen.

"Well, I've always helped at home," began Sharon.

"No, I said other people's houses," Lois interrupted. "It's not the same."

"Oh, right." Sharon blinked a little. This was a different Mrs. Meade from the one who came into the shop for groceries. "Well, when Mrs. Carr's been poorly, I've given their house a thorough going-through. O'course, they're both old now, and don't keep it as spick and span as it should be. Still, after she got better, she asked me if I'd clean them up every now and then, so I have. You can ask them if it's satisfactory, if you like."

"I will," said Lois shortly. Then she put her pen down and grinned. "You'll do, Sharon," she said. "What I don't know about you and your family would go on the back of a postage stamp. When can you start?"

She arranged times and dates, and then gave Sharon a friendly but firm account of how her business worked, what she expected of her cleaners, and what they might encounter in unfamiliar houses. She warned Sharon about finding it very different working as part of a team, respecting her colleagues and keeping strict confidentiality on anything she heard whilst at work.

Lois stressed this last point, knowing Sharon's reputation for gossip. But most women gossip, and Lois reckoned she could keep it in check, making it clear that

anyone breaking the rule would be out on their ear before
they could say sorry.

"Right," she said, showing Sharon back through the
kitchen, where Gran was sitting over a coffee. "See you
next week. Weekly meeting Monday midday. I'll tell you
the rest then."

"Thanks *very* much, Mrs. Meade," Sharon said, and
then smiled at Gran. "You feelin' better, Mrs. Weedon?"
she said. "Nasty old business that. Sandy was really
poorly." She blushed, wishing she'd not mentioned Sandy,
but she ploughed on. "Funny nobody else has got the bug.
I'd hear if it was round the village. Anyway," she added
quickly, remembering Lois's strictures, "you're looking a
bit peaky still. Just you take care."

"Bye, then," said Lois, opening the back door. "See you
on Monday, if not before."

"Have you set her on, then?" said Gran.

"Yes, she'll be fine," said Lois.

"Especially with earplugs in and her mouth taped up,"
said Derek, appearing at the door. "Just met our Sharon on
her way out, and she was all excited about working for
you. Hope you know what you're doin', me duck," he said.
"Young Sharon is not all she seems, so I hear."

"If I believed all you hear in the pub," said Lois, refill-
ing the kettle, "I'd have no cleaners at all. And, by the way,
did you hear Mrs. T-J's had a row with the vicar?"

"Lois!" exploded her mother.

Now she was alone again, Gran planned an afternoon dozing and watching television. But her stomach was
still churning. She had little appetite, and the pills the doctor had given her were useless. Maybe she should get some
fresh air. A stroll down to the shop. They might have some
of her usuals, or a good old-fashioned remedy like that.
She fetched her coat and locked up the house. The village

street shone in bright sunlight, the warm, dark gold of the stone houses giving an illusion of summer. But there was a chill in the wind, and Gran stepped out, pulling up her coat collar. The shop was full, with Sharon behind the counter, speedy and efficient. There was no doubt the girl was a worker. Old Mrs. Carr limped in from the back, and Gran felt sorry for her. She was getting past it, without a doubt.

"Afternoon, Mrs. Weedon."

Bother, thought Gran, just my luck to get the old woman. She had hoped Sharon might serve her, and then she could be back home in a few minutes. Her legs still felt shaky, and she was short of breath. "Afternoon," she said.

Mrs. Carr settled herself on a high stool, hands on the counter, ready for a chat. "Better now?"

Here we go, thought Gran. Perhaps if I wander about for a few seconds, I might get Sharon. "Just looking for what I want," she said, walking away and peering at shelves on the opposite side of the shop.

Mrs. Carr followed her. "What is it you're looking for, dear?" she said.

Gran sighed, and gave in. "Something for indigestion," she said. "I'm really quite better, but still get a few twinges. Have you got some of my usuals?"

"Temporarily out of stock," said Mrs. Carr. "But let's think. Yes, I've got just the thing. Just wait a moment while I get them from the storeroom. Here," she added, pulling a chair towards Gran, "perch yourself on that while you wait."

The shop door jangled on the old bell, and Sandy Mackerras came in. Sharon's face was the colour of the tomatoes she was weighing. "Hi, Sharon!" he said cheerily. "How're doing?"

"Fine, thanks," she answered, and dropped a tomato, then stepped on it, and in great confusion mopped up the mess.

Sandy grinned, and turned to Gran. "See what effect I have on the girls, Mrs. Weedon," he said in a mock whisper.

Gran sniffed. "Don't be so sure it was you," she said. "Young Thornbull's just been in talking to Sharon—John's brother—and he's a real he-man. Anyway," she added, with a smile to soften the blow, "never trust ginger hair, my mother used to say. You heard that one, Sandy?"

Discomforted, he went over to the counter and engaged Sharon in a low-voiced conversation. Gran heard the words "Saturday" and "Tresham" and judged from the ecstatic look on the girl's face that Sandy had asked her for a date. Huh, well, no good could come of that, in Gran's opinion. He must've been stood up. Some smart one with big boobs and plenty of experience would have been his first choice, that's for sure.

"Here we are, dear." Mrs. Carr was returning from the stockroom, carrying a box, from the top of which she was blowing a layer of dust. "Just the thing. My mother used to swear by these. Lucky for you we've got some left. Hard to find these days." She took out a rattling box and handed it to Gran.

"Never heard of it," Gran said. "And there's no price on it."

"One pound fifty to you," said Mrs. Carr, plucking a figure out of the air.

Gran paid, took the box in its bag and put it in her pocket, and returned slowly up the High Street. Jamie was waiting outside the house. "Where've you been, Gran?" he said. "You're not supposed to be out on your own yet. Mum'll be furious."

"Then we won't tell her," Gran said.

FOURTEEN

❦

M<small>RS. CARR'S REMEDY HAD NOT DONE GRAN MUCH</small> good. She'd sucked one of the big white tablets as instructed, and not only felt no calmer, but the reverse. She'd spent the afternoon trotting up and down stairs, and by the time Lois came in, she had her feet up on the sofa, looking very wan.

"Just making myself comfortable," she said, as Lois looked worriedly at her. She had no intention of telling Lois about the tablets. Self-doctoring was not allowed in Lois's house, and the medicine cabinet in the bathroom held Elastoplast, throat sweets, and not much else.

"I had a little walk, and managed fine," Gran lied. "Saw Sandy Mackerras, and he asked about choir practice tonight. I thought I might try to go along. It'd cheer me up."

"You are certainly *not* going down there to a cold church, standing on a hard floor for hours! For God's sake, Mum, use your famous common sense. Jamie can take an apology."

But when time for practice came, Jamie rang Lois on his mobile to say he and Annabelle had missed the bus from Tresham, and they couldn't get back until later. "Oh, sod it!" Lois said. She was tired, and looking forward to a quiet evening. "Can't you ring Sandy? Oh, all right, I'll go down and tell them. But just be a bit more responsible in future." She banged the telephone down, and pulled on her jacket. "Shan't be long," she called out, and marched off down the darkening street.

The lights were on in the church, and Lois walked smartly up the path. "Watch out, missus!" said a voice from the shadows. It was Cyril. "There's a bit of broken paving by the door," he added. "Frost, or summat. Don't want you goin' arse over tip, do we." His chesty chuckle masked the sound of voices warming up.

"Thanks, Cyril," she said, and tried to move on, but he blocked her way. "Didn't know you was in the choir," he said. "Thought it was your mother. Now, there's a lovely woman."

"Pity I don't take after her, then, Cyril," said Lois, and edged past him into the church.

"Ain't she better?" he called after her.

"Yes, thanks," she yelled back, and carried on into the chilly interior.

All heads turned towards her as she walked up the aisle.

"Mrs. Meade!" said Sandy, with a broad smile of welcome. "How splendid! Now, are you soprano or alto?"

"More like frog," said Lois flatly. "I've just come to bring apologies from Mum and Jamie. Mum's still poorly, and Jamie's stuck in Tresham. They said sorry and they'd be here next week."

Before Sandy could reply, Mrs. T-J burst out, "Stuck in Tresham? What d'you mean? How are they getting back? I don't want Annabelle put at risk in that place at night!"

Lois turned on her a full basilisk stare, and said "She's not at risk. She's with Jamie, and he's quite capable of looking after her. They're getting a lift, an' will be back about half-past nine."

She turned to go, but Sandy said in his best pleading voice, "Oh, do hold on a moment, Mrs. Meade. We're so short on numbers tonight . . . wouldn't you do us an enormous favour and sing a couple of hymns with us? Just this once?"

Lois hesitated. It was not true that she had a voice like a frog. She knew she could sing. Music was the only lesson she enjoyed at school, and several times she'd done solos at school concerts.

Sandy pounced. "There, look, if you could just sit in the alto pew, and we'll go straight into 'Lead us, Heavenly Father, lead us.'" This had been a regular at school, and Lois was surprised to discover she could remember the alto line. The old heady feeling of singing out lustily in a large space came back to her.

Three hymns later, they paused, whilst Sandy looked up a modern tune in the gold book. "You sing lovely, Mrs. Meade," said Sharon shyly. The altos were sitting in front of the organ, and Lois had been aware of music being played very well behind her. She was about to say something complimentary in return, when Sandy Mackerras suddenly dropped the book, and bent over double. "Ahhhh!" It was a cry of agony, and Sharon was out of the organ seat in seconds, bending over him and holding his hand.

Without stopping to think, Lois ran out of the church at speed and through the vicarage gate. She banged at the door, thanking God there was a light, indicating the vicar was at home. "Quick," she said, as he opened up, "come quickly. Sandy's collapsed. Looks like that stomach bug again."

The two of them ran side by side, and then Lois allowed Brian to go ahead up the aisle to where Sandy lay stretched out on the floor, with a kneeler under his head. He was very still.

Lois slowed up, and found herself tiptoeing forward. Nobody said anything, until a sobbing Sharon turned and saw her. "Mrs. T-J's gone for the doctor," she said. "He'll be OK, Mrs. Meade, won't he?"

Lois looked down at Sandy's white face, saw the purplish-blue line around his mouth, the froth trickling down his chin, and thought it best not to answer.

FIFTEEN

❧

AS DAWN BROKE ON A GREY, MISTY MORNING, BRIAN Rollinson sat beside a hospital bed containing the slight, white-faced figure of Sandy Mackerras, son of his dearest friend Gerald, and wept. The nightmare had continued throughout the long hours after Lois Meade had appeared at his door. The doctor had been all efficiency and calm, the ambulance men wonderfully strong and reassuring; but then that girl from the shop had been completely hysterical and upset all the other women in the choir.

It had been left to Lois and Jamie to bring some sense and order, ably assisted by Mrs. T-J. After Sandy had gone, Brian had found himself being organized. "Give me the key," Lois had said, "and Jamie and me'll lock up. You get going. Get your car and follow the ambulance. We'll take care of the rest. You can ring me if you want—let me know what's happening."

Mrs. T-J, coming into her own, had ordered lesser sopranos and altos to pack up their books and get along home. Bill, objecting to being bossed around by a tiresome old woman, had dug in his toes. "I'll stay, and Rebecca, and help Lois," he'd said firmly. "Goodnight, Mrs. Tollervey-Jones. Mind how you go. That broken paving is lethal." He'd bitten his tongue. Not the most tactful thing to say, when the apparently lifeless body of the choirmaster had just been stretchered out of the church.

Now a young nurse appeared at Brian's side. "Would you like a cup of tea, Rev. Rollinson? Perhaps you should have a break. There's really nothing you can do. We've got a machine in the corridor. Tea or coffee. Or hot chocolate, but that tastes of gravy!" She smiled gently, but realized that she was not getting through to the ravaged-looking parson huddled on an uncomfortable chair, tears streaming down his cheeks.

IN THE WARM, BREAKFAST-SMELLING KITCHEN, GRAN was busy with her frying pan. She had woken early, feeling much stronger, and decided things were back to normal . . . for her, anyway. That poor young Sandy was another matter. Lois would be down soon, telling her off for doing too much, and then perhaps there'd be more news. By the time Lois and Jamie had returned from the church last night, Gran had already gone up to bed. Derek had been snoring in front of the television. Lois always nudged him awake, but Gran hadn't the energy. She had made a hot drink and retired to bed with a book. Half an hour later, hearing raised voices, she had gone out on to the landing and listened. Lois and Jamie were both talking at once, and Derek was trying to calm them down. Then she heard her own name mentioned, and decided to find out what was up.

"Mum!" Lois had looked at her anxiously. "How are you feeling? No worse?"

Then they'd told her what had happened to Sandy, and she had reassured them that *she* was not about to collapse.

Lois now appeared in the kitchen, and Gran put up her hand in self-defence. "Before you start," she said, "I'm feeling fine. Never felt better. And the best thing you can do is sit down and have some of this delicious bacon I got in Tresham. Better than that stuff of the Carrs. Sometimes I wonder how long things are hanging around at the back of that shop."

"Yes, well," said Lois, sitting down reluctantly. She ate her breakfast without speaking, and then suddenly looked up at her mother. "Here Mum, you know what you just said?"

"What?" said Gran, pushing two slices of brown bread into the toaster. "What did I just say?"

"About the shop," said Lois. "You know, about stuff hanging around. Do you reckon it does? Past its sell-by date an' that?"

Gran shrugged. "Dunno," she said. "Wouldn't be legal, would it?"

"No, but they're a dozy old couple now. Not everybody notices the sell-by date, you know."

Well, I certainly don't, thought Gran. She was too old a dog to learn new tricks, and had never bothered with checking what she bought. Besides, those sell-by dates were nonsense. All her life she'd relied on common sense to tell her when stuff was going off and ready for the bin. She didn't need some stupid date mark to know when the green mould round the top of the jam meant it was time to chuck it out.

"Anyway," she said, "why d'you want to know? You buy all our food from the supermarket, so it doesn't matter, does it?"

"Well, no, not to us," Lois said slowly. "But that poor bugger last night looked very much to me like he'd been poisoned by something. And the doctor never said exactly what was wrong with you, did he. Food poisoning can be serious. Are you sure you've not had anything from the shop and not said?"

"It's not a crime to buy from the village shop!" said Gran crossly. "I don't need to confess to you every time I get meself an apple on the way home. Anyway, I've not bought any food on the quiet at all. What I had was a bug, plain as plain." Her offended look brought an end to the conversation, but when Lois sat in her office, juggling with her cleaners' duties, the thought niggled away at the back of her mind. Where had Gran caught the bug? And why had nobody else around except Sandy Mackerras had it? Usually these stomach bugs spread like wildfire.

She stood at the window, looking out at the sombre morning, and saw a familiar car pull up outside. Black with darkened windows. Anonymous and threatening, if you had any reason to fear the fuzz. It was Cowgill, she realized, her old friend and adversary. Chief Detective Inspector Hunter Cowgill of the Tresham police had lowered his window to look out at her house. She ducked out of sight, but not soon enough. He beckoned. She shook her head and turned away, her colour rising. It had been so long since they'd been in touch, and life had been peaceful and uneventful. And boring? She went to the front door, opened it and went down the path to the road. Cowgill was standing by his car, smiling now.

"And how are you, Lois?" he said, noticing her pink cheeks, and thinking that she hadn't changed a bit. Still his Lois. That was how he liked to think of her, though she'd never given him cause to cherish that claim. The reverse was true, he thought ruefully.

"I'm fine," she said. "What d'you want?"

"And very nice to see you again, too," he said mildly. She frowned. "Listen," she said, "if I'm seen talking to a policeman outside my own house, everybody will know there's something up . . . again. Is this just a social call, or do you want my help?"

"I want your help," said Cowgill. "You're quite right, Lois. Meet me at Alibone Woods, same place, at two this afternoon. Can you make it?"

There was a pause as Lois tried to come to a decision. It was not an easy one. Back in business with Cowgill meant hours of ferreting, treating everything she heard with suspicion, editing much of it to tell Derek, and at times fearing for her own safety and that of the family.

"I'll be there," she said finally.

Cowgill resisted the impulse to crush her in his arms, and got back in the car. He drove off at speed without another word.

Gran was waiting in the hall. "Was that that policeman?" she said sharply.

"What policeman?" said Lois, and disappeared quickly into her office.

AT TWELVE NOON, BRIAN ROLLINSON STOOD UP. HE rubbed his eyes and sighed deeply. He might as well go home. The doctor had been round again, and said that it was looking very much like an allergic reaction to something as yet unknown, and there was no need to worry now. Sandy's mother would be arriving soon, and Brian could not face her yet. He walked slowly out into the corridor and paused outside the door to say the necessary thanks to the gentle young nurse. He stopped suddenly, mid-sentence. They looked at each other, eyes wide. Then both turned and went back swiftly into the room.

A noise. There had definitely been a noise.

In the hospital bed, connected up to a tangle of tubes, Sandy Mackerras groaned again, and opened his eyes.

Sixteen

❧

"THAT YOUNG MACKERRAS, 'E WERE POISONED, y'know. Ole Willy Mellish all over again." Cyril was pensive, looking sorrowfully at the worn gravestone.

Lois sighed. She had taken a short cut through the churchyard in order to get home quickly and then be on time for Cowgill later, and had hoped to avoid the old man. But Cyril was wily. He'd seen her coming, and kept out of sight in the church porch until she was close. Then he had popped out like an arthritic jack-in-the-box and blocked her path.

"Nobody's said it was poison, Cyril," she said, "and as for being the same as the Mellishes, Sandy Mackerras isn't even married, so his wife couldn't have done the deed!" Maybe I'll be old and lonely one day, she thought to herself. I can spare a few minutes to talk to the old bugger.

"Don't need t'be married these days. All sorts set up house together . . . includin' them at the vicarage," he replied darkly.

Lois thought it best to steer him clear of that one. "Well,

what about my mum, then?" she said. "She had the same bug, as you know. We didn't poison *her*," she added with a smile. "We rely on my mum to keep us goin'."

"'Ow come nobody else's had it?" Cyril pronounced his trump card with glee.

"Yeah, well . . ." Lois was stumped for a moment. He was no fool, old Cyril. "Anyway," she continued firmly, "this is silly gossip, and we shouldn't encourage it. The lad's lucky to be alive, from what I hear, and now he's comin' home, and Mum is back on form, and so we should forget it, I reckon."

Lois would not forget it, of course. Was Cowgill concerned? But surely he couldn't have been alerted for what was either a very nasty bug or a case of food poisoning. Lowly stuff for him, surely. Mum was sure it was a bug. Sandy would have an answer, probably, and Lois meant to find out what it was in due course.

"You can forget it if you like, missus," Cyril said huffily. "There's none s'blind as those who won't see," he added enigmatically, turning his back on her and disappearing into the church.

Now what did he mean by that? Lois tried to dismiss the whole conversation as she hurried on, but wondered if Cyril was on to something. She'd learned from experience that the old people in the village knew everything that went on. They had time to notice things, and at whist drives and Darby and Joan club, gossip was exchanged and chewed over. She resolved to have another talk with Cyril, when she had time.

GRAN WAS IRONING WHEN LOIS CAME INTO THE kitchen. She was singing softly under her breath, and Lois recognized the tune from her childhood. *"Dashing away with a smoothing iron, she stole my ha-art away"* warbled Gran.

"Oh my God," said Lois in mock horror, "you must be feelin' better. I remember Dad said you had a voice like a nightingale with a sore throat."

"You're not the only one who can sing," said Gran defensively. "Sandy was very complimentary about my voice in the choir. Which reminds me," she added, "are you going to join?" She hoped privately Lois would say yes. She was sure it had been Cowgill in his car earlier, and strongly disapproved of Lois renewing contact. Singing in the choir was a lovely thing to do. Every time she went, she felt cheered up, and it could do that for Lois too. She needed something outside New Brooms and the family.

"I might," said Lois casually. "We'll have to see, when Sandy gets better. He's coming home today. I shall drop in when I come back from Tresham and see if they want a cleaner to go this week. If he's feeling weak and wobbly he might not want hoovering and raising dust."

"What're you going to Tresham for? It's not shopping day." Gran knew that expression on Lois's face. Secretive. Ominous.

"Just got to see a possible client," Lois replied. "Now, I'll get a sandwich and be off. You make sure you get something hot after you've finished dashing away with a smoothing iron. And, by the way, Cyril asked after you tenderly, very tenderly, so just watch he don't steal *your* heart away."

"That's quite enough of that, Lois Meade," snapped her mother. Her face crumpled for a second or two, and Lois remembered with a pang of remorse her father, and how much her mother must miss him.

ALIBONE WOODS WERE DAMP AND DARK. LOIS PARKED off the road in the usual place. She hadn't done this for several years, and was half-expecting the track to be overgrown and inaccessible. Not many people walked in these woods, and the footpaths had become a tangled mass of brambles that tore at her clothes as she squelched her way through mud and puddles to the meeting place. The broad, mossy stump of a felled oak tree came into view, and she saw Cowgill standing motionless, staring in the opposite direction. He looked round quickly as she approached, and then smiled.

"Good afternoon, Lois," he said with his usual punctiliousness.

"Hi," said Lois. "What d'you want?"

"Don't you ever observe the social niceties?" he said sadly, knowing he invited a smart put-down.

"God knows," said Lois. "Maybe I would, if I knew what you were talking about."

It was not worth pursuing. "Never mind," he said, "and thanks for coming, anyway. I'm glad to see you looking so well, and not a day older, if I may say so."

Lois laughed. "All right, all right," she said. She knew she should tell him to get lost, but she was curious. He explained then, and she listened carefully. It was unpleasant, if not sinister, and with all the potential of something very nasty. In various places around the country, reports of black magic, voodoo, and corrupted versions of the dark arts had surfaced. Now it was close to home. "Nothing really violent, yet. But in Tresham it seems closely associated with racism," Cowgill said. "Harassment is common, and now there are rumours of pointy hats and fiery crosses."

"Ku Klux Klan?" said Lois sceptically. "You bin seein' too many American films."

Cowgill shook his head. "No, I'm quite serious, Lois," he said. "The black and Asian communities are scared. And when people are scared, they match violence with violence."

Lois shook her head. "But why me? There's only one black family in Long Farnden, and they're completely accepted. Their kids go to the local school, he's a pillar of the church."

Cowgill smiled wryly. "An exception to the rule, Lois. No, the reason I'm talking to you is a report I've had of local undesirables, quite a mixed bunch, who are meeting regularly and targeting a particular victim. At the moment, it's mostly threats, and they make sure the victim is too scared to shop them." Lois stared at him in disbelief. "And before you deny any knowledge," he said, "one name that's come up as being associated with them is your Jamie's new girlfriend, the aristocratic Annabelle Tollervey-Jones."

"What!?"

"Not your Jamie, I hasten to say. Annabelle T-J has other friends, friends of her own class and a very unpleasant lot they are."

Lois frowned. "Haven't met her yet," she said, "but Mum says she's a nice enough girl."

"Maybe so," said Cowgill. "Anyway, you are perfectly placed to keep your ear to the ground. Brief young Jamie, if you like, in a casual way. We need to nip this in the bud before real harm is done."

Lois had no intention of involving any member of her family in any of this, and she told Cowgill sharply that he'd better try some other snout. he reassured her quickly that she need not even mention it to Jamie, if that was what she wanted. If she would just keep her own ear to the ground, he was sure that would be extremely useful. "We need you, Lois," he said.

"Oh, all right," said Lois. "Though I can't see much coming my way. Do I still get you on the same number?" He nodded, and put out his hand. She looked at it tentatively, and then shook it, feeling an unexpected warmth in his dry palm. "Can I ask you something?" she said.

He opened his eyes wide, and said, "You've never hesitated before."

"Do you know anything about poisons?" Lois looked at him intently.

"Of course I do," he said. "A policeman's lot is a very broad one, you know. Poisons we know about. Why do you ask?"

"Oh, no reason. Just curiosity." Lois could see no sign of special interest in her question, and decided he had had no ulterior motive for meeting, other than this black magic rubbish.

"I'll be hearing from you, then," he said. He dared to rest his hand on her shoulder for a second or two, and said, "Change your shoes when you get home—you feet will be sopping wet. Bring boots next time." He tried hard to keep his voice light and unconcerned, but he knew he'd failed when he saw Lois grinning.

"Who says there'll be a next time?" she said, as the footpath divided and they parted company.

SEVENTEEN

꩜

THE SOFA IN THE VICARAGE WAS NOT REALLY LONG enough for Sandy. He was half-sitting, half-reclining, and had a crick in his neck.

"Brian!" he yelled, and smiled as the vicar came running anxiously into the room. "Relax, relax," Sandy said. "Just give me a hand, will you? This ruddy sofa is doing me more harm than good. I'd be better in that big armchair of yours."

"Oh dear, well, I'm not sure. The doctor said—"

"Never mind what that idiot said. Here, pull me up." A tottering Sandy made it to the armchair, and slumped down, breathing hard. "Blimey, that was some bug or whatever! Thanks, anyway." Maybe he should cut down on the booze for a while. He'd had a fair bit of belly-ache lately, and the usual remedies hadn't worked.

He looked at Brian, and felt an unaccustomed pang of compassion for his companion. Brian had lost weight and looked more cadaverous than ever. If it hadn't been for this illness, Sandy had hoped to be out of the vicarage by now.

He hadn't told Brian, but a flat had come up in the better suburbs of Tresham, just right for him. Ground floor, with a patio for barbecues in the summer. Two bedrooms, all mod cons of a decent standard. He could afford it, and looked forward with excitement to being independent. Would he keep on with the church choir? He'd thought a lot about it in his hours of inaction, and decided he would. One or two promising things developing there, mainly concerning the lovely Rebecca Rogers. It amused him to annoy Bill Stockbridge, to see that he was not enjoying singing hymns nor being teased about it in the pub. Being a housemaid was enough! But Sandy knew why Bill kept coming to practices. Keeping an eye on his beloved . . .

The telephone rang in the hall, and he heard Brian answer. "Hello, Mrs. Meade . . . Yes, he's doing very nicely, thank you . . . How kind of you to think of checking, but I'm sure we'd be glad to have a good clean-up today. Sharon Miller? Late afternoon? Yes, that will be fine. I have a sermon to write, and shall have an incentive to finish it before she arrives! Yes, I had heard Sharon would be working for you now . . . Oh, certainly, a very pretty girl! Just what he needs? Well . . ." Brian's voice tailed off, and then he put down the receiver.

A couple of minutes later, the telephone rang again, and Sandy listened intently. Not Sharon cancelling, he hoped. But no, Brian said in his jolly voice, "Hello, Rebecca! How nice of you to call . . . Yes, he's doing very well . . . Difficult to keep him down, really!" Sandy's spirits began to rise. Could be an interesting afternoon. "Of course you can, my dear," continued Brian. "This afternoon? After school? Yes, I'm sure he'll be delighted to see you . . . No, he's got everything he needs. Just bring yourself! Goodbye for now, then."

When Brian came in to tell him about the call, Sandy had already perked up. "Right," he said. "No more of this

invalid stuff. I'm going to take a shower and a shave. Then
I'll get dressed and—"

"No, no, Sandy! You don't realize how ill you've been.
I promised to keep you quiet for several days yet. I shall
put off Rebecca if you won't listen to me. Your mother is
coming tomorrow, and what will she say if you're worse
instead of better?"

Sandy sighed. "Look, Brian." He was patient, making
an effort. "I know it was serious. Nearly snuffed it. But I'm
fine now, just a bit weak." He smiled his "this-is-your-
dream-home" smile. It usually worked. "You know,
surely," he continued, "that a cheery patient will get better
far quicker than a misery? Well, here I am, getting better
and with a lovely visitor this afternoon. Do me a power of
good. Please, Brian, give me a break."

BY THE TIME REBECCA KNOCKED AT THE DOOR, SANDY
was smartened up, and apart from a pallor in his cheeks
and a reluctance to stand up, he looked very much his old
self. "Mmm, chocolates!" he said. "Not allowed them yet,
but I'll save them up to make a pig of myself later on." He
turned to look at the hovering Brian. "Why don't you get
on with that sermon?" he suggested. "A good opportunity,
now Rebecca's here to keep me company."

Oh dear, thought Brian, and left the room. He just
hoped the excitement wouldn't be too much for the lad.
What excitement? he wondered. Rebecca was Bill's girlfriend—almost wife—and Sandy knew that perfectly well.
Sometimes Brian's affection for the lad was mixed with a
tinge of dislike. Sandy had his father's looks, but not much
of his character.

In the sitting room brightened with flowers from well-
wishers, Sandy looked across at Rebecca and liked what he
saw. Now that she was on her own, and had no reason to
challenge him, her expression was soft and concerned. Her

eyes were warm, and her mouth generous and bright. He was absorbed in imagining how wonderful it would be to . . . Wow! His colour rose, and she asked anxiously if he was OK. "Oh, yes," he said, "all the better for seeing you, my dear, as the old wolf said."

They talked desultorily about local people and the latest gossip at the pub, and how the choir was managing without him. He asked about Bill, and saw her face change. "He's fine," she said abruptly. She didn't add that Bill had no idea she was visiting Sandy, and would be far from pleased if he knew. At the one choir practice they'd had since Sandy's dramatic exit that chaotic night, Bill had been helpful, helping to choose suitable hymns and find alternative tunes. He'd located old choir robes in a dusty cupboard and pulled them out to be cleaned and used by new members. He had complimented a blushing Sharon on her organ playing, and handled Mrs. T-J with tact. Rebecca thought it best not to mention any of this, but said they'd all be really glad to see Sandy back.

"Why don't you take your coat off, Rebecca?" Sandy had had a tempting glimpse of a dress cut perhaps a little lower than was suitable for a schoolmistress. "It's warm in here," he added. "Brian's turned the heating up . . . killing me with kindness, and all that!"

Rebecca stood up and removed her coat. Sandy watched her, and said, "Oh, while you're up, could you pick up a book I dropped down here somewhere? I still feel dizzy if I bend down." It was a lie, of course. There was no book. But Rebecca obediently leaned over him and looked into the dark corner behind the chair.

"Gotcha!" he said with a laugh, and put his hands gently round her face. "You're beautiful," he said, and kissed her on her shining mouth.

Oh my God, what a plonker, Rebecca thought, but allowed herself to be kissed.

At this inopportune moment, a figure passed close by

the window, stopped and looked in, and then ran back down the path. Brian, standing at his bedroom window above, saw that it was Sharon Miller and that as she wrestled with the iron gate, she appeared to be in tears.

WHEN BRIAN ROLLINSON'S CALL CAME THROUGH, LOIS was in the bath. After a long afternoon of visits, checking that clients were satisfied with New Brooms' service, she had settled in to enjoy a soak before tea. Derek was home early, and when she heard the telephone ring, and then his footsteps on the stairs, she groaned. What now? Everything was in order, surely.

"Cor, any hot water left for me?" said Derek, handing her the telephone. She nodded, and indicated he should wait. "Hello? Oh yes, vicar. Nothing wrong, I hope?" As Derek watched, he saw her frown, then an expression of irritation flicker across her face. "Leave it with me," she said. "I'll find out what happened and get back to you. It's probably too late to send anyone else now, but you shall have an extra half hour tomorrow morning to make up for the inconvenience. So sorry. Bye."

Derek raised his eyebrows. "What's up?"

"That stupid girl! Her first job on her own, and she ducked out of it. Got as far as the vicarage, and then turned tail and ran! What on earth's the matter with her? No, don't answer that. You said I shouldn't take her on. Well, you might be right. Anyway . . ." She stood up, foamy water streaming down over her wonderfully soapy body. It was too much for Derek, and as a result, by the time Lois made an angry call to the Miller home, Sharon had gone to bed, saying she had a migraine and must be left alone.

"I'm going round there now," Lois said, dressed and refreshed. "She'll have more than a migraine when I've finished with her. Shan't be long, Mum," she added. "Back shortly with any luck." Gran protested that surely it could wait until tomorrow, but her words fell on deaf ears.

Walking quickly along the path to the Millers' house, Lois saw a car pulling away from the vicarage. The light was going fast, but she could just see it was a girl driving. The girl waved, and Lois was almost sure it was Bill's Rebecca. Yes, it was her car, no doubt about it. What had she been doing at the vicarage? Not too difficult, that one. Visiting the sick. Lois had not missed the signs at choir practice. Sandy looked very often at Rebecca, smiled especially for her, and complimented her on solos he'd asked her to sing. Lois had noticed Bill's angry expression and wondered if trouble was brewing. Now it looked more than possible. Silly girl! Bill was worth six times that bouncy little . . . little . . . Lois waved back, and hurried on.

Eighteen

❧

It was past midday when Marion Mackerras's neat little Peugeot drew up outside Long Farnden vicarage. Brian was standing by the window, concealed by a curtain, and saw with a sinking heart that it was a good five minutes before she opened the car door and got out. Priming her guns, no doubt.

"Your mother's here," he said, turning to Sandy, who was lounging on the sofa reading the property pages of the local paper.

"Do you think I should act pale and interesting, or big, strong and quite recovered?"

Brian shook his head. "Try to be serious, Sandy," he said. "Your mother has been extremely worried."

"Not enough to come and see me in hospital!"

"For a very good reason," Brian said sharply. "She has had a bad cold, and would not be allowed to carry infection. She relied on me to keep her informed."

"Huh!" Sandy clearly did not believe him, and the air

was still full of tension when Brian opened the front door and stood aside for Marion to walk in.

She nodded a brief greeting. "Brian," she said. "How is he?"

"Come through and see for yourself, Marion. He's doing very well indeed." Brian despised himself for his humble, apologetic tone. But Marion hardly looked at him, and passed on swiftly into the sitting room.

"Hi, Mother," Sandy said, "how's the cold?"

Excusing himself tactfully, Brian retreated to his study to the impossible task of studying his text for next Sunday. It seemed hours before the sitting-room door opened again, and he rushed out into the hall to offer refreshment. Sandy was on his feet, unsmiling, and Brian quickly offered tea or coffee, followed by an "Or I could rustle up a glass of wine?"

Marion shook her head, buttoning up her coat. "I have to get back," she said. "Now I can see for myself that Sandy's on the mend, I shall be able to sleep again." She gave him a hug, and turned to Brian.

"Please keep me informed," she said coldly, "if there's any cause for worry. Anything at all."

"I assure you, Marion," Brian began, but was interrupted.

"Never mind about all that," she said. "All I care about now is that Sandy is safe and well, and settled in a job he enjoys."

Sandy muttered, "I am still here, you know. Not in a coma any more. And I'm quite capable of looking after myself and living my own life." Marion's persistent questions on Brian's household were beginning to irritate him. He knew he had been planted by his mother on Brian Rollinson, and was fed up with reporting back on life at the vicarage. And now she had done all the talking, telling him things that had stunned him into silence.

"Well, nice of you to come, Mum," he said slowly. "I'll try to visit soon. Maybe bring a friend . . ."

Marion turned sharply. "What friend?" she said.

"Don't worry, it'll be a girlfriend. One of many, naturally."

"I'm very glad to hear it," she said, and drove off down Long Farnden main street on her way home.

"She's gone," Sandy said flatly.

Brian slumped down into the big chair and closed his eyes. "I wish she could have stayed," he said. His voice was so low that Sandy could scarcely hear him.

"What was that?" he said.

"Nothing, nothing at all." Brian straightened up with an effort. "And what's the matter with you, anyway? You don't look overjoyed at your mother's visit."

Sandy shook his head. "I'm all right," he said. "I think I'll go down to the pub for a while. The walk'll do me good. Sun's shining. I'll get something to eat."

"Don't be ridiculous!" Brian was shocked and anxious.

"I'm serious," said Sandy, and walked towards the door.

"Then I'm coming with you," said Brian, and followed behind a furious Sandy until they reached the pub.

DEREK WATCHED THEM WALK IN FROM HIS STOOL AT THE bar. "Morning, Vicar," he said. He looked curiously at the pair. It was the first time he'd seen them together, and in view of rumours still flying about, thought he would—without staring—see what he could pick up from how they were together. Might help Lois to get the right cleaner for them. That Sharon was obviously useless. What had reduced her to tears? The thought of working for a couple of blokes living together? But there'd been stories of Mackerras giving her lifts, having a date or two. Confusing. Well, he had warned Lois about the girl, and now she would have to sort it out.

The landlord's greeting was muted. He secretly wished

this new vicar wouldn't come in so often. It wasn't that he minded him having only a half of shandy, or that he insisted on standing at the bar instead of going to sit decently in a corner. It was just that the purest white dog-collar was inhibiting to his other customers. "Difficult to have a good curse, with 'im watching yer," old Cyril had said, and his viewpoint was echoed by other regulars. "So what can I do?" said the landlord. "Ban him from the pub? I can just see the headlines: 'Vicar banned from village pub—bad for trade, says landlord.' No, we'll just have to hope he gets fed up with it. He's not a real drinker, anyone can see that."

Today Brian Rollinson surprised him. "A large whisky and water, please," he said, "and what are you having, Sandy?"

Sandy glared at him, then shrugged and said, "Oh, well, if we're celebrating something, I'll have a Bacardi Breezer."

"A what?" Brian raised his eyebrows.

"It's the latest, Vicar," said the landlord, and gave them their drinks. They ordered food, and were told to sit at a table—the corner one—where the sandwiches would be brought to them.

"Quite happy here, thanks," said Brian, looking round. It was easier to be one of the crowd, sitting on a stool at the hub of the drinkers. Breaking down barriers, and all that.

"Come on, Brian," said Sandy, carrying their drinks to the corner table. "You're better out of the way, wearing that badge of office. Instant blight on the conversation. Anyway, I've got something to tell you." He had decided it was a good moment, and the sooner said the better. But here, in a public place, he was going to have to be tactful. Put on a good act.

"It's not that I'm not extremely grateful for what you've done for me," he began, "but the truth is that we don't hit it off too well together, do we?" He managed a rueful, self-blaming smile, and saw the dawning of a new anxiety in Brian's face.

"So I've done something about it, Brian," he continued. "There's this really promising flat in Tresham. A bit shabby, but in a good area. It's all settled, and I can move in more or less straightaway. Or after I've done some refurbishing, anyway." He took a deep breath and waited.

Brian passed a hand across his eyes and took a gulp of whisky. "A *fait accompli* then?" he said after a long pause. He knew it was part of the plan, but hadn't expected it so soon. "No consultation, no discussion, no request for guidance?"

Sandy shook his head and frowned. "Brian," he said firmly, "I am twenty-five years old, I have been working for my living for five years, and many of my friends are married with children. They make decisions on their own every day of the week. I have made some good friends around here. Some are even socially acceptable—entertained at the Hall—which should please you and Mother. As I said, I am more than grateful for your hospitality. I know what it has cost you, and I'm sorry for that. And," he said, making a huge effort to suggest the last thing he wanted, "I hope you'll give me a hand in choosing things for the flat . . . You've got really good taste. . . ."

At this, Brian Rollinson stood up. He barked out a mirthless laugh that caused heads to turn. "Good taste?" he said loudly. "Good taste in what? Curtains? Furniture? Pretty things for the sitting room? Certainly not in friends, apparently. Not in companions to keep the lonely hours at bay. No, Sandy," he continued, "I shall not help you choose. You can wash your hands of me, as has everyone else."

He shrugged on his coat, buttoned it up crookedly, and in total silence walked swiftly out of the pub.

Derek, sitting quietly nearby, finished his ploughman's

and stood up. He walked over to a miserable-looking Sandy Mackerras and said, "Mind if I join you, lad?"

Sandy shrugged. "Suit yourself," he said. "I'm having another—what can I get you?" The pub returned to its hubbub of conversation, and Sandy made his way back from the bar with their drinks. Derek settled in his chair and prepared to listen.

Nineteen

ॐ

"So what did *you* say?" Lois had just greeted Derek and heard some of what had gone on in the pub. She was still simmering about the Millers, and was only half listening. Sharon's parents had refused to let her see Sharon the previous evening, saying she was in bed and poorly. The silly girl! Just because she had a wandering eye, they'd made a fool of her, spoilt her rotten. No sense of responsibility. How had she managed in the shop? But then, the old couple had no children of their own and had made things worse, making her think she was something special.

"Say about what?" Derek was patient, waiting for Lois to come to the point.

"You know, Derek. When Sandy told you about the vicar and his mother . . . about them not getting on and all that. What did you say?"

"Oh, right, yeah. Well, I said all families were difficult at times. Told him about Gran livin' with us and it sometimes bein' a bit tricky. Said we'd all got to try a bit harder when things got difficult. That kind of stuff."

"But did he tell you *why* they didn't get on?" Lois wasn't sure why she felt so curious. After all, it was someone else's family business, nothing to do with her. And Sandy's illness had nothing to do with witchcraft or poisoning. Well, nothing to do with witchcraft, anyway? It was just . . . it didn't smell right. There was something about Brian Rollinson. He was outwardly friendly enough, but only up to a point. Then the shutters came down. Still, Lois reflected, all vicars were a bit like that. She supposed it was part of their training, like doctors and teachers, not to get too personally involved.

"Nope, he didn't say any more about them," Derek replied. "Just said they hardly spoke when she came to see him. The lad was really upset about something. Course, we all heard what Rollinson said when he stalked out. About everybody bein' against him. Anyway, me duck," he added briskly, "I just thought it might be useful info for you, deciding who you're goin' to send in there."

"Very kind," said Lois. "I might send Sheila in. Nice, motherly woman. And she's a good listener."

Derek looked at her suspiciously. "What're you up to?" he said. "Why d'you want a good listener at the vicarage?"

"No reason," Lois said hastily. "Just thought she might be a comfort to the vicar when Sandy moves out. You know, in case he feels lonely. He hasn't really made any friends in the village, has he."

"Give him a chance," said Derek. "He'll want to be up there with the nobs, I expect. Creepin' to Mrs. T-J. Which reminds me," he added, "Jamie rang. Said could he bring Annabelle to tea on Saturday, before they go to a film. I said he'd have to ask you."

Gran had come in during this last sentence, and said chirpily, "Of course he can, can't he, Lois? This is his home. Tell him yes, straightaway."

Remembering the ear she was supposed to be keeping to the ground, Lois agreed. "Don't go killing the fatted calf, Mum," she said. "It'll embarrass them."

Gran bridled. "I suppose I'm allowed to make a cake for them? Is that all right? Or shall we just have bread and scrape?"

Derek could see trouble brewing, and decided to change the subject. But just as he began to describe his latest job over in Ringford, there was a tentative knock on the front door.

"I'll go," said Lois. She had an idea who it might be, and was right.

"Um . . . hello, Mrs. Meade." It was Sharon, in the pink of health, but nervous.

"Ah, Sharon. Come in. Go in there, in my office." Lois followed her in and shut the door. She motioned Sharon to a chair and sat down herself behind her desk. "Right," she said. "Explain."

"I'm really sorry about yesterday. It's these migraines, you see," the girl began. "They come on very sudden, and then I'm often sick, and can't see very well. Only one thing to do then. Go to bed in a dark room and take a pill. Even that doesn't work sometimes. Anyway, I'm usually all right next day."

"Mmm," said Lois. "Sounds bad." She tried to look sympathetic, but couldn't help thinking Sharon sounded as if she'd got all that from a medical dictionary. Still, why should the girl lie?

"Why didn't you tell me this before?" Lois said in an even voice. "And how often do you have these attacks? Our clients rely on us turning up, and if you really don't know when they're coming on, it's going to be difficult."

"Oh, not very often! Luckily for me . . ." Sharon laughed, and then immediately stopped when she saw Lois's unsmiling face. "And sometimes I do get a warning . . . flashing lights an' that. If I take a pill then, I can sometimes stave it off. Anyway, Mrs. M, it isn't more than three or four times a year."

"Right," said Lois. She looked down at her revised schedules. "I'd like you to start with Mrs. Jordan on the new estate—"

"Oh, please!" interrupted Sharon, "can't I carry on at the vicarage? I'd really like to do that, and Rev. Rollinson said how much he was looking forward to me goin' there. An' what with Hazel expectin' the baby an' that, I thought . . ."

"You can safely leave the organizing to me, Sharon," Lois said acidly. She continued, "Well, I suppose you can have one more chance, if the vicar agrees." It might be useful, after all, to have Sharon at the vicarage, lovesick as she was. If Sandy was in with the Tollervey-Jones lot, archgossip Sharon might well pick up something about the followers of the Prince of Darkness. It was worth another try.

"Now, how about the shop?" Lois changed the subject. "Have you sorted that out, reduced hours an' that?"

Sharon nodded. "Oh yes. I'd like to work for you fulltime, but I can't let them down altogether. They've been kind to me, and it's all a bit beyond them now. I'm going in on Saturdays, and now and then during the week. I promised to tidy out that old store at the back. You should see it! Stuff in there from the year dot."

Lois sighed. "Just remember, Sharon," she said, "our rule about confidentiality. If you hear anything that worries you while you're cleaning, come straight to me. That clear?"

A huffy Sharon left the house and walked quickly down the garden path. Lois watched from the window, and saw Jamie draw up on his newly acquired motorbike. He took off his helmet proudly and smiled at Sharon. She saw them talking amiably before Sharon finally walked off.

Lois was about to see if Gran had heard any mention of

Sharon's migraines, when Jamie came into the kitchen and gave her a hug. "Hi, Mum. You OK?"

"Fine, thanks. Now, let's hear some more about Annabelle coming to tea on Saturday. What's the film, and can I come too?"

"Ha ha. No you can't, and it's a spooky film about the devil and black magic and that kind of stuff."

"Not for me then," said Lois, grinning. "Anyway, why don't you and Annabelle come a bit earlier, and we can have a good chat. Get to know her . . ."

Jamie frowned. What was his mother up to? All this good chat stuff was not like her at all. He shrugged. "Yeah, well, let's not get too heavy. Just make sure Gran bakes us a cake, then it'll be fine."

Gran's smile of triumph lit up the room.

TWENTY

As Cyril walked slowly up the road on his way to unlock the church for choir practice, he slid on a patch of slimy leaves, swore and shivered. It was quite dark, and the one light in the village street—a dim, low-wattage lantern outside the shop—lit up only a small circle on the pavement. A cold wind blew through Cyril's coat and chilled his old bones. He'd be glad to get home again by his fire. A load of good logs had arrived yesterday by tractor from the Hall. Say what you like about Mrs. T-J, he thought, as he opened the gate into the churchyard, she looked after them that were needy in the village. He'd offered to pay last winter, but she'd looked down her long nose and said, "I hope I know my Christian duty, Cyril. Those who have, should give to those who have not."

Cyril had not been too pleased at being thought of as an object of charity, but his countryman's instinct for prudence and common sense came to the fore, and he had thanked her kindly, touching an invisible forelock. He plodded up the path to the church, needing no light. He could have done it blindfold. He'd been verger for years, and his father before him. The church was an old friend, and he had no fear of the damp, cold interior which took hours to warm up, even with the heaters on full blast.

As he approached the porch, a shadowy movement down by the tower caught his eye. Vandals? There had been quite a spate of it in the village lately, and the Neighbourhood Watch had asked everybody to be on the lookout.

Cyril stepped on to the wet grass and made his way round to the back of the church, where broken tombs and headstones lurked in the undergrowth of untrimmed bushes and shrubs. No buildings overlooked this part of the churchyard, and nobody bothered with it. He realized with surprise that a flickering light eased his path. He began to walk forward, and then stopped dead. Gawd Almighty! Yards away from him a group of people, cloaked from head to foot in light-coloured robes, faced a single, much taller figure, who held aloft a pole, surmounted by a cross. It was a large cross, outlined against the dark sky and burning with a fierce Satanic fire.

Cyril gasped, and they heard him. He began to run, but twisted his ankle, and collapsed on to the grass. "Hey! You there!" He watched helplessly as they fled, leaving the fiery cross burning in the long grass.

Cyril attempted to get up, but the pain was bad. He tried calling out until he was hoarse, then fell back into the grass. After a while, he began to shiver as the damp cold penetrated his clothes. He tried again: "Help! Anybody there? Help! Round here!"

"Cyril! Where are you?"

Oh, thank God. It was Mrs. Meade, arriving on time as usual. "Here, missus!" he shouted, and in a few seconds Lois had found him. "Cyril! What on earth's been going on?" Then she looked past him and saw the fire still sputtering in the long grass.

"What the . . . Oh, Cyril, it's a cross!" Lois shuddered.

She took a step forward, but could not go any nearer. She stood transfixed in front of the burning image. Then she remembered the old man. First things first. She got him to hold on to her, and managed to help him round to the church door. Two narrow benches stretched either side of the porch, and she sat him down carefully. "Give me the key," she said. "I'll open up and put the heaters on, then we'll take you home. And I'll get Derek," she continued with sudden relief. Derek would know what to do.

They half-carried Cyril home, got him upstairs and into his bedroom. He firmly refused all help to get into bed, and said he would be fine. He had only wrenched his ankle. He'd see how it was in the morning, and get help if necessary. Lois and Derek returned to the church, and found other choir members looking down at the cross, now smouldering in the wet grass.

"That's nasty, gel," Derek said. "Very nasty." He bent down and gingerly picked up one end of the cross.

"Careful!" Lois said. "You'll burn yourself!" Or something worse, she said to herself.

Jamie, standing by his father's side, echoed her thoughts. "That's evil, Dad," he said, and shivered.

"Don't talk rubbish," said Derek. "Some kids muckin' about, that's all. Still, could have caused a real fire. Did Cyril see who they were?" he asked, turning to Lois.

"Nope," she replied. "He said they were all covered up, even their heads. What're you going to do with it?"

The rest of the choir stood by, watching silently as Derek moved the cross upright. Mrs. T-J came forward, ready to take charge. "I think you can leave this to me, Mr. Meade," she said. "Just lean it up against that gravestone, and I'll have someone deal with it in the morning."

"Oh no you don't," muttered Lois. She put a hand on Derek's shoulder. "You take it away, love," she said quietly. "Never know who might come back to collect it. Look there . . ." She pointed to the ashy mark on the ground. The grass had been burned into an unmistakable image of a cross. "That'll be enough for the police," she said.

Sandy Mackerras, who had been strangely quiet, now spoke in a voice of authority. "Come on, then, choir," he said. "Back to the church. Time to sing, and frighten the shadows away."

"Time for exorcism, don't you mean?" said Bill Stockbridge coldly.

Rebecca grabbed his hand. "Don't be silly, Bill," she whispered. "You heard what Derek said. Just kids, mucking about."

But Mrs. T-J, on reaching the church porch, stopped and turned to Sandy. "I think I must be on my way," she said distantly. "Enough time wasted already. I have a great deal to do, you know. If I were you, I should cancel tonight's practice."

There were murmurings of dissent, and Sandy said jauntily, "No, not at all! We won't let a few stupid kids mess us about, will we, choir? Sorry you can't stay, though," he added quickly. "See you next week, I hope."

Watching Mrs. T-J walk with hurried steps down the church path, Lois's thoughts were churning. She took out of her pocket a small screwed-up square of soft cotton she had picked up by the burning cross. Under the porch light she straightened it out and saw a letter embroidered in the corner. It was *A. A* for Annabelle?

"Sorry, Sandy," she said swiftly, "I think I'd better go and check on old Cyril, make sure he's done what he's told. I'll be here next week. Bye all." She slipped away and found Mrs. T-J at the church gate remonstrating with Derek, who had shoved the cross into the back of his van. "This is really unnecessary, Mr. Meade," she said, and Lois grinned to herself. Derek didn't take kindly to that kind of talk.

"Maybe," he said flatly. "But we'll let the police decide

that, shall we? Goodnight, Mrs. Tollervey-Jones. Are you comin' with me, Lois?" he added.

She shook her head. "I'll just check on old Cyril, then I'll be back home." Derek drove off without another word, leaving Mrs. T-J standing uncertainly by her car.

Lois walked quickly down the street, and, turning into a farmyard entrance, stopped in the shadows and took out her mobile phone.

"Hello? Oh, good, it's you. Sorry to interrupt your evening."

"I'm working, Lois. A policeman's lot is not a happy one." But Cowgill sounded quite jolly, and Lois wondered if he had a bottle at his elbow. No, not Cowgill, she decided, and gave him an account of what had happened in the churchyard. His voice became serious at once, and Lois was glad she had telephoned.

"Mrs. T-J wanted to hush it up," she said. "Tried hard to persuade Derek not to do anything. I reckon she knows who they were." Lois was reluctant to tell him about the handkerchief. Suppose it was Annabelle's? What would that do to Jamie? On the other hand, did she want her son mixed up with that disgusting lot?

"You still there, Lois?"

"Yes, I am. There is just one other thing . . ." And she told him. "Keep it safe, Lois," he said. "I'll collect it next time we meet. I know it's difficult, with Jamie, but I'll be discreet." I'd do anything for you, Lois, he said to himself, except break the law. Bend it, maybe.

There were no lights in Cyril's house, and Lois relaxed. He'd gone to bed, as instructed, and she would see him early next morning, first thing, before he could go off gardening or some other stupid thing.

NEXT MORNING, LOIS HURRIEDLY ATE A BOWL OF CORN-flakes, pulled on her duffel coat and shouted to Gran that she'd be back shortly. She half-ran down the street to Cyril's house, knocked on the door and waited. No reply. He'd probably not heard, being more than a little deaf. She knocked again. Still no answer. She frowned. The curtains of his sitting room were open. He lived mostly at the back of the house, sitting by the old-fashioned range in the kitchen to keep warm. She peered in and could see through the open door. No sign of Cyril. Damn! Surely the old man had not got up and gone out already? She knew he was an early riser, but not with a sore ankle? She knocked once more, and hearing no movement inside, tried the door handle. To her surprise, it opened.

"Cyril?" She stood at the foot of the stairs, and repeated her call. "Are you OK, Cyril? It's Mrs. Meade here . . ."

The silence was not right. Her knocking and shouting would have woken him by now, even if he'd been deeply asleep. Her heart began to thud, and she climbed the stairs slowly, calling his name as she went, more to break the awful silence than in expectation of an answer.

It was dim on the landing. A grubby net curtain completely covered the small window overlooking the back garden, and in the half-darkness Lois tried to remember which of the closed doors was Cyril's bedroom. She was fairly sure it was at the front, and as she pushed open the door, the old story of Goldilocks and the three bears surfaced ridiculously in her head. "Who's been sleeping in *my* bed?" Well, she could see who was sleeping in this rumpled bed. It was old Cyril, half-hanging over the edge. But he wasn't sleeping. He was quite clearly dead.

Twenty-one

ஐ

The most difficult task that morning for Lois was keeping Gran away.

"But I wasn't very nice to him! He tried to chat me up, be friendly, and I was sharp and not very kind." Gran was almost in tears, and Lois forcibly restrained her from running out of the front door, down the street and into Cyril's house, where by some miraculous afterdeath delay, his spirit could accept her apology and she could rest easy.

It had been a gruesome morning. Cyril had not had a calm release from this life. Those who would tidy him and arrange the ritual of the dead could not get away with "he passed away peacefully in his sleep." There was vomit everywhere. He lay screwed up in a tight ball, his face showing the agony which must have preceded his poor old body giving up the struggle. Lois had thought first of cleaning him up, giving the whole place a New Brooms going over. But then she remembered that nothing must be touched.

After her telephone calls, first to the doctor and then to

Cowgill, the village constable arrived in the vanguard of all the rest. Then a procession of bland-faced professionals marched through Cyril's cottage and made their examinations, wrote their notes and took their pictures. Last of all came Hunter Cowgill, his expression grim and authoritative.

"Morning, Lois," he said quietly. "Don't say anything now. We'll meet later. They'll take your statement. Stick to the facts. Leave it to us now, we'll make all the arrangements."

She mentioned Gran, and said she'd better be getting back home. Cowgill nodded, and added *sotto voce*, "Ring me this afternoon."

With one last glance at the cruelly twisted body of old Cyril, Lois said a silent goodbye, and a "sorry" on behalf of Gran, and left the cottage, walking back home with misty eyes. She passed the churchyard, and on impulse went in. Without thinking, she made her way to the small gravestone with the poisoner and her gullible husband just visible. "She done 'im in"—Cyril's voice echoed in her head and Lois shuddered. Who or what done Cyril in? The stomach bug, was it?

IN THE SHOP, SHARON WATCHED AS THE PROCESSION ARrived, and then, in dribs and drabs, finally left. "What on earth's going on, Mrs. Carr?" she said. It was her morning on duty at the shop, and tomorrow she was due to clean at the vicarage, an assignment she was looking forward to with mixed feelings.

"Old Cyril has passed away," the shopkeeper said. "Poor old man had that rotten infection that's going about." News spreads fast in a village, and what the village shopkeeper doesn't know isn't worth knowing.

"Then why all the police and that lot?" Sharon frowned. From her diet of lurid library books, she knew that an old man dying of a bug did not need the police. Doctor, ambulance, undertakers, certainly. But the police? She shook her head. "Something funny going on there," she said.

But Mrs. Carr said that it could be a matter of course, when circumstances were unusual. After all, hadn't Cyril been perfectly all right the night before? Sharon agreed. She had seen him after all that palaver up at the church, and apart from twisting his ankle, he was fine. "Last thing I heard him say was to Mrs. Meade, telling her to 'get those young buggers who were messing up his churchyard.' She took him home, you know, saw that he was comfortable and told him to rest until she came round in the morning."

"Perhaps she should have got him to a doctor last night." Mrs. Carr put the final tin on a pyramid of baked beans.

Sharon nodded. "Maybe," she said. "But he weren't complaining of stomach ache then, as far as I know."

"He was prone to indigestion," said Mrs. Carr. "I do know that. Used to come in here for milk of magnesia and tablets. A martyr to his stomach, he used to say."

Sharon laughed, and then put a hand to her mouth. "Shouldn't speak ill of the dead, should we," she said anxiously. "But he was a crotchety old man sometimes. He got quite cross with me one day when I couldn't find the thing he wanted. Can't remember what it was, now, but he had me nearly in tears."

"Ah well, he's gone now. We'll miss him, plodding up and down to the church. The Reverend will have to find someone else to open up, and generally look after the place. Not so easy these days. Folk aren't much interested in religion."

"There's other things going on up there," said Sharon. "Not exactly religion, either! Last night, when we arrived for choir—"

The door bell jangled, and Derek Meade came in. "Morning," he said.

Sharon blushed. She remembered Mrs. M's strictures about gossiping and hoped Derek hadn't heard her beginning an account of the fiery cross. Anyway, she reassured herself, she wasn't on New Brooms' duty, so that wouldn't count.

"All sorted out over there?" Mrs. Carr was casual, distantly interested as was her usual tone. She had long ago discovered that she elicited more information that way. Never appear too keen.

"No good asking me," said Derek shortly. "Nothing to do with me. Just sorry for the poor old sod, that's all. I liked him. One of the old villagers. He had a good memory, and I reckon knew more about Farnden than anybody."

Mrs. Carr inclined her head gently. "God rest his soul," she said. "He'll be up there with all his relations soon. Generations of them, Sharon. That was the way in the old days. Families stuck together, went on living in the same place, helped each other through good times and bad. There was a time when the whole village was like one family." She perched her ample behind on a stool and sighed.

Oh no, here we go, tales of the good old days, thought Sharon, and looked at her watch. Soon be time to go home, thank goodness.

"Them days is gone," said Derek, pocketing his Polo mints. "But I reckon someone should've made notes of Cyril's stories. It was a world away from nowadays." Mrs. Carr chuckled. "Probably some things he knew were not fit to print!" she said. "Some of our respected parishioners might not have wanted old Cyril speaking out . . ." She tailed off, and in the silence that followed, both she and Derek reflected with alarm on what that could mean. But before more could be said, Sharon had looked at her watch again and went off to get her coat.

Derek walked briskly to the door. "Thanks," he said.

"It'll all come out in the wash, Mrs. Carr. Best not to go makin' too many guesses." He shut the door and was gone, well aware that nothing he said would stop the speculation rife in the village by midday.

LOIS WAS FINDING IT DIFFICULT TO CONCENTRATE. SHE sat in her office after a scratch lunch—Gran was too upset to cook—and stared at a printed leaflet from the tax office. More changes. Why couldn't they leave anything alone? Didn't she have enough to do, organizing her cleaners and keeping them happy, not to mention the clients, some of whom could be extremely hard to please? She stared at the small print, but all she could see was old Cyril, smiling up at her before she left him last night, assuring her he would be right as rain in the morning. "We got to find out about that cross, Mrs. M," he had said. "Could lead to worse." She had made him a cup of tea, and he'd told her that this was not the first sign of something nasty going on. "I was up there late one night, in summer, but nearly dark, and heard voices. They was chantin'. Couldn't make out the words, but it was comin' from the back of the church. Round where we found the cross. By the time I got round there with me little dog—barkin' her 'ead off, she was— they'd scarpered."

Lois closed her eyes, and a tear ran down her cheek. If she'd taken him in to casualty last night, had them look at his ankle and check him over, he might be alive now.

She opened her eyes and shook her head. Might, might, if, if. She didn't, and that was that. She got up and looked out of the window. A small Jack Russell terrier trotted quickly by on the opposite side of the road. Oh no! Wasn't that Cyril's little dog? She rushed out and caught up with it. It stopped and looked at her enquiringly. Lois was sure it was Cyril's, and looked at the nameplate on its collar. "Betsy," clearly visible. Yep, it was Cyril's. Probably been out all night, and now on her way home, looking for her master.

Lois picked her up, and buried her face in the wiry coat. "Come on, Betsy," she whispered, "come home with me. We'll look after you." She ran back across the road and into the big kitchen, where Gran sat at the table, staring into space. "Here, Mum," Lois said. "Here's somethin' you can do for Cyril. He loved this dog."

"Are you mad, Lois?" Gran said in a flat voice. "What about Melvyn?"

Lois looked at the large cat fast asleep and totally indifferent to the snuffling terrier padding about the kitchen. "They've met," she said, grinning now. "Betsy knows who's boss, and keeps well away from Mel. No, it'll be Derek we have to worry about."

She was right. When Derek came home later, he exploded. "You're crazy, Lois!" he said. She thought it best to agree, and said it had been an impulse and she'd take Betsy to Tresham dogs' home in the morning. This had the effect she hoped for. Gran said there was no need to decide right now, and Derek nodded. "Best take her for a bit of a walk, anyway," he said, reaching for a ball of string to make a temporary lead. "Old Cyril always took her out beginning and end of the day. Up to the churchyard, eh, gel?" he added, and patted her on her small, warm head.

TWENTY-TWO

༜

SHARON MILLER LOOKED AT HERSELF IN THE MIRROR, and wondered for the first time for years whether it would, after all, be a good thing to have her eye fixed. She did not know if it was even possible. In her imagination, she saw masked faces in the clinical glare of the operating theatre. Her own body lay supine on the table, swathed in dark green wrappings. The surgeon, tawny brown eyes showing above his mask, peered down at her lovely face.

"I can't do it, Jim," he said, turning to his assistant. "This girl is perfect as she is. God has made her to His own design, and who am I to interfere with such loveliness?"

Sharon laughed out loud. I reckon I could write one of them books, she thought. I'm wasted doin' cleaning for the vicar. Still, she reflected, applying makeup and brushing her long, wavy blonde hair, at least it'll give me a chance to see what Sandy's up to.

She had finally convinced herself that her glimpse of Sandy and Rebecca kissing had been an affectionate greeting. Everybody kissed everybody these days. Especially the nobs. Mwa mwa! And all of them being careful not actually to make contact. "At least with us lot," she muttered as she went downstairs, "a kiss means something. Like love. Or lust!" She laughed again delightedly, and shouted goodbye to her mother. "See you later," she called. Then she ran back into the kitchen and planted a smacking kiss on her mother's cheek. "There," she said, and grinned at her expression of alarm. "Don't worry," she added. "Just because I felt like it."

BRIAN ROLLINSON ANTICIPATED SHARON'S ARRIVAL WITH something like dread. He had a lot to think about. An old sister of Cyril had surfaced in Tresham, and she and her unmarried daughter would be handling all the arrangements for the funeral. But it was not at all clear when that could be. The police were being very cagey, talking about an autopsy and coroner's verdict, all in a vague kind of way that left him unable to offer the usual comforting platitudes to reassure the bereaved. Once the sadness of the funeral was over, he would say, God and time would begin to heal the wounds of loss. It was actually not true. Most people found that the arrangements and excitement of the funeral—yes, excitement—and seeing friends and relations they'd not seen for years, buoyed them up until their loved one had been satisfactorily despatched. And afterwards, when there was nothing but emptiness where once someone familiar had been, they often felt the real pain of bereavement. But at least it gave him something to say in difficult circumstances.

This time, though, the old sister had never troubled about Cyril in life, and might not be so struck down by his death. She hadn't been in Farnden for years, it was said. There had probably been a feud. Yes, that would be it. Villages were full of feuds. The old thing would not be in the least distressed, and her daughter had more than likely been conditioned to believe Cyril was the devil incarnate.

"Devil incarnate!" Brian stood up suddenly, and put his hands to his head. Sometimes he felt that he was being pursued by the anti-Christ, and now here were rumours of him in Farnden's own churchyard.

"Sharon?" Brian opened the door and strode into the kitchen. She wasn't there, and he could hear the cleaner humming away upstairs. He'd surprise her with a cup of coffee on her first morning. Get the conversation round to the disturbance in the churchyard last night. Sharon was a friendly soul. He had to admit he was not sorry to lose Hazel Thornbull, née Reading. She was abrasive and suspicious, and though her work could not be faulted, she was a constant thorn in his flesh. Thorn . . . in the flesh . . . yes, well. It was very difficult being a vicar, Brian Rollinson decided. Words were against you. The parish was largely against you. And, sometimes, privately, he wondered if God was against him.

He called again, but the vacuum was still going and she did not hear. He walked upstairs, his footsteps cushioned by carpet, and saw to his surprise that the machine stood by itself, anchored to the banister by its flex, and through the open door to Sandy's room he could see Sharon lying on her back on Sandy's bed, eyes closed and a seraphic smile on her face.

At the same moment he heard the front door open and Sandy's voice calling him. Why was he home in the middle of the morning? What on earth was going on? He swiftly turned off the cleaner, noted Sharon rise up in alarm, and ran back downstairs to prevent Sandy from rushing up to find a blonde stretched out on his bed.

"Hi," said Sandy. "Left some papers behind—here, excuse me!" he added, as Brian stood firmly at the bottom of the stairs, preventing him from going up. "I left them in my room! Please, let me by . . . you got a woman up there or something?" His smile was mocking.

Brian forced a laugh. "Yes, as a matter of fact, I have," he said, noting with relief that the vacuum cleaner had started up again. "And of course you can go up. It's only Sharon, cleaning upstairs. I'm afraid I was miles away, Sandy. Not all of us move at the speed you do, you know."

He stood aside, and watched as Sandy ran up the stairs, two at a time. "Morning, Sharon," he heard, and then, without a doubt, the sound of a panting kiss. Oh God, prayed Brian, please don't let him seduce the servants! He relaxed, however, and with a small smile went off to his study.

Sharon operated her machine in long sweeps along the landing, and trembled. Passing and repassing his door, she watched as Sandy systematically undid all the tidying she had done in his room. A rush of desire had driven her to lie down on his bed, surrounded by the smell of him. Now she saw him toss aside piles of papers, swearing under his breath.

"Can I help?" she said, pausing for a moment.

"Did you see a folder with a red cover? Picture of a grand house on the front?" He would have to tell Sharon not to tidy up. Good God, he might never find it again! And the client waited outside in his car, on the way to clinch one of the biggest sales Sandy had had so far.

"Yes," she said in a shaky voice. She could still taste him on her tongue. "Here, look, you just missed it in this pile." She leaned in front of him and pulled the folder out. He put his arm around her and squeezed. "Good girl," he whispered, and nuzzled the back of her neck. Then he was off downstairs at the double, and out of the front door before she could breathe again.

Downstairs later for her coffee, Sharon perched on the edge of a kitchen chair and sipped elegantly from the thick china mug. "Nice of you to make coffee," she said. "But Mrs. M tells us we should do that as part of our duty. A little extra, to make people feel we care, she says."

"A bright woman, your Mrs. M," said the vicar. "It was she who found that burning cross in the churchyard, wasn't it?" He knew it wasn't, but thought it would get the subject going.

"No, no. It was Cyril, and Mrs. M heard him call out. She was the one to find him, poor old man. He was in a poor way by the time the rest of us got round there. Nearly crying, he was, with the pain of his ankle. *I* think," she said, warming to her story, "that he was in shock." People were always in shock in her library books. They said and did things, and had things done to them, whilst they were in shock.

"Did he say anything about the cross? Had he seen anybody who might have left it there?"

Sharon shook her head. "Not that I heard," she said. "But I reckon I know who did it," she added confidingly, lowering her voice.

Brian raised his eyebrows. "You do?" he said.

"Yep." Sharon leaned back in her chair with an oracular nod. "There's a nasty lot started comin' round here," she said. "They get in the pub sometimes. I was in there havin' a drink with your Sandy. He knew one or two of them." She watched the vicar carefully, waiting for his reaction.

"Oh, yes? Who are they?"

Sharon shrugged. "I don't know anything much more about them," she said.

Brian's heart sank. He wondered if these were the socially acceptable friends Sandy had talked about. Surely not! He had heard about racism and associated violence in Tresham. But that had been thugs. Neo-fascism, Nazism, any ism that caught the fancy of ignorant bigots. He sighed. "Well, we must keep our ears to the ground, Sharon," he said gently. "These things are best nipped in the bud. If you hear or see anything that bothers you, please don't hesitate to come to me."

She smiled happily. It had been a good morning so far. Kissed by Sandy, encouraged by the vicar. Even so, she thought, if she heard anything more, she wouldn't tell the vicar. No, it would need to be someone tough. Like Mrs. M. Yes, she'd tell Mrs. M if there was anything really bad to tell. Just like she'd said.

TWENTY-THREE

❧

GRAN HAD PUT A BLUE AND WHITE CHECKED CLOTH over the kitchen table, deciding that the scarred and stained top—especially the clear outline of a red-hot iron left by Josie in her teens—would not do. It wasn't every day that Jamie brought a girlfriend home for tea. In fact she couldn't remember a single time. He'd had loads of girlfriends, of course. First the pairing-off that goes with gangs at school. Then the dating, and fallings-out and jealousies and hopeless yearnings. All part of growing up. Gran smiled. Some things didn't change all that much. She remembered her own romance with Lois's dad. Alf Weedon had been a catch. All the girls lusted after him, but she had kept her distance, reeling him in like a fish on the hook. And then Lois, treating Derek with casual carelessness, but planning her campaign like a seasoned politician. Poor old Derek! He never knew what hit him when he first saw Lois in Woolworths in her mini-skirt and eyelashes!

Now it was Jamie. Her lovely boy, the baby of the family. But of course he wasn't a baby any more. He was a young man, tall, dark and handsome, gentle in his manners, but tough when he set his heart on something. Like the piano! Goodness, that had been a battle, with Derek scathing about his son poncing about on the piano keys. Jamie had taken no notice, and now here he was, on the verge of a career in music. Had he set his heart on Annabelle? That might be even more of a battle.

Gran filled the kettle, put milk in a seldom used jug, and looked happily at the table set with the best china, and in the centre a perfect Dundee cake, covered in almonds and baked to perfection.

The back door opened, and Cyril's dog rushed in, followed by Derek. "Brr! Brass monkeys out there, Gran!" he said. He handed her a bag of shopping from the village shop. "They hadn't got no lump sugar," he said. "No call for it, they said. So I reckon Annabelle will have to spoon it out like the rest of us." He smiled as he said it, not wishing to hurt Gran's feelings. She had gone to a lot of trouble to make a nice tea for Jamie and his girl, and though he knew Lois would tease her, he was touched.

"Here, what's this?" said Gran, delving into the shopping bag. She pulled out a packet of doggy choc drops.

"Ah, yes, I got those," Derek said defiantly. "Look, Betsy! Look what Derek's got for you." The little dog sat on its hind legs and begged. Gran and Derek both laughed delightedly.

"So she's staying, is she, Derek?" said Lois acidly, coming in and catching them red-handed. "No need for me to go to the dogs' home?"

Derek's reply was drowned by the roar of Jamie's motorbike appearing in the yard, with Annabelle clinging close behind.

"Lucky for you," repeated Derek, giving Lois a peck on the cheek. "Can't let Annabelle see me beating up the wife. Mmmm!" he added, sniffing behind her ear. "Your new scent? Blimey, perhaps I'd better put me best suit on." But he made do with swilling his hands under the tap and dry-ing them on the tea cloth. He turned to his smiling son as he came through the door, with Annabelle behind him. "Come on in, then," he said. "Too cold to hang about in the yard!" And he walked forward and planted a firm kiss on Annabelle's cheek. She beamed, took hold of Jamie's hand and walked confidently into the warm kitchen.

WHEN THE SALMON AND CUCUMBER SANDWICHES, homemade shortbread and Dundee cake had been demol-ished, Gran relaxed. Everything seemed to have gone very well, apart from Annabelle refusing milk in her tea. Gran had sniffed the milk, but it was fresh. Now, she reckoned her spread had been much appreciated. There was still an hour to go before the young ones needed to leave for the cinema, and Lois suggested they might move to the sitting room.

"Good idea," said Derek, getting up smartly. "We can get the results on the telly."

This was not what Lois had in mind. She planned to steer the conversation somehow round to the fiery cross and see what emerged. If, as Cowgill said, Annabelle knew something about it, Lois was sure she could get it out of her. She was very straightforward, and although she had the confident air of a girl whose grandmother was Mrs. Tollervey-Jones, she happily gossiped at the table about village goings-on with apparent enjoyment. Derek turned on the television and settled back in his chair. Lois had for-bidden her mother to do any clearing or washing up, and she and the rest sat comfortably warming themselves by the leaping fire.

"How cosy!" whispered Annabelle, as she snuggled up to Jamie on the sofa.

The local magazine programme unrolled inconsequen-tially in front of them. School football matches, fundraising bazaars, an old man of one hundred years clutching his telegram from the Queen.

Suddenly Annabelle gasped. The screen was showing an unsteady piece of film, obviously the work of an amateur running hard in half-darkness, following a fleeing group of young men, who were shouting and laughing and raising their fists. "Max!" she said involuntarily, and Jamie stared at her.

"Someone you know?" he said.

"No, no, just a mistake," she replied quickly.

The scene had changed now to a reporter standing in the same street, but in daylight, a group of children gaping behind him. "This is not the first incident of its kind here in the multi-ethnic area of Tresham," he was saying. "Broken windows, stones thrown, excrement dumped through letterboxes. These are daily occurrences for people like Mrs. Merrilees." The camera focused on a grim-looking, middle-aged black woman.

"That's enough of that," said Derek firmly, and switched channels. Talk turned desultorily on sports results and the chances of the Meades ever winning the lottery.

Jamie looked at his watch. "Better go," he said to Annabelle. "You OK?" he added, seeing her pale face in the firelight.

"'Course I am," she said, and with genuine enthusiasm thanked Gran and Lois for a lovely time. "Wish we could stay here in the warm," she said with a shiver, "instead of tramping around the streets of Tresham."

Lois looked at her closely, missing nothing.

"Come on!" said Jamie heartily, pulling her to her feet. "Exercise will do you good. Cheero, Mum, see you later."

After they had gone, Lois and Gran washed up together. They were quiet, until Gran suddenly said, "Who's Max?"

"That's what I was wondering," said Lois.

TWENTY-FOUR

❧

"REBECCA, CAN YOU SPARE A MOMENT?" THE HEAD
teacher at Waltonby school appeared at Rebecca's
classroom door.

The children stared. When Mrs. Thorpe came unexpectedly into the classroom, it usually meant trouble for someone. But she was smiling, so it couldn't be that. They
waited. Rebecca beckoned her in, told the class to get on
with their reading books, and began a conversation. Eyes
were turned down to books, darting up occasionally to
check what was going on. Several children—the usual
rebels—began to relax. Then Rebecca, her face flushed,
turned to the class and spoke.

"Mrs. Thorpe would like a few words with you, children. Pay attention, now."

All eyes obediently turned to Mrs. Thorpe, who began
pleasantly. "I have had a call from a Mr. Mackerras, who
works for an estate agent's in Tresham. He has launched a
competition—painting or drawing—for children in our
area, and the winner gets a giant construction set to build

his own model village! Sandy—he would like you to call him Sandy—wants to come and talk to you about it—well, to all the children in the school, but class by class, as there are various age categories—and tell you what you have to do. What do you think, children?"

"Yeah!" They reacted with one voice, and the rebels punched the air with small fists.

Mrs. Thorpe turned back to Rebecca. "Well, that seems pretty conclusive!" she said. "Such a nice young man. It will be a pleasure to meet him. Goodness knows what the agents are getting out of it . . . It's not pure philanthropy, I'm sure. Estate agents have such a bad name! But anyway, it's harmless enough. Right!" she added, "I'll leave you to get on."

BY THE TIME REBECCA HAD CALMED DOWN THE CHIL-dren, finished a day's teaching, called in at Farnden shop and noted that Sharon Miller was monosyllabic in serving her, she arrived home exhausted. All through the day Sandy Mackerras's competition had reared its head in the school. At lunchtime, the school secretary had enthused, and in the playground the children gossiped like old women. The news spread after school amongst the moth-ers and fathers waiting for their excited children. Rebecca was glad to be home in her quiet cottage, collapsed on the sofa and mindlessly watching television. However, it was too banal and irritating and she switched off. Why was Sandy doing it? Surely not just to have an excuse to see her for longer than the usual choir practice? No, that was ridiculous, although . . .

Bill came stumping in, his hands red and frozen from the cold. On his way home from cleaning at the Hall, he had helped the vet with a lamed sheep caught up in barbed wire, and he had scratched his wrist. "Got the kettle on, love?" he said, rinsing his arm under the tap.

Rebecca got to her feet. It would have been nice, wouldn't it, if just for once he had asked how *her* day had gone. She made the tea, and put his muddy boots on newspaper to dry.

Should she tell him about the competition? No, any mention of Sandy Mackerras seemed recently to prompt nothing but contempt from Bill. He would hear no good of him. Rebecca expected Bill to resign from the choir at any moment, but he didn't. Each week he attended with a grim face, sang his part with extreme accuracy and skill, and said nothing. But his face said it all. If—as often happened—Sandy smiled directly at Rebecca, or complimented her on her sight-reading, Bill's expression would radiate ill-will. And Sharon too! Rebecca was no fool. She knew Sharon fancied Sandy, and that he had taken her out once or twice.

Well, why not? He was attractive, unattached and trawling a new area. The poor girl was green with jealousy. If only she knew. Rebecca had heard tales of some of Sandy's more hair-raising exploits in Tresham clubland. Mind you, she reassured herself, not wanting to think badly of him, he had apparently been taken up by the Hall set. Perhaps he would have a go at Annabelle T-J next— maybe she should warn Mrs. M. Jamie Meade was known to be keen on the girl, though local gossips didn't give much for his chances.

Rebecca returned to the sitting room, ready to relate an amusing incident from school, nothing to do with Sandy Mackerras. But Bill flicked on the television, and slumped in his chair. "Sshh!" he said. "I want to watch this. Tell me later."

LOIS WALKED SWIFTLY DOWN TO THE SHOP. IT WOULD be shut in five minutes, and she needed stamps. The post office cubicle was closed all day, but Mrs. Carr always kept stamps in the till. The door was opening as she approached, and the vicar emerged. His usual smile of welcome was muted. "Hello, Lois," he said.

"Afternoon, Rev. Rollinson," she replied. For God's sake, he'd not been in the village five minutes before it was Christian names all round.

"I'm glad I met you," he said. "We have a date for Cyril's funeral. Next Thursday, half past two. I expect there'll be a big turn-out, and his sister has unexpectedly wanted to make a bit of a do of it. Asking for the choir, and some of Cyril's favourite old songs to be played on the organ. She also requests 'Abide With Me' to be sung as a solo. I said I was sure one of the excellent singers in the choir would be glad to oblige."

Oh ho, thought Lois. That'll put the cat among the pigeons! Our chief pigeon will certainly expect to be asked. But then there's Sandy's obvious yen for Rebecca, so he'll probably ask her. Should be interesting. She made a mental note not to miss choir practice this week.

"I shall certainly be there, but not as soloist," she said, smiling modestly. There was no answering smile. He seemed to be in a dream, but suddenly he turned on his heel and shot off without another word. As she opened the shop door, she noticed Sandy's car pass by at speed. The two of them still not getting on too well? None of your business, she told herself, and laughed.

"Afternoon, Mrs. Meade. Glad to hear you're cheerful. Most of my customers today have been very cast down." Criticism oozed from Mrs. Carr's tone. She made a great show of tidying up the shop, ready to close. "What can I get you?" she said, and her impatience at finding Lois wanted only stamps was clear. Lois felt her usual guilt at making infrequent use of the shop, when she bought almost everything at the Tresham supermarket. She was not alone, of course. Most people did the same. But she knew that village shops teetered on the edge of insolvency most of the time. She'd miss it if it had to close, and so would most of the rest of the village. From her point of view, it was a valuable source of information; gossip, Derek would call it, and so it was, most of the time. But in her work with Cowgill, it became more serious.

"I expect you'll be going to poor old Cyril's funeral on Thursday?" she said contritely.

This was too much for Mrs. Carr to resist, and she stopped brushing up the day's detritus from the floor. "Oh, goodness yes," she said. "Known him for years and years. He was my best customer. Bought everything from me," she added pointedly.

"Such a shame," Lois said. "He seemed in good shape, considering his age. Always out with Betsy, twice a day up to the church, regular as clockwork."

Mrs. Carr nodded. "I would have said there was not a lot wrong with him. Suffered a bit with his stomach— indigestion, trapped wind, all that kind of thing. But that's one of the blessings of old age, I used to tell him. You'll find the same one day, Mrs. Meade," she added with relish. "And anyway," she continued, "he never had it so bad as to kill him! He could control it with what he ate, and some of my specials." She laughed. "Could've made a fortune, if I'd invented them," she added.

"Specials?" said Lois incredulously. She knew her mother relied on tablets from the shop for bouts of colic. Harmless enough, she'd always thought, but not the cure-all Mrs. Carr seemed to imply.

"I swear by them," the shopkeeper said, picking up her broom. "Now, you'll have to excuse me, Mrs. Meade. *I* have work to do."

"Thanks," said Lois. "See you on Thursday, then. Should be a good do, according to the vicar. Old songs, an' that."

Mrs. Carr nodded. *"Moo . . . oon River"* she sang tunelessly. "That was his favourite, poor old dear." She wiped away a tear with the edge of her overall, and Lois made a quick getaway.

That's quite enough of that, thanks, she muttered to herself, and set off for home and sanity.

TWENTY-FIVE

❧

CHOIR PRACTICE WENT EXACTLY AS LOIS HAD ANTIC-
ipated. She arrived early to settle up with Bill for
honey he had brought for her from the gardener at the Hall.
She paid him, and noticed that he did not have his usual
smile for her. "Feeling all right, Bill?" she said. "Don't
want any more dramas at choir practice." He grinned
quickly, and said no, he was fine, it was the thought of putting up with that idiot for an hour. She did not need to ask
who he meant.

When all were gathered, Sandy announced the arrangements for next week's funeral, and before he could turn to
Rebecca, Mrs. Tollervey-Jones said with saccharine emotion, "*Dear* old Cyril, he loved that hymn. 'Abide with Me'
was his favourite. I often used to sing it with him while I
did the flowers and he cleaned up the church. Quite a duo,
we were! Yes, of course, Sandy, it would give me great
pleasure to sing it once more for an old friend."

Lois looked at Sandy, waiting for the next move. Was he
outsmarted? For a moment she thought Mrs. T-J had won,

but then Sandy smiled. "Just what I had in mind," he said, "and how appropriate that we should be able to produce a duet for Cyril, just as in the old days you remember so clearly!" An appreciative rustle came from the choir. What was he up to?

"I would like you, Mrs. T-J, to take soprano in the first verse, with Rebecca singing the alto part, then full choir on verses two, three and four, then Jamie and Bill finishing off with due solemnity in the last verse. Jamie will sing the tune, and Bill accompany . . . if you could manage the tenor part, Bill?" He looked maliciously at Bill, knowing that this would be difficult for him, being a bass.

But Bill stared back at him and nodded. "Fine," he said. "No problem."

Mrs. T-J spluttered and made a last-ditch attempt to regain the limelight. "But don't you think a soprano solo in the last verse would be more touching . . . and if Cyril's sister has specifically requested a solo?"

"No," said Sandy flatly. "But thanks for the suggestion. I'm sure Cyril's sister will be delighted. Now, let's have a go at it. Ready, Sharon?" He flashed a smile across to the organ, and Sharon returned it with enthusiasm.

"Usual introduction . . . first two lines?" she said.

"You're a wonder," said Sandy. "What should we do without our Sharon, eh?"

Mrs. T-J glared at him. "Perfectly well," she muttered, so that only her neighbour could have heard.

Finally, the others drifted away. Only Sandy, Sharon still at the organ, and Lois, who had dropped all her music, were left in the church. "Here, let me give you a hand," said Sandy. He knelt on the stone floor beside Lois, and reached out a hand . . . and quite deliberately let it rest warmly over Lois's for several seconds.

Ye gods, randy little devil! thought Lois. "I can manage, thanks," she said, scooping up the books and sheets of paper in an untidy heap and shoving it in the plastic bag that did duty for a music case. "I'm off," she said. "See you at the funeral."

Sharon watched her go. She had not been within sight of the two crouching figures and so had no idea why Mrs. M had gone off in what looked like a huff.

"Difficult woman," said Sandy lightly, coming over to the organ. "Not like my dear little Sharon . . ." He leaned over, and she turned to meet his kiss.

"You were a bit naughty with Mrs. T-J," she whispered. His hands were busy now, and she gulped.

"Old bag," he muttered. "Come on, Sharon," he added thickly, "let's go somewhere private."

"Nowhere more private than the church. Everyone else has gone." She was half-scared, but determined. At last life was living up to fiction. "Nobody comes in here after choir. And you've got the key, haven't you?"

He looked at her in admiration. "Right-o," he said. "You make us somewhere comfortable, and I'll lock us in." He pulled her up from the organ stool, and kissed her again. "Mmm, quick as you can," he grinned, and walked down the aisle to lock the big oak door.

Lois, halfway home, remembered she'd left her purse in the choir stalls in the church. Damn! She turned around and ran back through the dark street, up the narrow path and past the poisoner's gravestone. Puffing into the porch, she turned the big iron handle. Blast! They must have gone already and locked up. She stood wondering whether to get the key from the vicarage, when she heard an unmistakable high-pitched giggle, followed by a loud masculine shout. Sharon and Sandy. Well! Lois was not easily shocked, but the idea of the pair of them having it off under the noses of all those religious statues and stained glass saints took some swallowing.

·   ·   ·

BRIAN ROLLINSON LOOKED AT THE LITTLE CHINESE clock on the mantelshelf over the fire, and checked the time with his watch. Funny—Sandy should be home by now. He'd said he would come straight back after choir practice, as he had some office work to catch up on. No, he wouldn't be going down to the pub tonight. Brian had been pleased, thinking they could have a companionable couple of hours without television. Just the two of them, reading and working, and he'd make some creamy hot chocolate to keep them going. Sandy had been very cool with him lately. Brian knew there had been a hold-up with Sandy's plans for the flat, and guessed this might be the reason. He stood up, and went over to the window. It was dark, but he could see by the light over the gate that nobody was around. Perhaps he was coming back through the church-yard and in the back gate, by the vicar-only path. Could he have been delayed? And by what? Brian remembered the fiery cross, the ashy scar in the grass. "Oh, no," he said aloud. His imagination conjured hooded figures, hysterical chanting, human sacrifice . . .

Grabbing his coat, he left the house and went swiftly and silently through the churchyard, round to the back of the church. Nothing. All quiet there, then. He relaxed, and told himself he was a fool and should know better. Then he saw a faint light shining through the vestry window. Some-one had forgotten to switch it off? He could leave it until the morning—indeed, would have to, since Sandy had his keys. But where was Sandy? The choir had obviously gone home a while ago. Could it be burglars? There had been a spate of church burglaries lately, and parishes had been ad-vised to tighten security. Not that there was much to steal in Long Farnden church, Brian reminded himself. But still, it wouldn't look good if thieves had got in easily and trashed the place.

He walked over to the window, feeling his feet getting wet in the long grass. He was cold, and wished he'd never come out to look for Sandy. As he stood on tiptoe, he could just see into the vestry.

So that's it. He'd come out to look for Sandy, and now he'd found him. Snugly cushioned on a pile of choir robes lay Sharon Miller and Sandy Mackerras, clearly obeying God's injunction to be fruitful and multiply.

There was only one thing for it, and that was to go back home and pretend to know nothing. Sandy was a grown man. He was also Gerald's son, and all he had to remember his friend by, and he had no wish to alienate him. And although at the moment, he despised Sandy for his sacrilege, he knew this would pass. He retraced his steps, but went round by the front porch to check the lock—he wanted no one else to see them—where he collided with Lois Meade.

"Steady up!" said Lois, leaning against the wire door that kept birds out of the porch. "All locked up, vicar," she added, speakly loudly in an effort to warn. Thinking quickly, she had decided it was no business of hers to thwart amorous adventures, and a few instant pictures had unrolled in front of her mind's eye—peculiar places she and Derek had found for the same purpose. The unsuitability spiced it up a treat. She remembered that with warmth.

"In the bracken round the back of the playing fields was best," she said out loud to herself, but the vicar stared at her.

"I beg your pardon?" he said.

"Oh, sorry—miles away," she said. If she could keep him here talking, they could get away out of the vestry door. Sandy must have keys. "I'm glad I bumped into you," she said, laughing a lot—more than it merited—at the aptness of the phrase. "There was something I wanted to ask you."

"Couldn't it wait until tomorrow?" said Brian irritably.

He had to get back home before Sandy, so that he could keep up his pretence of knowing nothing.

"Won't take a minute," she said briskly. "Here, look, we can perch on these. No time like the present when there's something on your mind." She sat on the edge of one of the damp, narrow benches in the porch, and Brian reluctantly did the same. "It's about that cross. You know, the one poor old Cyril found. Have you had any idea who they could have been? Derek handed it over to the police, and he's heard no more."

Not a lie, Lois said to herself. Derek hasn't heard, though I have.

"I have not had time to follow it up yet," Brian said stiffly. "Cyril's funeral is my main concern at the moment." He had to get away. It had gone very quiet in the church, and any minute the young ones would be coming out.

"O'course," Lois said sympathetically. "It's just that . . ." She paused, adding vital minutes on behalf of the lovers. She began to splutter, thinking of what was going on inside, and decided to own up. "Well, I'm just delaying you—no other reason for sitting in a dark porch on a cold night, bums getting damper every minute. I thought I'd spare you the sight of Sharon and Sandy busily tidying things up inside and making a quick getaway through the vestry door." She collapsed, her shoulders shaking with laughter.

Brian stared at her dark shape against the porch wall. "I saw them," he said. "Through the vestry window." She stopped laughing. Then, to her surprise, he said something she would never forget. "I am angry with him," he said quietly. "It is not something I would have expected of him. But there it is. I must take him as he is, warts and all. I love him like a son, Mrs. Meade. Like my own son."

Then he stood up and touched her lightly on the arm. "You're right," he said. "The whole thing is ridiculous. But

I cannot find it funny. I'm so sorry." Whilst Sharon and Sandy silently locked the vestry door behind them and tiptoed off into the darkness, Brian and Lois walked side by side down the church path, Lois sober now, and for the moment they were in harmony.

It *was* ludicrous, of course, Lois was sure of that as she related the evening's happenings to Derek. But when she had finished constructing a suitably hilarious account, and Derek and Gran had stopped laughing, she said, "Mind you, I do worry a bit about Sharon. I reckon she's not been around much, unlike our Sandy, and if he lets her down, it could be nasty."

Derek shook his head. "That Sharon," he said, "keeps a secret or two, me duck. Not quite what she makes out. Ask 'em down at the pub," he added wisely. "They could tell you a thing or two."

"No doubt," said Lois sharply. "But she is one of my team now, and I don't listen to gossip, as you know."

Derek raised his eyebrows. That was a laugh. Lois not listen to gossip? But he caught Gran's warning look, and went back to his newspaper without comment.

TWENTY-SIX

❧

"WHEN ARE YOU GOING BACK HOME?" JAMIE AD-dressed his question to Annabelle, both of them warm and half-asleep on a sofa in the small sitting room at the Hall. Mrs. T-J had gone to London for a few days to supervise the redecoration of her Baker Street flat. "Flat" was something of an overstatement, since it consisted of one room with galley kitchen and shoebox bathroom, but she was redesigning and buying new furniture and generally fulfilling her creative spirit. She would not be back until the weekend, and her granddaughter was making the most of her absence.

"Dunno," said Annabelle, opening her eyes. "Why do you ask? Want to get rid of me?"

"Course not," said Jamie. "I just wondered. Aren't you supposed to be going on to some college, or something?"

"If Grandmother has her way." Annabelle combed her hair back with her fingers and sat up. "Secretarial. They don't think I'm up to anything more demanding."

"Don't you care?" said Jamie, who blindly considered

his love as one of the most witty, articulate and intelligent girls he had met. "And anyway, you haven't said when you're going home. Your folks must be back from America by now?"

"Yep," she said. "Had a card from NY today. Mum's back next week."

"And your dad?"

"Ah, yes. Dad. He's staying out there, apparently. With a lady called Dory. What kind of a name is that?" she added, and then to Jamie's horror, burst into sudden and desperate tears. He put his arm around her and did his best to comfort her.

"Never mind," he said, in what he realized was his mother's voice. "Could be just a temporary blip."

Annabelle shook her head and buried her face in Jamie's chest. "No," she said in a muffled voice, "Mum says she wouldn't have him back if he was Noah and the only man left above water." Jamie felt her shake, and feared more tears. But then she spluttered, and he saw she was laughing.

"That's better," he said with relief.

"Just the thought of Dad as Noah," she said, pulling away from him. "He's got a beard, you know," she added. "Looks more like an old goat than the brave sailor, though."

She got up and crossed the room to throw another log on the fire. "I do love fire," she said, spreading her hands to warm them. "It's clean, isn't it, the way it eats up everything."

"Leaves ash, though," said practical Jamie. "Somebody has to clear out the grate. My dad does at home, or sometimes Gran. I think she'd like one of them gas fire jobs, but we all stick out for the real thing."

Annabelle was silent for a minute. "You're a real family, aren't you," she said. "You always talk about 'we' . . . must be really nice. I wish I had a brother."

"You've got me," Jamie said gallantly. He stood beside her and they both stared into the flickering flames. "Talking of fire . . ." Jamie was hesitant, and did not look at her.

"What about it?"

"I just wondered . . . that half-burned cross we found that night behind the church . . . do you know anything about it? I mean," he added hastily, "have you heard where it might have come from . . . from your other friends, an' that?"

"What friends?" Annabelle was sharp. She frowned at him. "What are you suggesting, Jamie?"

Definitely a tinge of Mrs. T-J there, he thought. Might be best to change the subject. But Mum had asked him to keep his ears open, and anyway, he was curious himself. "Well, you know, there've been rumours—daft magic rites, like in the films. That kind of thing," he tailed off lamely. To his relief, she laughed.

"Oh, that," she said dismissively. "You mean that Tresham lot. Waste of space, most of them. I went along once, but I don't do that stuff. Dressing up and chanting and passing round this and that . . . half of them were high before it began. No, I shall steer clear of that lot. Pathetic, really, but they sound pretty nasty when they get going." She looked closely at Jamie. "Who wants to know?" she said. "Somebody on their tail?" He didn't answer, and she continued, "Because if there is somebody, I don't want to be the one who told. Not good news for me. So don't pass it on to anyone. Anyone at all," she repeated firmly. "And now can we change the subject? D'you want a drink? We can go and raid the fridge." Annabelle was cheerful now, efficiently plumping up cushions and putting the room to rights.

"Just one thing," Jamie said slowly.

"Oh, Jamie. Give it a rest."

But Jamie persisted. "You know on the telly the other night? When we were at my house. There was a news clip of thugs in Tresham, running away from some bit of bother. You said 'Max!' like you knew him."

Annabelle was silent. She looked suddenly very young, like a schoolgirl up before the headmistress. "So?" she said finally.

"Was he Magic Max, the one who asked you to go with them that once?"

For a moment, Jamie thought he had gone too far—she had an icy glint in her eye.

Annabelle said, "If you must know, yes, it was. But I told you, Jamie, I have nothing to do with them now. Either you believe me . . . or we'd better not see each other again. I am not a liar."

Jamie nodded. "I believe you," he said simply. "Come on, let's go and get tea. By the way," he added, "have you thought any more about joining the choir? You might like it. There's no practice on Thursday—tomorrow—'cause of Cyril's funeral. We'll have done enough singing. But next week . . ."

Annabelle opened her blue eyes wide, and laughed in the uncomplicated way he loved. It was still a child's laugh, spontaneous and loud. "Me?" she said. "Jamie darling, I can't sing a note!"

"Bet you can," he said, unwilling to acknowledge any possible shortcomings. "Anyway," he added, "let's raid the kitchen—come on—lead me to the crumpets." She relaxed, and said she reckoned he'd had enough crumpet for one afternoon. He patted her tightly jeaned bottom, and they raced downstairs like a couple of children without a care in the world.

AFTER A MORNING BUSILY SORTING PAINT COLOURS AND swatches of curtain fabric, Mrs. T-J cut herself a sandwich and went to fill the kettle. No water. A faint hissing in the tap, and that was all. She tried all the taps, but they were the same. The water supply seemed to have dried up completely. And the rain outside was torrential!

She checked with others in the building, but they were fine. No trouble with the water. Several offered her a bucketful to flush the loo. She returned to the flat and tried again. No water. Frustrated and angry, she telephoned plumbers from a list in Yellow Pages, and none were prepared to come out for at least a week.

There was nothing for it. She would have to go back to the country and try to organize something from there. She stormed out to her car, stepping in a deep puddle as she went, and set off for the motorway. Her right foot was sodden and cold, and she could hardly see beyond the car in front. She turned on Radio 3 and encountered a piece of modern music so assaulting to the ear that she snapped it off again straightaway. Radio 4 was no good. It was some worthy little drama about dreary miners and accidents down the pit. She drove on, and at last, with only one more junction to go, she began to relax. Then she felt a wobble in the steering. She was having trouble holding the car steady. It could be only one thing. A flat tyre.

Incandescent with rage, she managed to manoeuvre the car on to the hard shoulder and drew to a bumping halt. It was nearly dark now, and she took out her mobile phone. There was no signal. At this point, generations of Tollervey-Joneses, landowners, rulers, men of influence in all parts of the world, rose up before her. She narrowed her eyes, opened the door and set off in the teeth of a howling, rain-filled gale for help.

BY THE TIME HER TYRE WAS CHANGED AND THE MOTOR-way finally left behind, she approached the Hall in no mood to be trifled with. As she came into the entrance hall, she was surprised to hear voices coming from the drawing room. She frowned, and walked forward quietly to see who was in there. Visitors? No one was expected. The door was ajar, and she peered through. What on earth was going on? She could see Annabelle, piling butter and jam on to what looked like . . . yes, she was using the Georgian silver muffin dish always kept locked in a cabinet for display! And her companion? Of course . . . Mrs. T-J snorted now, and was heard. Of course, it was that village boy, turning round from the fire, still on his knees and clutching the precious toasting fork that had been her great-aunt's.

"Grandmother!" Annabelle was the only one not struck dumb. "Goodness, we weren't expecting you! But never mind," she continued, with a presence of mind that made Jamie vow to be true to her for ever. "Never mind, come in and have tea with us. You're sopping wet, poor thing!" And then she took control, fetching another cup, and dry slippers and a towel to rub wet hair. And to Jamie's amazement, Grandmother sat meekly by the fire, drank her tea and ate her crumpets, and said not a word. So that was all right, wasn't it?

JAMIE, ON RETURNING HOME TO HIS FAMILY, GAVE THEM an edited version of events. But when he came to the end, and described Mrs. T-J's apparent capitulation, he knew in his heart that it was not all right. In fact, he was quite sure it was all wrong.

TWENTY-SEVEN

⁓

THURSDAY MORNING, AND THE WHOLE VILLAGE PRE-
pared for Cyril's funeral; not just old friends and
neighbours, distant relations, civic dignitaries and repre-
sentatives of his old regiment, but also those who wanted
to be seen to be there.

The passing bell began to toll, and Lois shivered as she
made her way to the church. It was a mournful sound, one
bell ringing insistently, reminding the village that this was
no ordinary morning. It had been one of Cyril's duties, and
he had solemnly seen many an old friend on their way with
his doleful ringing. Out of respect for an old customer,
Mrs. Carr had announced that she would not open the shop
until two o'clock. Sandy Mackerras had been allowed time
off, and members of the choir had made arrangements to
be free for their part in the service. Lois had helpfully revised the cleaning schedules.

Bill, Rebecca, Jamie and Mrs. T-J were all in the vestry,
putting on their scarlet robes. Old Gladys, long-time friend
of Cyril and former organist, had let it be known that she

was extremely offended at not being asked to play, and arrived at the church early. She sat in a front pew, and glared disapproval at Sharon, already at the organ playing a selection of Cyril's favourite songs. "No idea how to play those old tunes," Gladys muttered to an old crone sitting beside her. "Making a right mess of 'Moon River'—got the timing all wrong!" She smiled nastily, cheered up by knowing she could have done better.

The church filled up, until folding chairs were hastily fetched and set out in a side aisle. Conversation was subdued but vigorous. There were waves of recognition from one side of the church to the other. Babies were soothed, coat collars turned up in the draughty church, comments passed on how much *older* so-and-so looked in the dusty light coming through grey glass windows. A few brave souls hummed "Moon River," and a tear or two fell, remembering old Cyril and his eccentric performances on his own Hammond organ.

Then silence fell. Sharon glanced around and received her signal from the undertaker. She brought the recital to a gentle close, and put her hands in her lap.

"Jesus said," a loud voice proclaimed from the porch, and heads were bowed. Brian Rollinson, tall and spare, his face shining with certainty that Cyril had gone to a far, far better place, began to pronounce the soul-stirring words: "I am the resurrection, and I am the life; he who believes in me, though he die, yet shall he live, and whoever lives and believes in me shall never die."

Lois looked around, her spine tingling, and saw the vicar heading the sad procession, his white surplice fresh and immaculate, his head held high. Undertakers bore Cyril's coffin, crowned with flowery wreaths, slowly up the aisle towards the chancel. Following were Cyril's sister and her daughter, and a small group of people, distant relations, who were complete strangers to the assembled villagers. As the coffin passed slowly, some choked and

fumbled for their handkerchiefs. Lois sniffed, told herself
not to be a fool, and was unable to stop hot, salty tears running into her mouth.

She turned her head again to the back of the church,
hoping to conceal her weakness from Gran. Her eye was
caught by a tall, pale-faced young man, dressed all in black
and wearing dark glasses. Who was that, then? He was
standing partly concealed by the stone font, and squeezed
into a corner by a group of local children drummed up
from the Sunday School, where Cyril had been an unpop-
ular helper. Lois felt Gran nudge her.

"Don't stare, Lois." Gran was dry-eyed, being no
stranger to funerals and death, and stood quite straight, her
expression calm. Lois peered at her through watery eyes,
and was amazed to see the ghost of a smile on her lips.
Gran handed Lois a tissue. "He'd love to be here," she
whispered.

Lois took the tissue and nodded. She made a mental
note to ask her mother if she knew the black-clothed young
man. In a church full of people wearing black, there was no
reason why he should stand out, but he did. The dark
glasses? Probably an affectation, but there was something
else. Something about the way he stood, chin jutting out,
hands gripping the back of the pew in front. Her attention
was taken again by the vicar, speaking in a pleasant voice,
with just the right amount of solemnity.

The service went smoothly. The choir sang, not too
lustily as befitted the occasion, and "Abide With Me" was
a success. Mrs. T-J held on to the ends of lines a fraction
longer than was necessary, as was her custom, and Rebecca kept her alto harmony respectfully muted.

Brian Rollinson had worked hard at the address. He
believed in portraying the departed in as true a light as possible, emphasizing good works and achievements, but also
raising an affectionate laugh at the natural blemishes in
every human character. Cyril was dealt with kindly, and

with good humour. The atmosphere in the church warmed up slightly, in spite of chilly gusts of air from the bell tower.

Finally it was time for the bearers to shoulder the coffin once more, and all were invited to take refreshment in the village hall after the committal. Not everyone went up to the windy cemetery, but those who did stood silently and tearfully as an old soldier from Cyril's wartime regiment sounded the Last Post from a high point among the graves.

Lois, standing by the cemetery gates, had a good view of the assembled mourners. There he was again! This time he had added a black overcoat against the cold wind. A piece of grit must have blown into his eye, and he took off the glasses, rubbing his hand across his eyes. Before replacing them, he looked across towards the gates and Lois recognized him. It was that thug! The one who'd been running away laughing with others on the television, when Annabelle had suddenly said, "Max!" So it was Max. Max the thug. What on earth was he doing at old Cyril's funeral?

Brian Rollinson, dignified and reassuring, said with absolute confidence that Cyril was "in sure and certain hope of the resurrection to eternal life," and the service was at an end. The small crowd began to drift away back to the village hall, and Lois kept an eye on Max. She saw him slip expertly between the cluster of people blocking the gates, and after that she lost him.

As she walked back down the quiet street, leaving Gran to join the others having refreshments, a car passed her slowly and pulled up outside the shop. When she reached it, Hunter Cowgill lowered the window and said, "Morning, Lois. A sad day. And by the way, before you say anything, I am asking you when the shop is opening today."

Lois glowered at him. "What are you *really* saying then?"

He smiled at her. She warmed the cockles, did his Lois. "I've been to the funeral," he said seriously. "Paying my respects. I noticed what we might call an outsider."

"Ah," said Lois. "So did I. Him with eye problems."

"More interestingly," he added quickly, seeing Gran approaching. "We know he's one of the Wycombe Society— black magic mumbo-jumbo lot I was telling you about. Keep your eye open for more sightings. Heard of him at all?"

Lois hesitated, which Cowgill noted. "Um, no, I don't think so," she said.

"Lois, Lois," he said. "You've not changed. Family first, as always. And quite right too. But I did warn you about Jamie's Annabelle. Oh yes, and poor old Cyril had traces of something not quite right in his stomach. More later." Gran had almost reached them, and he said quickly, "I'll keep in touch. You brighten my day." Before she could retort, the window was shut and he drove off, gathering speed until the car disappeared around the corner.

"Who was that, Lois?"

"Somebody wanting the shop. I told him Mrs. Carr was opening up at two."

Gran looked at her suspiciously. "Car looked familiar," she said, and left it there.

IN THE CHURCH, SHARON TIDIED HER MUSIC AND PUT it neatly in her case. She had played on after most people had left for the cemetery, enjoying the old tunes and thinking about Cyril. Now she heard footsteps in the vestry and sat quietly, breathing in the heavy scent of lilies from the pedestal by the altar. She recognized Sandy's voice, talking to the vicar. He must have come back to disrobe. She could hear one or two choir members, too, still there, and gossiping quietly. She had no reason to hurry. Mrs. M had rearranged her cleaning duties for the morning, and she would still be on time for the vicarage this afternoon. Out of sight of the main body of the church, she closed her eyes, allowing her thoughts to wander. She saw behind her eyelids the vestry, pictured the pile of robes on the floor and Sandy's amorous face close to hers.

In a daydream, she did not realize the church was now quiet. She snapped awake to the sound of two pairs of footsteps, clacking sharply on the tiled floor of the aisle. Although she could not be seen, she could see. It was Sandy and Rebecca, and at the door of the church they stopped. Frozen with horror, Sharon saw Sandy put out a hand and touch Rebecca's cheek. Neither said a word. Then he leaned forward and kissed her lightly. She did not move. He kissed her again, less lightly, and this time with her arms around his neck. Sharon sat as if turned to stone. She stayed like that until the long embrace ended and they disappeared. Then she blinked, stood up unsteadily, and made her way out of the church, walking awkwardly. She tripped on the uneven stone path and fell. Her head hit the iron support for the bird-proof gates, and she groaned, her music scattering over the path. She tried to get up, but felt dizzy and sick. Putting her head between her knees, she began to cry like a child with a grazed knee.

"What's the trouble?" A man's voice. Sharon looked up with difficulty against a reeling sky. A tall, black figure stood silhouetted in front of her. "Here," he said. "Let me help you up." She put out a hand and he lifted her to her feet. "What *is* a pretty girl like you doing sitting on the ground sobbing her heart out?"

She shook her head. "I fell. Hurt myself," she said.

"I've seen you around," he said in a friendly way. "In the pub, with young Sandy? Him that I just saw in a clinch with a dark-haired beauty?" At this, Sharon collapsed, and the stranger put his arm around her shoulders. "So sorry!"

he said. "Tactless fool . . . but never mind—Sharon, isn't it?—I'm just the person you need to put Sandy Mackerras straight." And he laughed unpleasantly. "Come on," he said briskly, helping her to pick up the music, "I'll give you a lift home, and tell you more."

Twenty-eight

❧

"DID YOU KNOW OLD CYRIL, THEN?" SHARON WAS feeling less dizzy, seated in the front seat of a low-slung sports car parked in a lay-by on the way to Waltonby. "Why were you at the funeral?"

"I knew him slightly," her companion said. "But I'm ashamed to confess I enjoy a good funeral—theatre, you know, all the drama and emotion."

Oh yeah, thought Sharon, and changed the subject. "Did you say your name? I'm afraid I didn't quite catch . . ."

"Maximilian is my name," said her companion. "Bit of a mouthful! I'm Max to my friends. Which I hope will include you, Sharon dear."

He sounded a bit weird, Sharon thought. Fancy enjoying funerals! And the way he spoke. Not like her friends, and certainly not at all like Sandy. Sandy could be one of the lads in the pub, talking their language, or he could be quiet and gentle, but he was always the same Sandy. This man sounded like one of the characters in her novels.

"I think I'd better be getting back," she said, as he turned his smile on her, and she noticed his teeth were crooked and discoloured. "I'm fine now."

"Oh, what a pity," he said. "I was going to give you lunch at a pub. Set you up for scrubbing floors this afternoon!"

Sharon glared at him. "Nothing wrong with cleaning," she said defensively.

"But I haven't told you my little plan," he continued, not in the least put out. "Between us, we can make your Sandy jealous, win him back from Bill's Rebecca. Does that appeal, Sharon?"

She was tempted, and intrigued by how much he seemed to know. "Tell me, then. But quickly. I've got things to do at home before I go to the vicarage."

He turned to her and took off his glasses. Nothing wrong with *his* eyes, then. She had sometimes thought of wearing dark glasses herself, to conceal the wandering eye. But she couldn't be bothered. And anyway, she repeated to herself, love me, love my eyes.

Max's eyes were small, grey and hard, and he looked at her closely. "Right," he said, in a different, more ordinary voice. "I'll take you to a sort of club I kind of run. Sandy comes sometimes, and that girlfriend of your boss's son— Annabelle whatsit. You can come with me, and I'll make a fuss of you—make sure Sandy notices."

"What do you do at this club?" said Sharon suspiciously.

"It's fun, but it's also more than that. We can give each other power, make things happen in a way outsiders can't understand."

Sharon frowned. "Sounds 'orrible," she said, but then added, "but when does Sandy come? And is he on his own?"

Max laughed, showing his nasty teeth. "Yes," he said.

"So far . . . Anyway, you might know some of the others. And if you don't like it, you can forget the whole thing."

Sharon thought for a moment. The idea of a jealous Sandy was appealing. "All right, then," she said, "just this once. When?"

"Next week? Friday evening. Sandy'll definitely be there. He's a vital part of the evening. I'll pick you up at seven. Wrap up warm. Sometimes we have a bonfire."

"A barbecue? Oh, that'd be nice," said Sharon, and smiled as he drove her straight home. He never even put his hand on my knee, she thought. I'll be safe enough with him.

LOIS HAD REACHED HOME AND SAT IN HER CHILLY OF-fice thinking about Cyril. Derek wouldn't have the central heating on during the day, and Lois shivered. What was it Cowgill had said? They'd found something wrong with the old man's stomach? Ugh! She remembered the mess in his bedroom. The police had probably taken samples. But what could they have found? His last meal would have been tea. Bacon and eggs, every day without fail. His menu was simple and routine. Breakfast: cereal and toast. Lunch: frozen fish fingers, or a burger from a packet, chips and peas. And for tea, bacon and eggs. Eggs? They could be a bit dodgy. Salmonella, was it? It was sometimes serious, Lois knew. Perhaps that was it. But the eggs came from the shop, and were new-laid, free-range from a nearby farm. And Cyril always fried them until they were like yellow pebbles. She'd teased him about it once, and he'd protested that his mother always cooked them like that, and that was how he liked them.

Gran came in with a cup of tea. "Not brooding, are you, Lois?" she said.

Lois shook her head. "No, just thinking."

"Dangerous business, thinking," said her mother.

Lois sighed. "Yes, well, do you remember Cyril saying anything about feeling sick the day he died?"

"No—well, not more'n usual. He was a martyr to his indigestion. I reckon he was Mrs. Carr's best customer for remedies. Mind you, those things she gave me had no effect at all. Made it worse, I reckon."

"Well, you had a bug, Mum. It wasn't just indigestion. And anyway, it didn't kill you."

Gran grinned. "I thought it was going to, at its worst! But no, you're right. Whatever done for old Cyril was something quick and powerful, poor ole bugger. If ever I should swear!" she added hastily.

Lois sipped her tea, which was hot and restoring. "I might go out this afternoon," she said. "Get some supplies from Tresham. I'll probably call in on Cyril's sister, just to pay my respects and see if there's anything we can do."

Gran looked at her suspiciously. "Hardly necessary, I'd have thought?" she said. "Still, don't take notice of me. You never do anyway!" She frowned and looked more closely at her daughter. "You're not up to anything, are you?" she said. "And by the way, I've remembered who that car belongs to. The one you were talking to this morning. Don't go forgetting the trouble that cop got us all into those other times."

Lois said nothing, and Gran turned to leave, saying as a parting shot, "And don't forget you have a very good husband."

Lois made a face at her mother's departing back, and got up to look out of the window. The street was back to its empty, quiet self. Not a soul in sight. Lois felt restless, plagued by Cowgill's hints and cloak-and-dagger games. He'd always been like this, and she supposed it jollied up a boring job. She should ignore him, tell him to get lost. That's what Derek would say. He was clearly hoping this latest contact with an old enemy would fizzle out. Still, he had a pact with Lois. She would tell him what was going on, and he would not try to stop her playing detective. He would even help, if he could, on the old principle that if you can't beat 'em, join 'em.

She saw a car then, a smart sports job, cruise down the street and stop outside the Millers' garage. She'd not seen that one before. Most local people used the village garage, and their cars were familiar. It didn't turn in, though, but pulled up by the kerb. The door opened, and Lois was taken aback. Sharon, carrying her music case, stepped out and waved goodbye to the car, now slipping away. Lois automatically made a note of the number plate, and wrote it down on her pad. Sharon was one of her team now, and everything she did was of interest. Not nosy! Lois answered an imagined, critical Gran. All part of my job. Well, Sharon was due at the vicarage later this afternoon, so Lois crossed her fingers and hoped all would go well.

She was turning back to her desk, when she saw another traveller along the street. This time she knew only too well who it was. She smiled, and then wondered why Jamie was coming home at this time of day. He'd gone straight from the funeral into Tresham, where he was working. Why had he come back so soon? He turned into the drive, and Lois went through to the kitchen to greet him.

"Hi Mum, Gran . . ." His voice was subdued.

"What are you doing home so early?" said Gran, not one to beat about the bush.

"Not feeling so good," he replied, and cleared his throat. "Maybe a cold. I've got a sore throat . . . think I'll take an aspirin and crash out for a bit."

"Don't you want something to eat?"

Jamie shook his head, and walked out of the kitchen. They heard him stump up the stairs and then his bedroom door slammed. Lois and Gran looked at each other. "Sore throat?" said Lois. "That wouldn't send him home in the middle of the day."

"Better go up and talk to him," Gran said. "Here—take him a cup of tea. See what's up."

Jamie sat on his bed, still in his biker's rig, with his head in his hands. He looked up as his mother came in. "Gran's cure-all?" he said. "Nice cup of tea?" And to Lois's horror, a tear plopped out of his eye and on to his leather jacket.

"What on earth's the matter?" she said. She sat down on the bed beside him and put an arm around his shoulders. "Hey," she said. "Big boys don't cry." It was an old phrase from his childhood, and he tried to smile at her.

"Sorry, Mum," he said.

"So what is it?" Lois spoke quietly, and waited. As Jamie appeared to be dumb with misery, she said, "Annabelle?" Bullseye. He nodded, and then began to speak.

"I rang her this morning to make a date." His hands, with their narrow, pianist's fingers, twisted together. "Mrs. T-J answered the phone. She said I couldn't speak to Annabelle, because she wasn't there." He sniffed, and Lois silently handed him the tissue Gran had given her earlier. "I asked when she'd be back, and the old witch said she wouldn't be back. She'd gone up to London to stay with friends, and would be there until her mother returned. She added that I was not to try and get in touch with her, because Annabelle had said she was fed up with me pestering her . . ." He choked, and it was a minute or two before he began again. "And that was one of the reasons she'd gone. I managed to ask her what the other reasons were, and she told me to mind my own business. End of conversation."

He turned to Lois and looked at her bleakly. "I know what the other reason was, anyway," he said. "I'm not

good enough for her precious granddaughter. Village boy.
No money. No car . . ."

"And mother a cleaner," said Lois bitterly, sick with
anger.

Twenty-nine

❧

Brian Rollinson had eaten a quick sandwich, and now sat without light in his gloomy study, dark even though it was still afternoon. He had been looking blankly out of the window, watching rain falling relentlessly on his sleeping garden. He was longing for Christmas, with its hopeful message of new beginnings. The winter had seemed so long, cold and cheerless. And today, consigning old Cyril to the next world, he had for once failed to find comfort in the familiar words.

He could always put on a good show, of course. That was his job, and he knew the village spoke warmly of his funerals. He sighed. Would his spirit ever be quiet? He had been drawn to the church as a refuge—probably a mistake, for a start—and had met men, young and old, who had the strength and peace of mind that he so coveted. They were an inspiration, yes, but he also envied them their tranquillity. Had any of them had a past such as his, a past that crept up on them in their dreams and gave them unquiet sleep? Maybe. Or perhaps they were as good as he at concealing inner turmoil.

A sharp knocking at the front door brought him to his feet. He looked at his watch. Sharon Miller, dead on time.

He opened the door and looked at her pink cheeks, yellow hair blowing in the cold wind, and was cheered by her big smile. Such a pity about the eye, he thought. Still, it hadn't put off young Sandy!

"Hello, my dear," he said. "Come in, come in. The wind's too cold to be standing about. Now," he added, once they were inside and heading for the kitchen, "you know the ropes, so I shall leave you to it. Work to do, you know. Oh, and by the way, you played the organ beautifully for old Cyril. He would have been so touched to hear all his old favourites."

"Maybe he did hear," said Sharon, buttoning her overall. "Up there, you know, watching us all." Brian suddenly saw through her eyes a childlike vision of old Cyril, clad in a pure white robe, perched on a cloud and observing them all with his evil grin. He laughed, his optimism returning, and strode off with a lighter heart to write to Sandy's mother. Sandy was no letter-writer, and so he had promised Marion he would keep in touch. He told her only the good things, of course, and made absolutely no mention of Sandy's lustful tryst with Sharon Miller in the vestry. No, no, he wouldn't shop the lad, however much he tried his patience.

Sharon's mind was not on cleaning this afternoon. She dusted and polished in a dream. How many people had seen her getting out of Max's sports car? Lots, she hoped. When she had finished downstairs, she looked at her watch, and tapped on the vicar's study door. "Time for a cuppa?" she said.

Brian smiled at her. "Lovely, thanks Sharon," he said. The sermon had gone well, and he thought perhaps a short break, a chat with Sharon, would be timely. It had worried him a little that Sandy was such a butterfly in his affections. He would hate to see this innocent—well, perhaps not so innocent, but certainly naïve—young girl with a broken heart.

He'd done his share of breaking hearts, he reminded himself. And more seriously than Sandy. Much more seriously. He looked at his letter to Marion, neatly sealed and stamped, and wondered if he could ever forgive himself—if, indeed, there had been any other path he could have taken. Marion and Gerald had been the perfect couple. Everyone said so. A handsome pair, with every prospect of a happy married life.

Brian shook his head violently, as if to scramble unwanted thoughts, and stood up. Useless to brood on the past. He pushed back his chair and walked through to the kitchen, where Sharon was busy with mugs and teabags. "Let's sit down for a few minutes," he said. "Take a short break. I'd like a little chat about next Sunday's hymns." This was an innovation in Long Farnden church. Consultation and compromise, these were Brian's bywords. His tutors had shown him how to achieve his goals without resentment and animosity—at least, that was the aim. They hadn't told him about such as ex-organist Gladys Mary Smith, of course, but she seemed to have subsided into a simmering resentment that he hoped would fade.

"Now," he said, opening the hymn book, "I thought that after the second lesson we might have number seven: 'Christ, whose glory fills the skies.'"

Sharon nodded. She was quite happy to play whatever he suggested, and was anxious to get back to her daydreaming. Would Max pick her up in the sports car to go to the meeting? She must make sure to mention it to the Carrs, so they could look out of their window.

"By Charles Wesley, this one," said Brian. "It has been described as 'one of his loveliest progeny.'"

"You what?" said Sharon.

"Well, one of the best of his hymns. He composed a great many, you know."

"Right." Sharon took another biscuit. She could do without this togetherness.

"The words are full of light and darkness imagery," ploughed on Brian. "So lovely to start the morning in the light of Christ's glory . . ." He looked at Sharon, who was staring out of the window.

"Oh, look," she said. "There's the dairy van. That's good. Mrs. Carr was hoping they'd be there today with the new yoghurts. She was running short, she said."

Brian gave up. "Here," he said, putting the list in front of her. "See what you think. I'm always happy to change them if you or the choir disagree. Now I must get on."

Funny bloke, thought Sharon. Still, all vicars are a bit odd. Rotten job, anyway, dealing with the likes of Mrs. T-J and old Gladys. She resumed work, going into Sandy's bedroom briskly, determined not to think about him at all. Just another room to clean. Then she picked up a sweater from the floor and the smell of his aftershave wafted under her nose. She held it against her cheek and closed her eyes. Sod him, she thought, but was comforted by the possibility of the small revenge that Max had dangled before her.

As Sharon emerged from the vicarage into the darkening street, a car pulled up beside her, and she looked round, suddenly excited. But it was only the boss, Mrs. M, who lowered her window and said, "Everything all right, Sharon? Jump in, I'll give you a lift."

"No, it's OK thanks, it's only a few steps."

"Come on, girl, I want a word."

"She who must be obeyed," muttered Sharon, and got in. She'd had enough of little chats for one day.

"Was everything all right at the vicarage, then?" repeated Lois.

"Yep, fine," said Sharon.

"Did the vicar say anything about this morning? Old Cyril, an' that?" Lois's tone was casual.

"No, not about Cyril. He just thanked me for playing the songs. Said Cyril would've bin pleased. But I'm not so sure about that!" Sharon laughed. "He was a miserable old sod most of the time. Mrs. Carr says we have to make allowances, because of his indigestion. Enough to make anyone bad-tempered, she says. He's got a good heart, she says." She paused, and added, "*Had* a good heart, I should say . . ."

"Yes, well, it wasn't a good end, Sharon. Poor old man must've been in great pain that last night. Did he complain at all . . . more than usual? In the shop, I mean?"

Sharon shook her head. "No, he'd been in for some more tablets in the afternoon, and I opened a new box. He went off quite cheerful . . . for him . . ."

They were outside the Millers' garage, and Lois stopped. "There you are then," she said. "Don't forget the team meeting on Monday. Twelve o'clock sharp. Enjoy the weekend."

Sometimes, thought Sharon, as she opened her front door, Mrs. M could be quite nice.

THIRTY

> ❧

At noon on Monday the sun was still low, and shining through Lois's office window, where it filled the fish tank with light, dazzling the ghost goldfish hiding behind an immersed pottery ashtray remembered fondly by Gran as Ash Cottage. Fishy-Wishy had been golden once, but age and a tumour at the base of his tail fin had rendered him colourless, except for an ugly red patch of scaleless skin. Lois stared at him. "You're a survivor, F. Wishy," she said. "A lesson to us all." Wiser than the vet, nature had taken pity on the fish and cured the tumour without aid. "No such luck for Cyril," Lois muttered. "Perhaps he'd have done better to go easy on the tablets."

Tablets for indigestion. A new box opened by Sharon that very afternoon. Something that Mrs. Carr kept just for her favourites. Lois wrote a memo to herself. *Shop: ask about tablets.* She picked up her mug of coffee awkwardly and it slipped from her hand, spreading scalding liquid over her desk and on to her legs. "Bloody hell!" She gasped, jumped up and ran to the kitchen for help. Gran was not around, so she grabbed cloths and a kitchen roll and ran back. Luckily, only her memo pad was soaked, and she threw it quickly into the bin. The skin on her thighs was beginning to sting, and when she had finished mopping up she rushed upstairs for the burn cream. She was still smoothing it over the tender skin when a knock at the front door signalled the start of the weekly team meeting.

"Coming!" she yelled, and pulled on a dry pair of jeans. She felt dizzy and queasy.

"Mrs. M? Are you OK?" It was Bill, standing foursquare and reassuring on the step. She remembered his nursing experience in Tresham General, and explained.

"Shock, probably," he said. "Go and sit down and I'll make you a drink."

At this moment, Derek arrived back from a job he'd finished early, took one look at Lois and made for the cupboard in the corner. "Brandy," he said. "That's what you need, my girl."

When Bill returned with a cup of hot, sweet tea, an argument ensued. Derek stuck by the brandy, and Bill said it was not right. They became so heated that Lois realized she was totally forgotten and stood up.

"Derek! Bill! Shut up the pair of you! I'm fine now, and we've got work to do. Gran's around somewhere, Derek, and she'll get your dinner. Bill—sit down and wait for the others. I'm just going for pee. Back in a minute."

The two men looked at each other. "Right," said Derek. "That seems to be that. She's like that, Bill. Might as well leave her be."

Bill nodded. "Yeah, well, you're right. Still, I'll keep an eye during the meeting. Just to be on the safe side."

"Fine," said Derek, and left the room.

When they were all there, Enid Abraham, Sheila, Bill, Sharon, Bridie and Hazel with her bump, Lois picked up her pen and said, "Morning everybody. Let's get the schedules sorted, and then we can go over anything else you want to talk about." She shifted uneasily in her seat.

"Sure you're all right to carry on?" said Bill, unwisely.

"Forget it, Bill," snapped Lois, and took them through the week's jobs at a cracking pace.

Enid was the first to speak up. "I wonder if I could make a suggestion?" she said mildly. Enid Abraham had gone through dreadful family troubles, but had come through with increased confidence. Lois had a soft spot for her, and remembered how kind she had been in giving Jamie his first piano lessons.

"Of course," she said, and moved her legs, wincing.

The others looked sideways at each other. If any of *them* had offered suggestions, they'd have got a dusty answer, especially this morning, when Lois was clearly suffering.

Enid continued, "I have been wondering if it would be a good idea to suggest—for the spring—a special package to our existing customers? Spring cleaning, in the good old-fashioned way. A good turn-out and airing throughout the house. It was always done in the old days, and I remember as a child how sweet my grandmother's house smelled after she'd gone through it like a tornado!"

Again the others exchanged glances, waiting for the explosion. The thought of extra work, more organizing, would surely bring forth a storm. But Lois smiled at Enid, nodded her head, and said, "Great! Why didn't the rest of us think of that? Thanks, Enid, you're a star."

Bill frowned. Had Lois flipped? Was this what happened with shock and a large brandy? He cleared his throat, and said, "If there's nothing else, perhaps we should let you go and have a rest, Lois. Scalding can be very nasty." He braced himself, waiting for another snub, but Sharon spoke up first.

"Um, there was one thing before you go, Mrs. M. I've been invited to a sort of party, and need to get a new dress, an' the buses aren't that good, an' I thought I'd go in on

Thursday afternoon—the party's on Thursday—and see what I could get. Trouble is," she carried on without a pause, "I'm supposed to be at the vicarage." She stopped, smiled brightly at Lois, and waited.

Lois realized she was feeling distinctly odd now, and said quickly, "Fine, Sharon. Whatever. I'll cover for you. Now, if there's nothing else . . ." And then she fainted and was caught by swift action from Bill, who carried her upstairs to bed.

When she surfaced later, and sat up in bed drinking tea and trying to reassure an anxious Derek, she realized she could remember nothing from what had happened at the meeting. Something about spring cleaning? Ah well, she'd ask Bill. He would fill her in, and then she could get on with her week's work.

Gran quietly cleaned the coffee stains off the carpet, emptied the soggy waste paper from the bin, and polished the top of Lois's desk. "Takes on too much, that girl," she muttered to herself. "Expect she was miles away, not thinking what she was doing. Just like those other times when she got mixed up with that cop. Damn it all!"

REBECCA WAS HOME FROM SCHOOL AND COOKING. THE kitchen was full of steam and warmth, and Bill put his arms around her waist and kissed her floury face.

"Pooh!" she said. "You smell of cows!"

Offended, Bill withdrew. "Never bothered you before," he said. "Anyway, it's part of my job. Once I'd finished at the Hall, I had to help with one of old Giles's cows in trouble. Sebastian sent an SOS. That's why I'm a bit late."

"Hadn't noticed," said Rebecca. She was remembering the good smell of Sandy Mackerras, the clean masculine scent that surrounded her when they kissed.

"I'm out tonight," she said. "We'll have supper early. That's why I'm well on with it now."

"Where're you going? You never said anything this morning . . ." Bill was instantly suspicious. Did she think he was a fool? All those lecherous looks from Sandy in church, returned with blushes and smiles from his Rebecca . . . Yes, *his* Rebecca! Maybe it was time he said something. But what? He and Rebecca were not married. She was free to go anywhere and with anyone, and if he didn't like it, he could leave. It was her cottage, after all. She'd lived there before he joined her, coming down from Yorkshire in determined pursuit. No, his commonsense told him it would be best to ride it out, unless it became too unbearable.

"Governors' meeting," she said quickly. "Probably go on later than usual. A lot to discuss, what with the new classroom extension and all that. Don't wait up for me."

This was too much. "Go on that late?" exploded Bill. "Come on, Rebecca, I wasn't born yesterday. What're you up to?"

She gave him an icy look, and said, "Don't ever say that to me again, Bill Stockbridge. We have an open relationship, remember? Respect each other. Trust each other." She felt a pang when she said this. Still, nothing had really happened with Sandy. Mild flirting, that was all.

MAX WEDDERBURN (OR DARREN COCKSHUTT, AS HIS mother knew him) sat in his cramped bed-sitting-room in Tresham, staring at the television. He had come home from work—a mundane job in the office of a second-hand car showroom—and put in his favourite video, fast-forwarding it to the sequence he had played over and over again. He loved the Coen brothers' films, with their strange twisted plots and spooky violence. This one, a tale of the Deep South, featured three convicts escaping, and had the most exciting scene of all. He peered closely at the screen, where a black friend of the convicts is dragged by the Ku

Klux Klan to a huge and fearsome gathering of figures in white robes and pointed hoods, a giant fiery cross towering over them. Their leader, a bigoted, racist local, harangues the chanting multitude in violent and inciting language, and tension rises like the leaping flames from the cross.

Max huddled close to the screen, his fists clenched. The next scene, where the black guitarist is rescued, was not to his taste. He licked his lips and reached for the off button.

His mobile rang.

Who the hell? "Hello, Darren?" It was his mother, asking him to collect his washing next time he was round that way, and would he like to come to tea on Sunday, when his Auntie Doris would be coming and she'd love to see him.

THIRTY-ONE

❧

"WHERE'RE WE GOING, THEN?" SHARON HAD FI-nally decided on jeans and a new top, with a scarlet leather jacket and her hair in a swinging ponytail. She looked clean and fresh, and very young.

"You'll see," said Max, glancing at her approvingly and smiling. They continued along the dark country lanes in silence for a while, Sharon trying not to notice that the glamorous sports car was the most uncomfortable ride she'd ever had. Max drove well, but she felt every bump in the rough road surface.

"Max," she said tentatively.

"Yes?" He could see that she was looking at her own re-flection in the dark window.

"You know about my eyes?" she continued slowly.

"What about them?" Max's thoughts were elsewhere.

"Well, one of them wanders around a bit," she said, turning to look straight at his profile. It was a good profile, and you couldn't see his teeth in the dark. "I thought I might see about getting it fixed. Now I'm getting out and about an' that." His reaction startled her.

"No!" he said violently, then lowered his voice quickly. "No, don't do that, Sharon. You're perfect as you are. Our Sandy wouldn't have anything to do with you unless you were special, you can be sure of that!"

She blinked. "Oh. Right, then. Thanks."

A near thing, that, thought Max. The strangely independent eye had been the very thing that had attracted the Wycombe Society. Eyes like Sharon's had magical properties, gave mystical power to their owners. It was in the lore. Not that the likes of Sharon would know about that, of course, but she would be shown how to make the most of her gift.

"Oh, I know where we are!" she said, changing the subject with relief. "It's Mrs. T-J's! We used to play Trespass in there when we were kids. Is she a member of your lot?"

"Not really," he said evasively. "But her granddaughter, Annabelle—you know her?—comes along. Mrs. T-J is abroad at the moment, inspecting her racing stables in South Africa. A woman of many parts, our Mrs. T-J!"

The car approached the house, then turned off on a curving drive to where the outbuildings huddled round a courtyard. Lights were blazing in one of them, and Max pulled up outside. He went quickly round to the passenger door, and helped Sharon to struggle out. Not very elegant, she said to herself. I shall have to practise that. She looked through the lighted window and saw a dozen or so people, all in animated conversation, full glasses in hand. Suddenly she felt frightened. What was she doing here? It was not her world at all. But it *was* the world of her novels, of her dreams. And so she braced herself and followed Max into the meeting.

•   •   •

THAT AFTERNOON, LOIS HAD TURNED UP AT THE VIC-
arage as substitute for Sharon, as arranged. It had been a
strange couple of hours. She sat now in front of the fire,
cup of tea in hand, and watched Gran's fingers busy with
her knitting. Derek had said he would be late, and the two
had eaten earlier.

"Everything all right with the vicar?" Gran had decided
Brian Rollinson would do. She found him a bit secretive,
withdrawn sometimes, and had said so to Lois, who'd
agreed. But both had said they liked him and thought he
was doing a good job.

"He was fine," Lois said. But that was not altogether
true. He was friendly enough, as always, but had followed
her about the house like a dog, starting sentences and not
finishing them, leaving questions hanging in the air. What
had he wanted to know? More than once he had asked
where Sharon had gone. When she'd mentioned a chap
with a sports car, he had frowned, and said he thought that
Max Wedderburn was one of Sandy's less desirable
friends. Lived in Tresham and was known to the police.
Had been involved in some racist secret society that
plagued the black community in town and left threatening
messages scrawled on the homes of known . . . er . . . gays.

Suddenly Lois remembered the contorted face on television news, and Annabelle's sudden "Max!" blurted out
and then swiftly retracted. Oh my God, she thought now,
watching the flames flicker in the grate, what is our Sharon
up to now? True to form, the overprotected precious
daughter was the most likely to go off the rails—and in
Sharon's case, right off and into a bog, if Cowgill was
right. Lois sighed. Better have a word with him. She finished her tea and said there were one or two things she had
to clear up in her study. Gran looked hard at her. "Derek
will be home soon," she said. "You promised him ice
cream, and there's none in the freezer."

"OK, OK! I'll go next door and borrow some as soon as

I've cleared up." She left the room, and only just stopped herself banging the door. Sometimes Mum was a bit too ever-present. You bet she'd have her ears flapping for the sound of the telephone.

"Hello, is that Inspector Cowgill?" It was, and he was delighted to hear from Lois. However, he kept his delight out of his voice, and asked her crisply what he could do for her.

"You asked me to keep my eyes open—something to do with that Wycombe lot. Well, I need to ask a question or two. I can't help unless you squeeze the tiniest bit of information out for me."

Cowgill ignored the sarcasm, and said, "Fire away. What d'you want to know?"

"How many, where do they meet, what do they do, and is one of them called Max?"

He gave her details that made grim listening. Up to thirty had been seen gathering in twilight on Tresham Common. They liked fires, and were not averse to a spot of chanting. Nothing had been proved, but they were thought to be behind a lot of the racial disturbances in town. And not just blacks. Chinese, immigrants, gays. They were not fussy. Max Wedderburn was their leader. "A very nasty piece of work, too," added Cowgill. "We're watching them closely, but they're smart. Always out of the way by the time we arrive, and careful not to infringe any by-laws at their meetings. Kind of sad mixture of good old-fashioned black arts, and the KKK, which is infinitely worse, and why we're more than interested in Mr. Wedderburn-cum-Cockshutt."

"Well," said Lois, a catch in her voice. "That's not too good, because our Sharon Miller has gone to a party with the said Max Wedderburn, and I have no idea where it is."

"Ah," said Cowgill.

"One more thing," said Lois. "Are they dangerous?"

"Yes," said Cowgill bluntly. "Every instinct in my old

policeman's body tells me they're dangerous, so sit tight, Lois, and I'll keep you posted. Bye."

But this was not good enough for Lois. She felt a reluctant responsibility for Sharon, and pulled on her coat, yelling out to Gran that she was just off to borrow ice cream. That would do for the moment.

The street was dark, and a cold wind made Lois wish for her scarf. She passed old Cyril's house, shut up now, with its mullioned windows blank and dead. Like Cyril, really. Lois knew there was something about Cyril at the back of her mind she'd meant to follow up. His sister? No, that had been a false trail. The old girl had hardly known him for years. Big show for his funeral, but no help in guessing what took him off so violently. Ah, well, it would come back. Right now she had to find out where Sharon had been taken. She turned in at Miller's garage and knocked at the house door.

"Is Sharon in?" she said, as Mr. Miller answered the door.

He shook his head. "Gone out to a party," he said. He peered out into the darkness. "Mrs. Meade, is it? Come in, won't you. It's a chilly night again." He stood aside to admit Lois, and took her into a warm, cheerful sitting room.

Mrs. Miller stood up, smiling. "Hello," she said. "What brings you out so late? Nothing wrong with Sharon's work, I hope?"

"No, not at all," said Lois. "She's fine. I'd nipped out to post a letter, and thought I'd have a quick word about tomorrow's client. Save a phone call. But she's not here?"

"Gone out with the new boyfriend," Mrs. Miller said. She frowned, and added, "Not sure I like this one. Too smarmy by half. Now that Sandy, he's a nice lad. Bit flighty, from what I hear! But that's right and proper at his age. No, this new one is a different kettle of fish all together."

"Do I know him?" said Lois innocently, taking the chair offered by Mr. Miller.

"We didn't." Sharon's father was unsmiling. "Just appeared suddenly. Turned up at Cyril's funeral. God knows why. Our Sharon took a tumble and he steadied her. Now it's Max this and Max that, and we don't hear no more about Sandy Mackerras. I know which one I prefer," he added glumly.

"Ah, well, our Josie was the same," said Lois, remembering her own daughter's involvement with serious crime. "And look at her now—couldn't be more respectable and settled! Still, if you think there's something not quite right, perhaps we should at least find out where she's gone?"

"Chance'd be a fine thing," said Mr. Miller. "We asked, but she didn't answer. 'Where're you going?' we asked, but all she said was 'Out!' Slammed the door and was gone. All done up in her best, hair washed, lots of makeup. Isn't that right, gel?" He turned to his wife, who nodded.

"Like a cup of tea?" Mr. Miller said, suddenly reluctant to let Lois go.

But Lois's niggling worry had turned to anxiety now, and she stood up. "Better not," she said. "Derek'll be wondering where I've got to. Cheerio—and don't worry too much. We all go through it!"

If only I was as sure as I sound, she thought, hurrying back up the street. There was one person who might remember something, with a little prompting. Brian Rollinson. Sharon must have rabbited on as usual to him, and it was unlikely she'd keep a party to herself. She would ring him straightaway.

"Good evening, Mrs. Meade. What can I do for you?" Brian tried to keep irritation at bay. He'd been in the middle of a really good play on television—a rare enough happening—and almost left the phone to ring. But it could have been Sandy. He had said he didn't know what time he'd be home, but not late. It wasn't Sandy.

"Did Sharon mention a party? No, I would have mentioned it to you, wouldn't I? But she does run on, so it's possible I wasn't listening. With Max Wedderburn? Ah, now that's the one we were talking about, isn't it. I don't know much about his haunts . . . where they meet, get together and do whatever it is they do. Mumbo jumbo, Sandy said, but he did go once or twice. Something there that attracts him, I suppose. Now, let me think."

Lois waited, fingers crossed. "Yes, this might help," Brian continued more confidently. "I believe your son knows Annabelle—granddaughter of Mrs. T-J—up at the Hall. Gone away? Oh, I didn't know that. But she was certainly one of the group, or society, or whatever they call themselves. Could be they meet up at the Hall sometimes? There's plenty of secret places on the estate, if that's what they like. You know, my dear," he added confidingly, "I had my suspicions that the burnt cross we found in the churchyard had something to do with that lot."

Lois remembered the small handkerchief with "A" embroidered in the corner. "Thanks," she said quickly. "Thanks a lot, vicar. See you." And rather to Brian's disappointment now, the phone clicked off. Then he heard Sandy's key in the lock and forgot all about Lois.

"Ah, there you are." Brian looked at Sandy's flushed face. "Are you all right?"

"Fine. Might go out later. There's a good programme on telly I'll miss, but you can record it for me." Sandy went straight to the fridge, looking for a beer. He turned to Brian, his breath revealing that it wouldn't be the first that evening. "Thought I asked you to get some supplies?" he said crossly. "Been looking forward to one all the way home."

"Sorry," said Brian. "I'll go down to the pub. Won't take me long."

"OK," said Sandy. "But don't be long. I've got one or two things to do, and then I'll be off. And I don't want that programme missed." His belligerent tone depressed Brian, but he promised to be back and left.

Sandy completed his task quickly, sniffed at his hands, then washed them and changed into fresh clothes. He slumped down on the sofa. It shouldn't be long now before he had his own place. Maybe he could tempt Rebecca to join him . . . a woman's touch about the place, and all that . . . God, he was tired! Funny way to make a living, flogging houses. And what on earth had Brian got on the telly? Some God-bothering programme. He turned down the sound and leaned back, eyes closed. A quick cat-nap would do no harm, then he'd be on his way. Brian would be back in a few minutes and he'd wake him. He began to snore gently.

"Lois!" It was Derek, back home in a gust of cold air. "For God's sake, woman, get off that phone. I'm expecting an important message about a big contract, but they'll never get through at this rate."

"And hello duckie to you, too," said Lois. She had not taken off her coat and, planting a moist kiss on Derek's cold cheek, said she'd be back soon. "Just off to clinch a job with a woman on the new estate. She's only there in the evenings." Then she was gone.

"Is that you, Lois?" called Gran. "Did you get the ice cream?"

Derek walked into the sitting room. "No, it's me," he said. "Your daughter has flown the coop, and as far as I know, taken the ice cream with her. What's for tea?"

Lois's car was slow to start. Damp, probably. It was not old, and had served her well so far. A smart white van, with New Brooms in gold lettering, it had been her proud purchase a couple of years ago. After one more attempt it fired, and Lois was on her way to the Hall. She found herself going faster than usual in the narrow, twisting lane. And what am I going to do if I find them? she asked herself. March in and demand to take Sharon home? She's not a child, for God's sake. But she kept going, and finally turned into the long drive up to the Hall. There were no lights in the house itself, but security lights snapped on as she drove into the stable yard. Nothing. No cars, nobody in the outbuildings. Everything quiet and still. They'd not met here, then.

Lois got out of the van and looked around. The stable yard was muddy with the rain, and a whinny from one of the loose boxes reminded her that Mrs. T-J kept a couple of hunters for her own use. Lois walked over to check on them, and stepped straight into thick mud. She looked down, furious with herself. New shoes, too! Then she saw the tracks. The security lights were bright, and she identified quite clearly the tracks of a car. And over in the shadows more showed up. Soon she realized they criss-crossed the entire yard. A number of cars had been here then, and quite recently. Damn! Must have been a short party . . . unless it continued somewhere else.

A stab of panic hit Lois. Where had they gone now—and why?

THIRTY-TWO

༄

THE WYCOMBE SOCIETY WAS ON THE MOVE. SHARON, back in Max's car, was feeling decidedly peculiar. "Am I a bit out of it?" she asked Max, and giggled. Had she had too many glasses of that stuff, whatever it was? She couldn't remember. She felt a bit sleepy, and not able to focus properly. But at the same time, she felt marvellous. She'd been the star of the party! They'd all crowded round her, asking Max to introduce them. After a while, she'd begun to see herself as the heroine of one of her novels. Little village mouse makes it into the big time! Now she knew the sky was the limit. She felt invincible. Max had shushed them all, and had made a speech, while they all hung on his every word. Something about perverts? She didn't really approve of that kind of language, but Max had sounded so grand. She was going out with somebody really important! If only he'd do something about his teeth. Sharon giggled again, and Max found her hand, squeezing it and sending lovely shivers through her. If only Sandy had been there, like Max had said.

"Where're we going?" she asked again.

"You'll see," he said. "We'll have that barbecue I promised you."

"Isn't it a bit cold?" Sharon was sober enough to know her leather jacket was smart, but too short to keep her warm. "No, I'd rather go home," she said. "If it's all right with you. Or . . . we could go to the pub?" Her voice was bright. She felt intelligent and sharp. Equal to any of them, she reckoned. What was it that Annabelle had said just now? Something about Sharon only being there for the power. Only she'd said it in capital letters: The Power.

"Hey," she said suddenly. "I thought that Annabelle had gone back to London? Mrs. M said her Jamie was a bit upset." Lois had said nothing of the sort to Sharon, of course, but she had eavesdropped. Useful stuff you could pick up that way. She giggled again. "Bit out of his league there, anyway," she added.

"Annabelle came back to look after the horses," Max said shortly. He negotiated a sharp corner, and then Sharon realized where they were. Back in Long Farnden, outside the village hall, and all driving very slowly with no lights, into the car park. Engines were switched off, and there was complete silence. Sharon heard an owl hoot to its mate at the bottom of the playing field. "What're we doing?" she said, a quaver in her voice.

"Sshh . . ." Max put his finger to his lips. Silence again. Sharon shivered. "But . . ."

"You'll see," he whispered. "Not long to wait, but we have to be quiet . . . Your moment will come very soon." He grinned at her, but she could not see in the darkness. There was usually a security light at the back of the village hall. Why hadn't it come on?

Suddenly Sharon felt afraid, and reached for the door handle. "Locked," whispered Max. "Sit quiet, there's a good girl. Not long to wait now," he repeated, and silence fell once more.

•   •   •

THE PUB WAS WARM AND WELCOMING, AND BRIAN obediently ordered himself a half of Best.

"Evenin', vicar," said a friendly voice. It was Bill
Stockbridge, and by himself, Brian noted. They fell easily
into conversation. Bill talked about his church back in
Yorkshire, and asked Brian questions which he evaded
without trouble. It was so nice to talk to a young man
without having to watch every word, reflected Brian. He
relaxed, and ordered another half.

"And what are you having?" he asked Bill.

"Same again, thanks," said Bill. "Aren't you having
another?"

"No, I have to get back," Brian said, but Bill wasn't
having that.

"Give the vicar another half," he called to the landlord,
as they made their way to the chairs by the roaring log
fire.

"Good for business for you, a night in the pub," said
Bill, with a grin. "Mix with the locals, and all that."

"I suppose that's true," said Brian. "But I do have to get
back." His full glass arrived, and looked inviting. Sandy
hadn't said what time his programme was, but the ones he
wanted to watch were usually pretty late on. A little longer
wouldn't matter. Bill was a very good-looking lad. Better
watch it, though. They talked on, and refilled their glasses.
Brian forgot about the programme, but realized Bill was
getting fuddled, and worried about him driving back to
Waltonby. He supposed he should offer him a lift, but
thought he should soon be getting back. There was a reason, wasn't there? He shook his head to clear it, but he
couldn't remember. For the first time, he felt relaxed and
accepted in the pub. And it was quite pleasant to be away
from Sandy's constant sniping. He'd been getting worse
lately, no matter how Brian tried to please him. Brian
laughed louder than necessary when Bill said he did not

know how the vicar put up with that little squirt who lived with him.

"Sandy, you mean?" What had the boy done to make Bill so virulent? Ah, now he was saying something about Rebecca. All was becoming clear. Sandy had made several passes at Bill's girl, and she was reciprocating.

"Not the same at home at all," said Bill thickly. "She's not my loving Rebecca any more. I could kill him, nasty little—"

"Hey, hold up!" said Brian. "He's my godson, you know. I have to defend him, I suppose. Though I agree he has a few faults. But he's done wonders with the choir. You must give him that, Bill. Got a roving eye, yes. But he's young, still looking around."

"He'd better look somewhere else then," said Bill belligerently. "Took up with Sharon Miller and then dropped her again, poor kid."

"That's being young, isn't it?" said Brian wistfully. "Got to play the field until you find the right one."

Bill stood up. "Well," he said, clenching his fists, "Rebecca's the right one for me, and until your Sandy came along, we were very happy. So you can tell him . . ."

At that moment, Rebecca walked into the pub. "Thought I'd find you here," she said shortly. She took one look at Bill and ushered him out like a naughty schoolboy. Brian, now mellow and full of goodwill to all men, began another conversation with young farmers up at the bar.

Much later, to his surprise, Rebecca was back. "He's escaped," she said, "silly fool. I've searched everywhere. Could you possibly help me find him? He's in no fit state to be out on his own." She looked at Brian, swaying slightly on his feet. "My God," she said, "what on earth have you two been up to?"

The end of a perfect day, she thought bitterly, as she took the vicar's arm to steady him. The governors' meeting had ended in acrimony, and then Sandy hadn't turned up to their rendezvous. And now this. Perhaps it's time I moved on, she thought to herself. Ah well, first things first. Got to find that big idiot, before he does something stupid.

THIRTY-THREE

❧

THE RAIN HAD STOPPED, AND THOUGH IT WAS LATE
and there was no moon, it was not completely dark.
As the unlikely pair trudged slowly arm-in-arm back to
the vicarage, Rebecca suddenly stopped. "Hey!" she said.
Brian had his head down in a vain attempt to see where
he was going. "Hey, Brian! Look at that!" She started off
again, at a quick trot, dragging him behind her. He looked
fuzzily to where she had pointed and was sober in an
instant.

Fire! And coming from the direction of the vicarage.
Even as they began to run in earnest, Brian could hear
crackles and shouting, and saw showers of sparks shooting
up into the air like unseasonal fireworks. Oh, my God!
Sandy!

A crowd had gathered, and Mr. Miller from the garage
came running up to the vicar. "Thank God you're safe!" he
said. "Fire engine's been sent for. We don't know how long
it's been alight, but a while, from the look of it."

Rebecca pulled away from Brian, but was immediately

grabbed. She screamed. "He might be in there! Sandy might be in there!"

"You're going nowhere," Brian said. "Leave it to me." He got as far as the path to the front door, and was held back at once by several bystanders. He struggled, suddenly enormously strong, but could not break free. He began to sob. "I left him in there," he said. "He could still be there . . . gone to sleep . . . Oh God, please keep him safe," he moaned.

Then the fire engine could be heard in the distance. But before it reached them, Brian saw a shadow moving across an upstairs window. There, against a fiery backdrop, was the unmistakable silhouette of his godson. Sandy was trying desperately to open a window. It was locked, Brian thought dully. And the window keys were in the kitchen, in an old Ovaltine tin, on the shelf. He fell to his knees, and his captors released him, standing back and staring at the window. Then there was an explosion and a burst of flames and they watched helplessly as the black figure fell back, disappearing into the inferno.

THIRTY-FOUR

❧

LOIS WAS IRONING. SHE HAD RETURNED HOME UN-easy and not sure what to do next. Gran was in the middle of a television programme Lois did not want to watch, and Derek was, as usual, snoozing with the newspaper over his face. Ironing was always useful. It was a chance to think uninterrupted. She had the radio turned down low, with soothing music helping her to concentrate.

Nothing more I can do tonight, she decided. Just cross fingers and hope Sharon comes to no harm. Maybe it was just a party, and she would be returned home unscathed. But tomorrow there would be work to do. She intended to find out much more about Max Wedderburn for a start. Gran was bound to know somebody who knew somebody who knew his mother. After all, Gran had lived in Tresham for years, and Lois had been born there. Gran remembered it when it had been a pleasant agricultural market town, with little crime and a strong community spirit. It was already changing in Lois's childhood, but now she hated to think of those neat rows of houses in the old back streets, where *her* grandmother had lived, being terrorized by fascist thugs.

And she would talk some more to Sharon. Lois was beginning to realize that the naïve dizzy blonde stuff that Sharon projected was not the whole picture. There was a hard centre to Sharon, sly and with more than a little cunning. She could slide away from an awkward question more skilfully than most. Yes, some serious talking to Sharon would be bound to produce something.

Lois picked up another shirt. Derek always changed into a clean shirt when he came home after work. Same as his father before him. "Sets a man up." That was his answer, when Lois counted the dirty shirts and complained. Most of the time, Gran did the ironing, but Lois liked to help out. She began to button and fold in the way Gran had taught her. At this moment, a face appeared at the window.

"Hey! Who's that!" Lois saw the figure pass on to the back door, and then thunderous knocking followed.

"Mrs. Meade, is Derek at home? Can he come, quick? The vicarage is on fire, and we need all the help we can get. It may be too late, but . . ." It was a breathless Mr. Carr, from the shop. He was not the swiftest of messengers, but all that could be spared.

Derek had already arrived in the kitchen, awakened by the knocking. He pulled on his jacket in seconds and was on his way out, followed by Mr. Carr, still panting.

"Mr. Carr, what d'you mean, it may be too late?" said Lois quickly, switching off the iron and reaching for her coat.

"There's somebody inside," he said. "Probably that young Sandy. Vicar's in a terrible state. Come on, then, let's get back."

It was a nightmare scene. The acrid smell of smoke, the hoses playing on smouldering, wet timber, flames still leaping from the destroyed roof, the silent watching crowd. For the older ones, it was a scene etched in their minds by newsreels of bombed-out, burning cities, bodies on stretchers, desperate searchers.

There was only one body here. It was carried carefully and gently from the ruins by ambulance men, and as Lois watched, the tall, angular figure of the vicar rushed forward and put his hand on the blanket covering the still shape of the young man he had loved. The ambulance men stopped, and not a sound was heard from anybody present. The chilly wind blowing black smoke into their eyes reminded them that this was not a newsreel. It was happening to them, in Long Farnden, right here and now.

After a minute or two, Brian Rollinson lifted his hand from Sandy's body and, head bowed, walked slowly away. One or two made to say something to him, tried to stop him in his tracks. But he brushed them aside and continued to walk, quickening his pace.

"I'm going after him," Lois said quickly to Derek. "See you later."

Brian was heading for the place he knew best, the church. He had the key in his pocket, and when he reached the door he unlocked it and walked into the darkness. He made no attempt to lock the door behind him, or to put on the lights. So when Lois came up and saw the door ajar, she pushed it open silently and tiptoed inside.

Her eyes were accustomed to the dark now, and she could see the outline of Brian's kneeling figure up at the altar. There was no sound. Well, he was praying silently, she knew. No need for words. She crept into a pew and sat down, still as a mouse. After a while, Brian stood up, crossed himself, and turned around.

"Who is that?" he said.

"Me, Lois Meade."

"Ah, Lois." He began to walk down the aisle, and came to where she was sitting.

"May I?" he said. She made room for him, and he sat down. They said nothing, but Lois felt an overwhelming presence so tangible she was sure she could touch it. Not just the vicar himself, but more. Something surrounding him.

After a minute, Brian said, "I have to find the strength to tell his mother. He was in my care, and I allowed him to die."

Lois said nothing, but reached out and gently took his hand.

"She hates me already, you see, Lois. I stole her husband. I stole Sandy's father away from her."

Jesus, thought Lois blasphemously. I'm not sure I want to listen to all this. Not unless it's something to do with what's been going on with that Wycombe lot. And how could it be? She contemplated making an excuse to get away. But the vicar was talking again, and she knew she had to stay.

"He was my best friend, you see. When they married, I tried to keep my distance. But Gerald was always ringing up, suggesting meetings. Marion didn't trust me, and she was right. I should have ended our friendship the moment they were married."

Lois's heart sank. She knew now what was coming.

"After Sandy was born—and Gerald had to fight for me to be godfather—we saw less of each other for a couple of years. Then one day I was walking home and Gerald appeared out of nowhere. He said we had to talk. He had realized, he said, that he was gay. He'd always known it, really. But he was fond of Marion, and had wanted a family and all the trappings of a conventional life that went with it. He'd been in an agony of indecision, but now he had made up his mind."

Go on then, said Lois silently. Say it, and let's get home. She was cold, and had begun to worry about Sharon again. Fire. That word swam in and out of her mind, and she wanted to connect it with what Cowgill had said. Something to do with the KKK?

Brian began again. "It was a Thursday. I remember it so clearly. Thursday evenings I went to Bible study group. Always a strong member of the church, Lois, though not a vicar then. But that Thursday I did not go. I loved Gerald and I agreed to the theft. He and I talked until midnight, and finally decided. I would steal him away from Marion, and we would set up house together. Move away, a long way away, and make a new life. Sandy was only two and a half, and there would be plenty of time to work out how to explain it all to him. I could not resist Gerald, Lois, any more than I could resist Sandy. Both of them could ask anything of me."

"And what happened?"

But Lois did not find out. Not then. There were steps outside, and in the church, up the aisle to where they were sitting.

"Mr. Rollinson, sir?" A policeman stood beside them, and behind him a familiar figure spoke. "Is that you, Lois? Cowgill here. We're here to help. Would you mind coming along with us, Mr. Rollinson? A number of things we have to clear up, and we can help you with what you will need to arrange. But first of all, are you in touch with Sandy Mackerras's parents?"

"His mother, yes," said the vicar in a whisper.

"Then you would be the person to talk to her." The authority in Cowgill's voice reached the vicar, and he stood up obediently.

"I'm ready," he said, and then turned to Lois. "Thank you," he said simply. "I'm glad you came."

He could have been thanking her for coming to his cocktail party. His voice was light and polite. But Lois knew what it was costing him, and nodded. "We'll see you tomorrow," she said, and followed after the little group. She would find Derek, and see what else could be done tonight.

THIRTY-FIVE

~

A FTER MOST BYSTANDERS HAD LEFT AND THE VIC-
arage was reduced to a stinking, blackened mess, Lois
and Derek—and Jamie, who had been mustered with the
pub contingent—walked slowly home. Lois looked at the
Millers' house and wondered if Sharon had returned, but
then forgot her as Jamie turned his head to follow a passing car and stopped dead, exclaiming, "Annabelle!"

"Where? I don't see her," said Derek. "You're imagining it, lad. Come on, time to get some sleep. We're all
exhausted."

"It *was* her . . . it was her car!"

"Well, she could have come back to visit her grandmother . . . ?"

"Mrs. T-J's away," said Lois, remembering the dark
Hall and the snickering horses.

"Well, *I* don't know," said Derek impatiently. "In any
case, she obviously doesn't want to see you, Jamie. Better
to forget it. Plenty more fish. Come on, I need my sleep.
Big match tomorrow."

"I offered the vicar a bed for the night," Lois said. "Maybe to stay until he gets somewhere." Nobody else had seemed to come forward, and Lois had pitied him.

"Fine," said Derek stoically. "Good gel."

Gran was waiting on the doorstep. "Is it bad?" she said.

"Very bad," said Lois gently. "The vicarage was burnt out. And . . . well, young Sandy was trapped inside. They couldn't get to him in time." She put her arm around her mother, and they stood silently for a few seconds.

Gran disengaged herself, took a deep breath, and said, "You'll need a hot drink. I'll go and see to it. The fire . . . oh! Well . . . I was going to say the fire's still in, so go and warm yourselves." She disappeared, and the others followed into the sitting room.

They talked desultorily about practical things, and then Jamie said, "Mum, how did it happen? Anybody say anything? I saw that cop friend of yours was there."

Lois frowned and shook her head. "Too early to say. There'll be investigations, of course. It doesn't look good, does it, with Sandy still in the house. If it had been a chip pan fire, or a coal jumped out on to a rug—that kind of thing—he'd have been able to stop it. No, it doesn't look like an accident . . ."

"But who would . . . ?" Jamie stopped, and his eyes had a guarded look.

"They'll find out," said Lois flatly. "We can all help. Try and remember what we noticed around the vicarage, or something somebody said in passing or in the pub. It'll come out."

THE MILLERS SAT IN A CHILLY ROOM AND SPOKE IN LOW tones. They were anxious not to wake Sharon. It had been difficult to calm her down and get her upstairs to her bed. Both mother and father had had to manhandle her in the end.

"She wasn't frightened, though. Or sad, even." Mrs. Miller looked across at her husband slumped in an armchair. "It was just . . . well, just . . ."

"High," he said. "She was high on something. Couldn't stop giggling. Then the shivering. We shall have a bad night, gel," he added. "She'll not like coming down again."

Mrs. Miller's alarm was in her trembling voice. "How do you know all this?" she said accusingly. "It's never happened before to her. How do you know she hasn't got a fever, or something like that?"

"I know," he said flatly. Then added, "Come on, now. We'd better get to bed. We'll get some sense out of her tomorrow." He stood up, took his wife's hand, and together they put out the lights and went upstairs.

AT THE HALL, IN ONE OF THE EMPTY COTTAGES ON THE estate, Annabelle looked around her. This would have to do. She was in no mood to sleep in the echoing great house. She took a couple of rugs and a cushion out of her car and stretched out on an old sagging sofa left behind by long gone tenants. Sleep would not come. Images of fire, sounds of chanting and screams of fear returned relentlessly. Finally, she went back to the car and found the little pack of pills that Max had given her. She'd never needed them before, but now she swallowed one with difficulty. It got stuck in her gullet and she choked. It went down in the end, and she returned to the cottage. In minutes she was in a deep and troubled sleep.

MAX WEDDERBURN, ON THE OTHER HAND, WAS TOO elated to sleep. He had left the society early, before the last part of his cunning plan was put in place. Some of the others had muttered that he was looking after number one, scared of being caught. But he ignored them. He was sure everything would have gone like clockwork. He was too smart, and his planning too exact for any danger to the society. Unless Sharon . . . She was the weak link, without doubt. She was new and stupid. But the eye would have worked. Perhaps the girl had enough sense to know how vital it was to keep quiet. He'd told her very firmly, several times, before he left. She'd been pretty dopey, but seemed to understand. Next time, they'd have to be more careful what they gave her. And Annabelle. Not to forget Annabelle. She'd been in the tack room of the stables that night when he'd talked to Sandy. Could well have heard something. Still, he could easily fix the pair of them.

He looked at himself in the spotted mirror over the brown-tiled fireplace. His face glowed. He smiled, and admired his cool grey eyes. Perhaps his teeth needed fixing a bit. He'd see to it tomorrow. Sharon had possibilities. He felt a twinge of desire. That fresh, dewy look had always appealed to him. But he knew now that she was not all that fresh, thank God.

The silly little tune of his mobile shrilled into the dreary room. "Hello? Oh, it's you, Mum."

"Of course it's me, Darren. I bin trying to get you all evening. Where were you?"

"Out. What d'you want?"

"It's her next door. She's sayin' things about you. Can you come round tomorrow? Get it straight, an' that?"

"No," said Max shortly. "Tell the old ratbag to mind her own business. Cheers, Mum."

HUNTER COWGILL SAT IN HIS CAR IN LONG FARNDEN High Street and pondered. The relatively simple investigation into a bunch of sad misfits involved in routine misdemeanours had changed. He'd known there was potential danger, of course, probably as a result of escalating violence, but this was something different. That little toe rag,

Darren Cockshutt, or whatever he called himself, was a suspected arsonist from schooldays. Curtains in the staffroom set alight, minor explosions in the science lab. And always he'd been too clever to be caught. But fire was his passion.

There'd been no sign of any of that lot tonight, of course. Cowgill did not expect it. But this time, if it *was* Cockshutt and his cronies, they had gone too far.

Cowgill had no doubt in his mind. This was murder.

THIRTY-SIX

ॐ

Marion Mackerras stood at her window, staring out at the quiet, surburban road. Everything was
familiar. The garden, neat and tidied for the winter, with
the trees that Gerald had planted. The sundial, with its
small cherub telling sun time. She remembered when they
bought it, she and Gerald. She had been pregnant with
Sandy . . .

She turned away from the window, consumed with
grief. It was a terrible pain, doubling her up and increasing,
instead of fading away. She moaned and ran from the
room. Where could she go? Into the kitchen? The bedroom? Sandy's old room, with all the tangible memories of
his boyhood? There was nowhere to escape from the unac-
ceptable truth. Sandy was dead. Her only son, only child,
was dead. The second death.

Brian's telephone call had come early. She had not recognized his voice, and had to ask several times who it was,
ringing her before breakfast. He had finally mastered a
sudden stutter, and said the awful words. God, oh God,

they were such awful words! If she had not answered the phone, or slammed it down when she knew who it was, she would have had a little more time. But sooner or later . . . She wrenched open the back door and screamed loudly in a desperate effort to erase the picture from her mind's eye. Sandy caught in the flames, his clothes on fire, his lovely hair and strong limbs . . . Oh God, oh God, oh Jesus Christ help me!

Her screams floated out over the garden and into next door, where her neighbour was hanging out washing. A face appeared over the fence. "Marion? What on earth's the matter?"

THEY PACKED MARION'S BAG. THERE WAS NO QUESTION of Marion driving, and her neighbour insisted on taking her to the station. "Just give me a ring when you're coming back, and I'll meet you," she said. She leaned over and kissed Marion's cheek. "Are you sure you'll be all right?" she added anxiously.

Marion nodded. She felt completely numb now, but reassured her neighbour that she would be able to do what was necessary for the journey to Long Farnden. Brian had said he would be there to pick her up. He was the last person she wanted to see, but there was no one else. Brian Rollinson . . . and two deaths, first her husband and now . . . Oh, Sandy . . . She shivered. She could stay in a hotel in Tresham, she supposed. But the thought of an anonymous hotel room, with its television and Jerusalem Bible, was worse than contact with Brian Rollinson. After all, he could have been the last person to talk to Sandy.

"Are you all right, missus?" An old man with a battered suitcase sat opposite her in the train.

With a huge effort, she said, "Yes, thank you. Thanks." After half an hour or so, she closed her eyes and tried to doze. But the pictures behind her eyelids began again. This time she was looking down into Sandy's coffin, seeing his friendly face, his reddish curls. But as she watched they blackened and shrivelled, and she opened her eyes with a gasp.

"Here, you're not well," said the old man. Marion shook her head, but could not control her tears, which were now spurting in a rush.

There were only two of them at the grimy table, and other passengers dotted around the carriage were busy with their newspapers and mobile phones. The old man silently handed her a spotless white handkerchief. She took it and mopped at her face, but the tears would not stop.

"P'raps you'd better try and tell me what's up," the old man said quietly. "But not if you don't want. Nobody's goin' to mind you havin' a cry."

Marion began to speak, but choked. She tried again, and this time said, "There's been an accident. A fire . . ."

"Somebody hurt?"

No answer, but a nod of the head.

"Close to you?"

Again the nod.

"Yer Mum?"

"My son." Marion clamped her lips together in a vain effort to stop the tears.

"Dear God," said the old man. He reached out and took her wet hand. "Don't say no more, dear. You just sit there, an' I'll talk. You'll not be interested, but that don't matter. I'll tell you about my old lady, her what's in a home in Tresham. That where you're goin'? Yep, well, it all come about like this . . ."

When the train drew into Tresham station, the old man was still holding Marion's hand, and he looked at her sadly. He would have to wake her now. Still, at least that bit of the journey had been got through. But she still had a long way to go, in a manner of speaking.

She opened her eyes, and looked puzzled. Then, with a

pain in the pit of her stomach, she remembered where she was, and looked out of the window. Brian Rollinson stood on the platform, and she hardly recognized him. His face was a mask, grey and hollow-cheeked. He raised his hand, and moved away to the carriage door.

"Is he meetin' you?" The old man had struggled to his feet, clasping his suitcase. "Right then," he continued, "I'll be off now. Goodbye, me duck. Chin up." And he moved surprisingly swiftly to the door and disappeared.

"Where's he gone?" said Marion urgently to Brian, who took her case.

"Who?"

"The old man! I must thank . . . Oh well, I suppose it doesn't matter. He was so kind." She looked at Brian, forcing herself to meet his eyes. Then she put out her hand and touched his arm. "It couldn't be bloody worse, could it," she said.

THIRTY-SEVEN

❧

Halfway to Long Farnden, Marion said suddenly into the silence between them, "Where are we going to stay? Isn't your house . . . ?"

"Completely ruined," said Brian. He seemed glad of a chance to speak about something practical. "But there's a very nice woman—runs a cleaning business in the village—has offered to put me up until I find somewhere to rent. She's got spare beds now her children have left home."

"What about me?"

"Room for you, too. It's a nice old family house, used to belong to a doctor."

"What's her name, this cleaning woman?"

"Um, she's a bit more than that, Marion. A business woman, really. Lois Meade, she's called. One of her staff cleans—er, used to clean—the vicarage. Sandy took the girl out once or twice." There, he had said his name. It had just come out naturally, and Brian was glad. Perhaps now it would not be so difficult.

Marion was silent. She felt unreal, as if all this was hap-

pening to somebody else, somebody she was inhabiting by
mistake. She heard herself say, "Sandy taking out a char?
Doesn't sound like him." And then wondered how she
could say something so awful.

Brian sprang to Sharon's defence. "I don't think he saw
her as a char," he said. "Just a pretty girl, and fun to be
with. She works in the shop sometimes, too. Her father has
a garage in the village. Very respectable folk."

The initial warmth between them was chilling rapidly.
Well, thought Brian, it was more natural. It wouldn't be
long before Marion got around to blaming him. Perhaps
rightly? He had not slept at all, although Lois and Derek
had been so kind when he had knocked at their door. It
had been late, but their welcome was warm. Gran had appeared, too, and in no time he was shown to a pleasant bedroom and told that he could sleep as long as he liked next
morning. All night long he had gone over and over his ac-
tions before he went to the pub. Had he left an unguarded
fire? No. Sandy had accused him of neglecting it, of nearly
letting it out. The fireguard was definitely put back. The
kitchen, then? Had the cooker been on, with something
boiling dry? He could not remember. He wondered if he
would ever remember.

Now this morning his thoughts were still confused. He
was uncomfortably aware that he had drunk more than intended. His head ached, and beside him in the car Marion
was silent again. When they drew up outside Lois's house,
she peered through the window and then curled up in her
seat like a child. "I can't go through with it." Her voice was
muffled by her hands. "I can't do it, Brian. I want to go
home."

He leaned across and gently took both her hands. "Marion, my dear," he said. "We have to go through this together, somehow. You have every reason to hate me. I took
your husband away, and now I have failed to look after
your son. But I loved them both. We have that in common.

It is all we have. Useless to ask you to trust me, but I will do my best to make it as easy as possible for you. The Meades and Gran Weedon are good souls."

She stared at him, her eyes full once more. "All right, then," she said finally. "Let's go."

LOIS WAS NOT THERE TO MEET THEM, BUT GRAN HAD A gift for making people comfortable, and Marion and Brian found themselves settled in armchairs in the warm sitting room, with cups of coffee and the door shut tactfully as Gran retired to the kitchen.

Marion spoke first. "There'll be arrangements to make." She could not bring herself to say "the funeral."

"The main things, date and time and so on, are taken care of," Brian said. The cup rattled as he put it down into the saucer.

Marion noticed. Good, she thought. He's very shaky. Suffering, no doubt, all over again. Well, that's justice.

"I was sure you'd have details you wanted to discuss, about the service—readings, hymns, that sort of thing." Brian was terrified. He was usually so good at this bit, consoling the bereaved with his confident expertise. Now he was on tenterhooks, waiting for Marion to burst out at him, accusing him of . . . well, of the worst thing she could think of. He ploughed on, suggesting suitable music, and perhaps a reading or two she might approve. "The girl I was telling you about, Sharon Miller, plays the church organ, and I'll ask her to pop in so we can discuss it."

Suddenly Marion stood up. "We're not planning a bloody party!" she hissed. "So just shut up! You've ruined my life twice now, and I don't ever, ever want to talk to you again! Sandy will be buried in our town, next to his father, and I'll find another parson to take the service. You can stay away. As far away as possible. I never want to see you again. Ever!"

She rushed blindly out of the room, looked wildly about her in the hall, and ran down the passage towards the kitchen.

"Ah, there you are, dear," said Gran, wiping her wet hands on a towel. "Now, sit down in this old chair—move the cat—and we can have a bit of a chat. That's it, put the cushion behind your back. Now, I'll just get this in the oven and we can relax."

Lois had received a telephone call from Cowgill early on. She'd reluctantly agreed to meet him in Alibone Woods, but said there was nothing to tell him. This was not strictly true, as she knew he would be interested in the party in the Hall stables. He'd want to know about Annabelle, too, and what she was doing back in Farnden when her grandmother was away. She wondered whether to tell him the vicar was living temporarily with them. It would sharpen his interest, without a doubt. There'd be questions he'd want her to ask. She could not deny that a tiny part of her charitable offer had been self-interest. With Brian Rollinson in her own house, much was bound to emerge in casual conversation. There would be no need for formal questions.

At breakfast, after the vicar had gone to the station, she had asked Gran casually if she knew anybody in Tresham called Cockshutt. Her reaction had been instant. "Do I!" she said. "If it's the Cockshutts who used to live down by the river, then there's quite a lot I could tell you."

"Could be them," Lois had said, and listened to a succinctly told tale of generations of Cockshutts following in the family tradition of sailing close to the wind in numberless nefarious practices. "So Darren is no exception," she'd said. Gran didn't know exactly which one he was, but there were rumours of a Cockshutt who'd made good, unlikely as it seemed. "Well, made money, maybe," Lois had muttered, "though not much good."

All of this she could relay to Cowgill, who probably knew most of it anyway. Cockshutts had doubtless been known to the Tresham police for years.

She parked off the road in her usual place, and thought how much more visible a white van must be than her old brown car. She shrugged. This meeting would be a quick one, and after that he'd have to find another place to meet. But not that barn behind the playing field! That had caused enough trouble several years ago . . .

He was waiting for her, by the old tree stump. His face lit up, in spite of himself, and he said, "Ah, Lois. Good morning." Even in an old anorak and Wellington boots, with her dark, shiny hair tied back severely from her face, she scrambled his mind so that for a second he couldn't think what on earth he wanted to ask her.

Lois sniffed. She pulled a handkerchief from her pocket and something fell to the ground. She bent down to pick it up, and said, "Go on, then. You start."

Never gives me a chance, thought Cowgill ruefully. But that was right. She wouldn't be his Lois any other way.

She was staring down, and he said, "What've you got there? Looks like a ball . . ."

It was a ball. A very small, plastic ball, muddy now, but discoloured by smoky black soot.

"I picked it up. I remember now," Lois said. "I trod on it near the vicarage. It was dark, and I put it in my pocket. Then forgot it." She rubbed it against her jacket to get rid of the mud and soot.

"Ugh!" she said, looking more closely. "It's an eye! It's horrible!" She held it up, and Cowgill could see now quite clearly. It was an eye, realistically made in clear plastic, with a rolling inner eyeball, the white part delicately laced with scarlet veining, and in the centre a menacing blue pupil with black iris. As Lois turned it in her hand, the eye-ball swivelled appallingly so that it still stared at her.

"I've seen them before," he said with distaste. "The grandchildren had one, and my daughter took it away from them. She put it in the bin, I think. Very nasty indeed."

Lois wasn't listening to him. She was thinking about eyes, about a wandering eye that swivelled independently from its fellow. Sharon Miller.

"It might be nastier than you think," she said slowly. "Think where I found it. Nobody at the vicarage has children. Why should it be there? Doesn't it remind you of something . . . somebody?" She hesitated. Perhaps she would speak to Sharon first, if he didn't respond.

"No, it doesn't," he said, puzzled. "The most likely thing I can think is that children were playing with it in the churchyard and it bounced over the wall. These things are extremely bouncy. Dangerous, really. Another reason my daughter—"

"Fine," interrupted Lois. "I'm sure you're right. Anyway, let's get on. I've got things to do."

He asked her a number of questions then, about the people seen watching the fire and what she knew of Sandy Mackerras. He said they had found mercury in Cyril's stomach, and were still working on the mystery of how it got there. It had been only a trace. Had she heard any more about the old man's movements before that night? And what about Sharon Miller and the Cockshutt lout?

She told him about the party at the Hall, but kept to herself her vague thoughts about the eyeball. Speak to Sharon first, and then maybe she'd have something to tell him. But there was something else.

"We saw Annabelle Tollervey-Jones," she said. "She drove past us as we walked home from the fire, Derek and Jamie and me. Jamie saw her, and got upset. I thought she was supposed to have gone back to London, and so did he. Her gran's away, so she wasn't visiting her. Funny, her being back on the night of the fire. I don't know if she saw us, but she gave no sign."

"Annabelle?" Cowgill was all attention. "Are you sure it was her?"

"I told you," said Lois impatiently. "Jamie saw her, and he was sure. He should know, shouldn't he?" Why was Cowgill suddenly so interested in Annabelle?

"Right," he said, and took her arm. "Time to go. You're busy, and I must make a call. You've been very useful, Lois, as usual. We'll keep in touch."

But not by holding on to me, thought Lois, shaking off his hand. "Next time," she said, "find a nice quiet, warm place where nobody goes. This wood is not good for old bones," she added, and regretted it at once. Poor old sod, he'd never done her any harm, never overstepped the mark. "Not that that applies to either of us," she said quickly.

Too late, Lois, Cowgill reflected sadly. Professionalism took over, and he went rapidly to his car. They left more or less at the same time, and she noticed that he branched off at the turn to the Hall.

Thirty-eight

❧

How could he have been so stupid? Brian Rollinson sat where Marion had left him, close by the fire in Lois's sitting room. What had made him think Sandy's funeral would be in Farnden? He sighed. Wishful thinking, probably. Or just general derangement. He had an odd sensation of floating just above the ground, not properly connected to what was going on. Should he follow Marion and apologize?

He got up and opened the door quietly. He listened. There were voices coming from the kitchen. Gran and Marion. He heard Gran laugh gently. Oh well, it was probably all right then. For the moment. Perhaps they wouldn't mind if he joined them.

Gran looked up as he stood in the kitchen doorway. "Come on in, Vicar," she said. "Coffee's still hot. I'm sure you could do with another cup. Sit yourself down."

Marion didn't look at him, but stared down at the table.

"We were just talking," continued Gran. "Marion was telling me about where she lives. Sounds a very nice place.

We shall go, of course. Lois and Derek will want to, I know."

"Go?" Brian said stupidly.

"To the funeral," said Gran. "We can give you a lift if you like."

He glanced quickly at Marion. "Well, I'm not sure that I'll be able to . . . er . . ."

She looked first at Gran and then at him. "I'm sorry, Brian," she said flatly. There was a pause, and then she continued, "I'd like you to be there. I'd like you to take the service . . . if it wouldn't be too . . ."

"Oh . . . oh, well . . . yes, of course, Marion . . . um, er, thank you."

Gran nodded approvingly, and said that it was time she got on with cooking the dinner, and maybe they'd like to go out for a breath of air. They could walk out of the gate at the bottom of the garden, round the footpath to the stream, and come back without having to meet anybody.

She watched as they disappeared down the garden path, and shook her head sadly. Marion had told her everything. Or nearly everything. Poor woman. It must have been hard for her, bringing up Sandy on her own. He'd been only two and a bit at the time of Gerald's accident, and Marion had found it easy enough to give a convincing account of that. Later, with Brian's co-operation, they'd managed to keep his and Gerald's brief love affair secret from the boy. Gran thought that Marion had told her all, but of course she had not. She had kept to herself that impulsive moment when she'd thought it time a convalescing Sandy should know the whole truth.

The plan for Sandy to lodge with his godfather for a while had been Marion's. "If only I'd had second thoughts about that," she'd said sadly to Gran. "He'd still be here, wouldn't he?" She'd swallowed hard. "I don't know why I suggested it. Well, yes, I do know," she had added, in an attempt at perfect honesty. "I thought Sandy's presence—

and he did look very like his father, you know—would disturb any peace of mind that Brian had managed to find. Not a praiseworthy motive . . ."

It was going to be a long haul for everybody, and the most useful thing Gran could think of was to make sure they were all well fed. Jamie hadn't eaten much at breakfast, and she planned a sustaining meal for this evening. Something up with the boy. He hadn't forgotten Annabelle, she was sure of that.

AT THE MUSIC SHOP IN TRESHAM, JAMIE WALKED through to the little office and spoke to the plump, kindly proprietor. "You don't look so good, Jamie," she said. "Feeling all right?"

He shook his head. "I think it might be a touch of flu," he said. "Sore throat, shivery, achy bones, that stuff. I wonder if I could slip off now . . ."

She was a motherly soul, and sent him away immediately. "Let me know if you need more time," she said. He hadn't been himself for a while. She'd noticed he was distracted, and had made one or two mistakes in the shop. He'd sold an empty CD case to a stroppy woman who'd demanded that "that oik" should deliver the missing CD to her that day. Something was wrong with Jamie, and she guessed it was not flu.

It had begun to rain as Jamie started up his motorbike and set off for Farnden. Then, at the turn to the Hall, he branched off and, like Cowgill, followed the little lane until he came to big stone pillars at the Hall entrance. The gates were open, and he drove steadily up the long drive, curving round to the stableyard. There was no sign of life. Mrs. T-J must still be away, then. He parked his bike and peered through all the windows. The horses greeted him with pleasure, nuzzling his hand, looking for food. Somebody must be looking after them, he guessed. A pile of dung steamed in a barrow by the stable door.

He was convinced Annabelle had been here, but could see no trace of her. Then he remembered the empty cottages. It was worth a look. Best to walk, he considered, rather than advertise his presence on the bike. It would be safe enough here in the yard.

He set off down the grassy track, noting encouraging tyre marks. As he approached the cottages, he stopped. There was certainly a car outside. In fact, there were two cars, and one of them was Annabelle's. The other he did not recognize. He quickly pushed through the hedge and continued through the spinney bordering the track. Close now to the cottage garden, he heard voices, and two figures appeared. One was Annabelle, and his heart leapt. The other was . . . wasn't it? . . . yes, it was. Mum's cop. What on earth was he doing here? Whatever it was, Jamie judged it best to keep himself hidden.

"I'll be in touch, then," he heard Cowgill say, quite kindly. "Let me know if you go anywhere where you can't be reached on your mobile. And don't forget what I said. Be careful."

Jamie watched as the big car slid away down the track, and then he emerged. "Annabelle!" he shouted, and she turned back from the cottage door. She saw him, and hesitated. Then she was flying down the path and out along the track to meet him. He held out his arms, and she ran straight into them, burying her face in his jacket and clinging on to him as if the hounds of Hell were in pursuit.

Which, of course, in a way, they were.

THIRTY-NINE

❧

THE FAMILY WAS NOW BACK TO SIZE AROUND THE BIG kitchen table, to Gran's delight, with Brian and Marion digesting a good meal and trying to contribute to the chat. Conversation did not flow easily. The Meades were awkwardly avoiding talk of the fire and the funeral, and Brian and Marion found it difficult to escape from private thoughts.

Jamie was totally silent, and Lois was beginning to wonder what was wrong when he suddenly blurted out, "Mum, I'm thinking of going away for a few days." His face was scarlet, and Lois and Derek stared at him.

"Away?" they chorused.

Jamie nodded. "Um, up to London. Thought I'd do a concert at the Albert Hall. Meet a friend . . ."

"What friend?" said Lois sharply. She need not have asked. She knew whom he would be meeting, though did not expect him to tell them. "Just an old friend from school. Interested in music. I'll be back Monday or Tuesday."

"How nice," said Brian politely, and Marion managed a smile.

"I used to go to Promenade Concerts in my youth," she said. "Stand and queue with Gerald for tickets. That was before . . ." She stopped, then said, "Oh, sorry . . . excuse me . . ." and walked quickly out of the kitchen.

Brian stood up. "Better go and make sure she is all right," he said apologetically, and followed.

Silence reigned for a minute or two. Then Derek, fed up with all this, said firmly, "Right, now then, young man, why the sudden need to go to London? We're not fools, you know."

"I don't see why he shouldn't . . ." Gran started to say.
"Just keep out of this for the moment, Gran," Derek said preemptorily. She snorted, and got up to clear dishes.

"Well, why shouldn't I?" said Jamie loudly. "I'm studying music, and there's bugger-all in the way of concerts in the great metropolis of Tresham!" He was shouting now. "I'll be on my own soon at the uni. Shan't have to ask your permission to go away for a couple of days then! You don't know how lucky you are," he added, speaking directly to Derek. "Most of the boys I was at school with are clubbing and fixing and dealing, and have no plans for the future, and cost their parents a fortune . . ."

Derek glared at Lois, as if it were her fault. She put a hand on his arm. "Leave it, Derek," she said. "We'll talk later, Jamie. Don't forget we've got a guest who's lost her son in a bloody awful fire. Let's think of her first."

"I'll be going in the morning," Jamie said, and left the room.

LOIS CREPT UPSTAIRS A FEW MINUTES LATER, WHERE THE only sounds came from Jamie's room. She tapped lightly. "It's Mum."

He opened the door and she went in. He had a backpack on his bed, and had begun throwing in a few clothes.

"Right," she said briskly. "Sit down, and tell me the truth. That way we'll not waste time."

Jamie did not sit down. He walked over to the window and stood with his back to her. "You know, don't you," he said.

"Annabelle." Lois's voice was neutral. "You're going back with her. That's fine by me, for a few days, but I have a good reason for wanting to know more. Tell me why you've suddenly decided to go, when you spoke to her, what she said. Not private things, o'course. But anything else. And, Jamie," she added, "I want an address of where you'll be, and for you to make sure you have your mobile switched on at all times."

Jamie sat down now, and sighed. "I wish I knew what was going on," he said quietly. "You're mixed up with that cop again, aren't you? Something to do with the fire. Still, fair's fair. I'll give you Annabelle's address. She's sharing a flat with a girlfriend. And yep, I'll keep me mobile on."

"Go on," said Lois.

"Go on with what?"

"Tell me what she said. And where you saw her."

Jamie told her about the cottages, but did not mention Cowgill. "She'd come down to look after the horses while her Gran was away. Stayed in a cottage from choice. Doesn't like the Hall when nobody's there. Says it's haunted." He smiled indulgently.

"And what else?" persisted Lois.

"Nothing else," said Jamie, and Lois knew he lied. But there was nothing more to be done, and so she left him and went off to placate Derek.

IN THE TIDY LITTLE HOUSE IN WALTONBY, BILL AND RE-becca sat at either end of the long sofa and stared blankly at the television screen. After a few minutes, Bill reached for the remote control and switched off.

"Rebecca," he said quietly, "we've got to talk."

She did not answer, and shrank back into the cushions, closing her eyes.

"It's no good, I know you're not asleep," he said, after more minutes passed in silence. "For goodness sake, talk to me. Say anything, but please say something!"

She stirred and opened her eyes. "Who started it?" she said in a low voice.

"Who started what?"

"The fire, of course. Somebody started it. It couldn't have happened by itself inside the house. Sandy was there, wasn't he? He'd have smelt the smoke, or seen it. It must have got hold too quickly for him. So who did it?"

He stared at her. "Why are you looking at me like that? You don't think . . . ? Bloody hell, Rebecca, you can't think it was me?"

She looked at him with hate in her eyes. "You were drunk," she said, "and you were away for ages. You could've done it, if you'd found something to get it going—paraffin, or petrol—in the vicar's garage."

He thought he would hit her. But he couldn't, wouldn't, and turned away.

"If that's what you think," he said, and she thought he sounded shifty, "then it's over, isn't it. I'll get out as soon as possible. Probably go back to Yorkshire. But don't forget, Rebecca," he added in a warning voice, "it was you who started it—not the fire, but the trouble between us. You and him. And mostly him. You're probably not interested, but I'll tell you anyway. I've always loved you, and still do."

She heard him clumping up the stairs and the spare-room door banged shut. She began to sob silently to herself, curled up in the corner of the sofa.

FORTY

ANNABELLE COLLECTED JAMIE NEXT MORNING. SHE did not get out of the car, but sat waiting for him. He kissed Lois and Gran, smiled reassuringly, and ran down the drive. They were gone in seconds, leaving the two women staring out of the window at the vanishing car.

"Sod it all," said Lois, and went quickly into her office, shutting the door firmly behind her. Gran shrugged, and went back to the kitchen. If Lois did not want to talk, fine.

IN HIS MOTHER'S UNTIDY HOUSE IN TRESHAM, DARREN Cockshutt sat on the edge of a chair and drank beer from a smeary glass. "God, Mum, don't you ever wash up?" He polished the rim with a clean handkerchief from his pocket.

"Oo . . . er, too posh to 'ave a drink in our mum's house, are we?" Mrs. Cockshutt smiled to soften the criticism. After all, it wasn't often that Darren, or Max, or whatever he called himself, came to see her. He'd parked the sports car outside her tiny terraced house, and she could see the neighbours' curtains twitching. Let them look! Her Darren had done well for himself.

"Beer's flat," said Darren. "How long have you had it? Anyway, what did you want me for?" he added. He had scarcely surfaced since the fire, keeping to his room and sleeping most of the time. It had all been very exhausting, and he just hoped it had gone to plan. He had made sure no nosey-parker could say he'd been there. He'd have to check there'd been no hitches. But everyone knew what they had to do. He looked around him in disgust. Why couldn't his mother clear up a bit? Rubbish everywhere. The sooner he got out of here the better. What had she wanted? Something to do with bloody old Auntie Doris . . .

"Is that the paper?" He reached out and picked up the local newspaper from the floor.

"Yesterday's," Mrs. Cockshutt replied. "Nasty old fire, that, at Farnden."

Darren looked at the front page story, and half-smiled at the picture of the vicarage ablaze. So everything was fine. Then he saw the headline:

LOCAL MAN DIES IN FIRE

He read on, and the sub-heading was like a blow:

YOUNG CHOIRMASTER
TRAPPED IN THE BLAZE

His face contorted and his colour drained away. He stood up, spilling his beer over the dingy carpet.

"Careful, Darren! 'Ere! Where're you going?" Mrs. Cockshutt stared at him. "You only just got here! Darren, we haven't had our talk . . . what'll I tell Auntie Doris?"

But Darren, or Max—young man about town—was gone. Mrs. Cockshutt heard the gears grating, and then the wheels spin as he took off at speed down the street, narrowly missing a child who ran out after a ball.

MARION HAD GONE OUT EARLY, ASKING BRIAN TO GIVE her a lift into Tresham. She was going to call in at the estate agent's where Sandy worked, to collect one or two things he had left there. She said she would like to see where he had worked, and been happy. She would be out most of the day. Brian, too, had a number of things to attend to, and would not be back until tea-time. Gran, relieved of duties for the moment, set off for the shop, savouring the consoling sunshine which filled the village.

"Morning, Mrs. Weedon." She looked up, and saw Sharon Miller.

"Morning, Sharon," Gran said. "You look a bit pale. Feeling better?" Lois had told her crossly that Sharon was off colour and would not be able to work for a day or so.

"I've asked Mrs. Miller to tell Sharon I want to see her as soon as possible," Lois had grumbled. "Silly woman tried to say she couldn't disturb her. *I'll* disturb her when she turns up!" Gran knew better than to disagree.

Now Sharon smiled weakly at Gran and nodded. "I'm much better this morning. I'm just going to see Mrs. M. Is she in? I hear the vicar and Sandy's mother are staying with you. How's that going? I'd like to meet Sandy's mum, if that's all right."

"Hold on, one thing at a time," said Gran sharply. "Yes, Lois is at home. Yes, the vicar and Mrs. Mackerras are staying with us for a day or two, and no, you cannot meet Sandy's mum because she is out all day, and going back home tomorrow. I'm not sure she'd want to meet anyone else, anyway, poor woman. And how it's going is none of your business."

Sharon bristled. "There's no need to be like that! I was only making conversation," she said.

"Mmm," said Gran. "Sounded like gossip to me. You need to watch it, Sharon. Anyway, you'd better get going, else you'll not catch Lois before she goes out."

That was not like me at all, thought Gran, as she opened the shop door. She felt the usual stab of pain in her stomach, and went over to look at the remedy shelves.

Mrs. Carr came over, and said, "How are you, Mrs. Weedon. A bad business, all this. And how's Mr. Rollinson, and Mrs. Mackerras?"

"All right, under the circumstances," said Gran. Blimey! Is this all the village is talking about? Of course it is, she told herself. Best thing that happened to the gossips for years.

"Your usuals?" Mrs. Carr said, taking a packet off the shelf.

Gran shook her head. "Got anything else?" she said. "And not those things you gave me last time. They nearly killed me."

Mrs. Carr laughed. "Nonsense!" she said. "That was a bug going round the village. Nothing wrong with those tablets. Been selling 'em for years."

Gran hesitated. "Oh, all right then. I chucked the last lot away. Maybe I'll give 'em another try."

When she returned, Lois was still in her office, and Gran could hear Sharon's voice. They seemed to have an awful lot to say. Time for coffee and a biscuit to help the tablet down. Lois came through to the kitchen and said, "Ah, coffee, good. Sharon's a bit upset."

Gran looked guilty. "Nothing I said, I hope."

"Good heavens, no," said Lois. "I'll tell you later. Here," she added, picking up the tablets. "What're these?"

"For me indigestion," Gran said. "Got them from Mrs. Carr. She swears by them."

Lois turned the packet round in her hands and looked closely. "Mum," she said. "Where did she get these from? There's no sell-by date, and I've never heard of them."

"She's had 'em for years," Gran said. "Keeps them in the storeroom and gives them to favoured customers. Cyril was one, and I'm another," she added smugly.

Lois put the packet in her pocket. "You're not to take these," she said. "On no account, Mum. Stick to your usuals. Now, I've got to get back to Sharon, but we'll talk later."

Gran frowned, but admitted to herself that she was relieved. She hadn't forgotten that terrible bout of sickness. Perhaps Lois would find out a bit more about them. Meantime, the coffee and biscuit seemed to have done the trick. She cheered up, and went into the garden to fill up the bird feeders.

"So, Sharon, is that all, or are you hiding something? Something that might change my mind about employing you?"

Lois had never seen such a shifty performance. Sharon was clearly still under the weather, and her tale of a party that went wrong was unconvincing. The party had happened, all right. Lois knew that. But the rest? Sharon said she'd been introduced by Max Wedderburn, and hadn't known any of them. One of them had kept her glass topped up, saying it was fruit punch, nothing alcoholic. She'd believed him, until she realized she couldn't see properly. Lois had exploded, and said surely she was old enough to know better. Sharon had dissolved into tears.

Now she sipped her coffee and, sniffing reproachfully, answered Lois's questions.

"It was all blurry," she said. "After that, I don't remember much. I've told you what I remember. An' I'm really sorry I couldn't go to work. Can I go now?"

Lois said nothing. Then she opened the drawer in her desk and took out something. Something small and round.

She held out her closed hand and said, "Here, Sharon, have a look at this."

Sharon stretched out her hand to take it . . . The blood-shot eye looked at her.

Her scream ricocheted round the room and reached Gran in the kitchen.

"Give it back, then," said Lois, and quickly put it in her drawer.

Gran put her head round the door looking anxious. "What was that?" she said. "My God, Lois, what's the matter with the child?"

"She'll recover," said Lois acidly. "And she's no child."

When Sharon had gone, fussed over by Gran, who insisted on walking part of the way with her, Lois lifted her telephone. "Cowgill? Is that you? Yes, it's me. I've got a couple of things to tell you, and I'd like you to have a look at some pills. Analyse them, if that's what you do. Yeah, OK, I'll be there. You do? Well, maybe you're not so bad yourself."

Had she really said that? Well, it was a joke, in answer to his. The old thing was getting quite a sense of humour in his dotage. Lois collected her jacket and set off for the new meeting place. He had suggested an empty house on an estate in Tresham, due to be demolished. "All been re-housed," he'd said. "Number thirty-seven, at the end of a cul-de-sac. Nobody ever goes there. Vandals occasionally, but never during the day. We keep watch." She hoped he was right. She couldn't risk Derek hearing any gossip. Not again.

FORTY-ONE

❧

ANNABELLE AND JAMIE SETTLED INTO A COMPANION-able silence until they reached the motorway, and then Jamie said, "I feel a bit guilty about Mum and Dad."

"Why?" Annabelle had never felt guilty about her parents in her life. It was they who should feel guilty about her, pushing her around from place to place, school to school. She wondered what it would be like to have a family like Jamie's, rooted and solid.

"Well, I couldn't tell them much. I'd promised you. I lied about going to a concert with a friend at the Albert Hall. Mum soon sussed that one. And she guessed I was meeting you."

"What did she say?" Annabelle was curious. She was used to doing much as she liked, unless Grandmother was around, and then she found it easy to deceive her. The old dear was so busy with her good works, and manipulating people who didn't realize what she was up to.

"Not much. But she was nice. Practical, as ever. Said she'd make it right with Dad, but I was to let them know where you live . . . and keep my mobile on all the time! They think London is full of muggers just waiting for hicks from the country with money in their pockets." He didn't admit to Annabelle that this thought had occurred to him too. He was still sore about Annabelle's account of Mrs. T-J's tirade about "that village boy." There'd been a lot on the same theme before she had more or less sent Annabelle packing back to London.

Annabelle laughed, and turned into a service station. "Need some petrol," she said.

"I'll pay," said Jamie, feeling in his pocket. "Don't be silly!" Annabelle said. "I'll use my card—Dad settles it for me. Makes him feel better about being a rotten dad, I expect."

They decided on a cup of coffee, and sat in the café staring out at the rushing cars. "It's really nice of you to come," Annabelle said, looking at Jamie with warmth. "I don't know why, but I do have this scared feeling. Something to do with the vicarage fire. I'm really nervous about being in the flat alone. Sarah will be back in a couple of days, so you won't have to stay long."

She had told Jamie a strictly edited story about her involvement with the Wycombe lot. Said she'd been to one or two of their meetings out of curiosity, and had thought them a joke. "A sad joke," she had said, describing their fatuous rituals and chanting. They had wanted somewhere private to meet, and she had said without thinking that they could use the stables when her grandmother was away.

"Annabelle," Jamie said now. "Were you at that party the night of the fire?"

"What party?" she said quickly.

"Well, Mum said Sharon had gone to a party with that horrible bloke who comes from Tresham."

"Sharon Miller? Scraping the barrel, aren't they?" Annabelle laughed again, and looked away from Jamie, wishing he would change the subject.

"You said you'd been frightened when I saw you at the cottage. Noises in the night, an' that. I wondered if you'd heard something from the party. In the stables, maybe. Was it them that frightened you?"

Annabelle stood up, pushing her chair back with a loud scrape. "Going to the loo," she said.

"Again?" said Jamie quietly, watching her sadly as she walked across the crowded café.

THE ROAD INTO THE DESERTED HOUSING ESTATE WAS full of potholes. Lois drove slowly, doubting whether this was any better than Alibone Woods. Still, what did she expect? A reception area in the police station set aside for informers? Coffee machine and cushions? She peered around the dilapidated houses and saw Cowgill's car parked inconspicuously up against a garage door.

"Ah, Lois, good, you found it," he said briskly. He didn't feel brisk. He felt soft-centred, like a peppermint cream. He had watched her lope across the road and wondered if he should finally give up meeting her. He was a man who liked being in control. But where was the harm? If Lois showed in any way that she reciprocated . . . Well, then it would have to stop. Meanwhile, he might as well enjoy seeing her, feeling half his age again, being insulted by her, and making use of the undoubtedly useful information she brought him.

"Right," she said, following him through the back door of a damp, dirty kitchen.

They perched on a couple of metal chairs, and he said, "What have you got for me?" Straight to the point. Competent policeman, wasting no time.

She smiled sideways at him. "Something important, I think," she said. She described Gran's dodgy indigestion tablets and said Cyril had been on them, too. Could they have had anything to do with his death? She handed him the packet. "Look," she said, "no sell-by date, label all faded and creased. How long has that woman had them in her storeroom at the back there? They could've gone off, been dangerous, anything! If Cyril had taken too many, or woken in the night and forgotten he'd already had some . . . Could there be a connection? Gran had been really sick, and they'd all said it was a bug. But . . ."

"Well done," said Cowgill, pocketing the packet. "I'll get them looked at. We shall find out. Sounds very possible to me. I've never thought there was much foul play in Cyril's death. Who'd want to kill the old bugger, irritating as he was? No, Lois, I think this may be it."

"There's more," she said, looking pleased with herself. "It's our Sharon. Sharon Miller."

Cowgill's eyes narrowed. "Go on," he said quietly. Lois could feel the sudden tension in the air. So this was what he really wanted to know. "She came to see me. Looked terrible, and was nervous, jumpy. I tried out the 'orrible eye on her, and she nearly had a fit. Not just a natural reaction. Much more than that, screaming and blubbing. Mum calmed her down, and then I let her go." She looked closely at Cowgill, who was silent and frowning. "Well?" she said finally. "Any good?"

He nodded. "Yes," he said. "Very useful. Very useful indeed. And now I have to warn you, Lois, to be careful. If Sharon Miller knows something she's not telling you, you can bet it's to do with Darren Cockshutt, and he is nasty."

"Nasty? Is that all?" said Lois.

"No, he is nasty and dangerous, especially if he cannot trust Sharon Miller to keep her mouth shut."

"Sharon couldn't keep her mouth shut if it was stapled together," said Lois baldly. "Sounds like it's her who's in danger, not me."

"Anyone who knows anything about the night of the fire, and just what Max-cum-Darren was up to, is in danger. *Anyone* . . . and that probably includes your Jamie."

"Jamie? Why? Because he knows Sharon? That's a bit far-fetched, isn't it. Anyway, he's safely out of the way. Gone to London for a day or two with Annabelle T-J."

"Has he indeed?" said Cowgill. "Annabelle T-J. Mmm . . . not a sensible idea . . ."

"Don't talk in riddles," said Lois crossly. "Why don't you just arrest Maxie-boy, and put him away? You think he started the fire, don't you?"

"Yes, I do," Cowgill said, getting up and offering Lois a hand, which she ignored. "But I don't know why," he added, "and I need to know more. He's a slippery customer, Lois. Don't underrate him."

FORTY-TWO

༜

Max Wedderburn returned to his untidy room, bed unmade, remains of a hasty meal in the wash basin that doubled as a sink, and thought hard. How had it all gone so wrong? God, if he was found to be mixed up in it, he'd be for the high jump this time. He shivered uncontrollably, and couldn't straighten out his thoughts. The weak links. That's what he had to concentrate on. Slowly he calmed down, and reminded himself he'd always come up smiling before. And would again. He'd made some decisions already, hadn't he? Swift to act, always one move ahead, that was Max Wedderburn. He shook himself and stood up. It would soon be time for him to go. His most trusted henchman was looking after the local end, and he had reserved London for himself. Yeah, the weak links were priority. Sharon and Annabelle T-J.

It was a pity it had to end in this way, but if the society went undercover for a while they could start up again when it had all been forgotten. Maybe move away, set up somewhere else. One of his mates, just released early for good behaviour, had let him know of an isolated place in Wales. That was something to look forward to. Meanwhile, there was a job to be done.

As he hastily tidied the room, he caught a glimpse of himself in the tarnished mirror. He stopped and had a good look. He straightened his shoulders, narrowed his eyes and allowed himself what he hoped was a small, heroic smile. Yes, that was better. All would be well.

He looked at his watch. She should be there by now, and by herself. She'd let slip that her flatmate was away, stupid bitch. It was because she *was* a stupid bitch, and let things slip, that he was now on the way to make sure she kept her mouth shut. North London, wasn't it? Annabelle had given him the address at the party—after the necessary persuasion—and he put an A-Z map in his pocket. Should be easy enough to find. He'd have to fill up with petrol before he got to the motorway. Much too expensive once you were on it. The cut-price filling station just outside Tresham would do.

He looked out of the window at the street below. A bloke who'd been in his class was walking along the pavement. He was in clean, dark blue overalls, and had a bag of tools in his hand. He put his tools in the van, then walked around to the front and wiped the headlights clean. He climbed in and drove away. What was his name? Max could not remember. He was a nerd, anyway. Always top of the class. And where had it got him? A plumber. Nice little council flat, nice little wife, nice little baby. A traitorous voice in Max's head said, "And a nice little business of his own, with a regular income and good mates. Plumbers in demand, security and a loving home. What's wrong with that?"

Everything, answered Max. He had his own boring job, but his real life in the society was different and special. He saw himself as an instrument of a higher power, the dark power that could blaze with a wonderful flame. He felt no guilt at what he and the society had done in the past, only exultation. And now? said the voice.

He forced it out of his head, looked at his watch again, and left the room, locking the door behind him. Head up, shoulders back, Max Wedderburn, man with a mission, was on the warpath.

THE AFTERNOON SUN SHONE THROUGH THE BIG WIN-dows in Annabelle's flat, and Jamie relaxed, stretched out on a sofa in the sitting room. It was on the ground floor, and had long French windows leading out into a pleasant, walled garden. Annabelle had unlocked and opened them to air the room, and a blackbird sang from an old apple tree, bare of leaves now, spreading its branches wide. As Jamie gazed out lazily, waiting for Annabelle to bring in coffee, a squirrel ran from one side of the tree to the other, dropping down out of sight into next door's garden.

The coffee was good. "Real coffee," said Annabelle. "None of your instant for Sarah. She has style, my flat-mate."

Jamie wondered if he would like her. He got on easily with Annabelle most of the time, but on the odd occasion when they had met her friends in Tresham, he had been stupid and tongue-tied.

Now he returned to something that bothered him. "Annabelle," he said. "You know that party, the one Sharon went to . . ."

"Oh, drop it, Jamie!"

"It's just that . . . oh, I dunno. There's something wrong somewhere. You must've heard something going on. The stables are not that far from the cottages."

"For God's sake! Why this inquisition? Come on," she added, stroking his face and nuzzling his ear. "Let's go to bed. I really want to . . . and so do you . . ." She laughed confidently.

But Jamie pulled away from her and got up. "It's not on, Annabelle," he said, a stubborn, Lois-like look on his face. "You're not telling me the truth, and if you don't trust me enough I'd best be going home now. I'd do most things for you, you know that. But not if you're playin' me along."

"Oh, Jamie, *please*," she pleaded, taking his hand and pulling him back towards her. He shook his head and went to sit down by the big marble fireplace.

She walked across the room and stared out at the garden. It was chillier now, and she pulled the French windows shut, struggling with the lock. Then she hunched up on the sofa and stared at him like a thwarted child. "Oh, all right, then," she said finally. "I *was* at the stupid party. Max had persuaded me to go. Said they had something very special on. So I turned up, had a couple of drinks, and chatted to stupid Sharon Miller—who was, by the way, three sheets to the wind."

Her eyes told him that was not all. "And?" he said.

"And nothing else," she said impatiently. "Now come here, and let's forget it." But Jamie did not move.

After a minute or two of silence, Annabelle spoke again, softly this time, almost to herself. "Max made a sort of speech. Like a call to arms, or battle, or something. He's very good when he gets going. But then it turned to a rant, and the others started chanting and stamping."

"What were they chanting?" said Jamie.

"Well . . . um . . ." She took a deep breath and said, "It was 'Fire!!' over and over again. That's what it was. I was frightened, Jamie. I tried to leave, but Max had locked the door. He told one of his oiks to look after me."

"Where did you go?" Jamie's face was pale. He knew what was coming, and realized he had no idea what to do next.

"The vicarage," she answered. "I managed to hang back, pretend I was going to be sick."

"And Sharon Miller?" Jamie's hand curled round the

comforting shape of his mobile in his pocket. "Was she still with them?"

"Yep, right out in front, eyes all over the place!" The shadow of a grin crossed Annabelle's face. "She had something in her hand, held up high. I couldn't see what it was, but they all started a horrible kind of whispering. It was like one of their chants, but whispered. I suppose they didn't want people to know they were there. Then Sharon threw whatever it was—it looked like a little ball—towards the vicarage. And then it started . . . I *was* sick then, but they'd all run off, and people had started appearing, so I hid for a while in the churchyard." She stopped and shut her eyes for a moment. Jamie waited, knowing there was more to come.

Annabelle rubbed her eyes, and continued, "There were crowds of people and the fire engines arrived. I was trapped, so I stayed put until everyone had gone and the fire was out, and then I sneaked off home. Most people had gone by then."

"That's when we saw you. Going home," said Jamie. "When you said 'it started,' did you mean the fire?" The light was going outside the window, and Jamie shivered.

Annabelle nodded. "It was so quick, Jamie. I don't know how they got it going so quickly."

They were both silent and still. Then Jamie said, "I'll put some lights on. And get some heating going." He looked out into the garden, and saw a black cat creeping along the branch of the apple tree. A sudden squawk and a blackbird flew off in alarm. The cat slunk away, over the wall. Jamie shrugged. This was London. Anything could happen.

Annabelle called from the kitchen that rotten Sarah had left nothing to eat. Could Jamie fetch a couple of take-aways from the Chinese round the corner? Jamie checked his cash, and thought he'd probably have enough. "Which way?" he said. It was going to be further than just around the corner, he discovered, more than ten minutes away. But Jamie was glad of some air and walked along at a good pace, happy to be doing something useful, feeling he belonged.

FORTY-THREE

❧

FOUR MILES OUTSIDE LONG FARNDEN, A SELDOM-USED farm track branched off and quickly became rutted and muddy from an overflowing ditch. Down here, an anonymous dark green car moved slowly, juddering as it negotiated the rough surface. The driver peered through a dirty windscreen and frowned. "Bloody awful place," he muttered. "Is this the best Max could suggest?"

His passenger, Sharon Miller, shivered, not from the cold wind, but with fear. She had been on her way to work at the shop after lunch, already feeling sorry for herself after her session with Mrs. M, when this bloke had pulled up beside her, opened the door and told her to get in. When she had protested, he'd said roughly that if she didn't do as she was told, she'd regret it. He had a message from Max Wedderburn, and people always did what *he* told them. And she could call him Stan, he added, glancing lasciviously at her.

"Just for a minute, then," Sharon had said, glancing up and down the street, hoping that someone would see her.

But there was nobody in sight. Then to her horror, the minute she got in the car, the man, whom she vaguely recognized from the party at the stables, had driven off at speed, with a squeal of tyres. Now they were in a barnyard, with no house in sight, and he was telling her to get out.

"In there," he said shortly, pointing to the barn. "We have to talk." By now, Sharon was in a state of terror. She was only too familiar from her novels with kidnapped beauties left to the predations of no-good villains . . . or mutilated so that . . . Oh my God, what was he going to do?

He turned her round, and then tied her wrists together behind her back. "Just in case you feel like doin' a runner," he said. "Now then," he added, pushing her down on the dirty straw, "let's see how much you remember of that night. Party night, Sharon . . . And shut that row, else I'll make sure you never make another sound . . . ever."

She choked, and was silent. "What d'you want to know . . . Stan," she stuttered after a minute.

"Everything you can remember," he said. "Starting with when Max brought you into the party."

"I got given a drink," she said.

"Did you know anybody?"

Sharon shook her head. "Only Max," she said. "I met him at Cyril's funeral. He was nice to me when I tripped over." She was shaking now, her whole body trembling in terror. Was he going to rape her? How much should she tell him? She was canny enough to realize that if she owned up to remembering everything, he would have to find a way of silencing her.

"I enjoyed it," she said lamely.

"You'll have to do better than that," he said, and lit a cigarette. "Such pretty hair," he said, taking a handful and stroking it. He put it to the lighted end of the cigarette, and laughed when it sizzled. "Horrible smell!" he said, and took it away again. "Good thing hair don't feel nothing.

Plenty of bits of you that does, though," he added, and sniggered.

"I remember them making a fuss of me, goin' on about my eye and sayin' it had power, an' all sorts of rubbish," Sharon said quickly.

"Rubbish?" he said, his smile vanishing. "What else was rubbish?"

"Nothing . . . Stan . . . It was soon after that I began to feel funny. Not faint, nor anythin' like that, but I couldn't see properly. Everything was a bit fuzzy. I felt good, though. Sort of powerful, as if I could do anything. But that's all I can remember. Just the feeling."

"Mmm." The man looked closely at her. "What was the next thing you do remember? Did you go anywhere after the party?"

Sharon shook her head. "Um . . . next thing I remember is my mum waking me up in my bedroom at home. I felt terrible. Real terrible. I've never felt like that before. I was screamin' and shouting, and Dad had to hold me down."

After several minutes, when Sharon began to think he was satisfied and she might get off lightly, the man said, "Right. Now see here, Sharon, you got to forget all of it, even the bits you do remember now. Put them right out of your head. If we hear that you've been blabbing anything about that night, everything you bin thinking I might do to you now . . . it will be done. See?" He waved his cigarette in her face, coming dangerously close to her eyes.

"Stop, Stan!" she screamed, and he put his hand over her mouth. She recalled what she'd said to Lois about the party, and began to mumble. He took his hand away. "I really don't remember anything else," she insisted. "When I heard about the fire next day, I thanked God I'd bin with you lot, well away from it all. If I'd seen poor Sandy . . ."

She began to cry bitterly, and the man sat back on his heels, staring at her. Finally he pulled her roughly to her feet, gave her push and said, "Get going. I'll take you back

now, and don't forget what I said. Any peep from you
about the party or Max, or anything else, and we shall
know. And you'll be sorry." He reckoned he'd done
enough, and dropped her back outside the shop with a clear
conscience. Max would be pleased with him, and that was
all that concerned him.

MAX WAS CERTAINLY FEELING PLEASED WITH HIMSELF.
He had drawn up outside the right house, checking the
road name and house number. That was fine. So far so
good. Yes, and there was Annabelle's car, parked a good
couple of feet from the kerb. Typical! Idiots like her who
were allowed to drive were a menace—kids just out of
school and with no idea at all. Stupid rich kids, whose parents bought them new cars as soon as they'd passed the
test. He remembered his own first car, a small, battered
Ford that shook and rattled, and had raised a laugh from
the likes of the plumber. He'd had to work for this beauty.
He patted the dashboard affectionately and felt good.

He cruised down the road and found an empty space,
parked immaculately, turned off the engine and got out.

The road was quiet, a cul-de-sac of substantial houses.
The cars already parked were prestigious, all the right
names and models. For a moment Max felt overawed, and
his confidence ebbed. Then he noticed an old Mini, with a
jumble of kids' toys and old newspapers. A terrier on the
loose, nosing in the gutter, cocked its leg against the Mini's
dirty wheel, and a stream of yellow pee carved a path
through accumulated dried mud.

Max laughed aloud and felt cheered. He walked jauntily
along the path and stopped outside the house where he
would find Annabelle. He checked in his pocket for what
he would need, and opened the gate.

The door opened after a few seconds, and Annabelle
said, "Jamie, that was quick! Oh . . . oh, my God," and

tried to shut the door. But Max had his foot inside and pushed hard against her. All those expensive hours in the gym paid off, and he forced her back easily. He stepped in and closed the door behind him, checking that the lock was on. Annabelle retreated fast and had her hand on the kitchen door into the garden, but Max was there at once, wrenching her hand away and locking the door, pocketing the key.

He pulled her arm round to her back, and she yelled. "Shut up!" he said sharply. He pushed her through to the sitting room and, still holding on to her, closed the curtains on all the windows. Then he made her sit down on the sofa. As she tried to get up again, he pulled his shiny blade from his pocket and held it to her throat. She subsided, her eyes staring with contempt.

"That's better," he said. "Now we can make ourselves comfortable. Have a nice chat." He smiled at her, then remembered his rotten teeth and banished the smile.

"You were at the party, weren't you?" he said conversationally. "Talking to those chinless wonder friends of yours from Waltonby, the ones we could do without? And you stayed . . . to the end?"

She shook her head. "I was at the vicarage for a while, but I went home early. And anyway, you left before me. I saw you go." Where was Jamie? Would he be back in time? She glared at Max, hating the smell of him, his cheap scenty smell. Yob. Still, better play along until she could think of a way out.

He menaced her again. "Never mind what I did," he said. "It's what you did, what you remember, that I've come about."

"I know there was a fire, but I'd gone by then. I know some of your lot were whispering a sort of chant, but that's nothing new. I didn't listen. I was too busy being sick. Those disgusting drinks, I expect. So you needn't worry. I saw nothing to bother you. What's more," she said, crossing her legs and relaxing, "I couldn't be less interested in what goes on in Long Farnden. Boring little hole. Only there to please Grandmother. She's quite rich, you know. Worth keeping on the right side of. Lots of influence, too. So I'd be careful, if I were you, Max Wedderburn."

"Your gran don't frighten me," he said violently, his accent slipping.

"And you don't frighten me," said Annabelle, and yawned.

JAMIE HURRIED BACK WITH THE FOOD, ANXIOUS FOR IT to stay hot. He turned into Annabelle's street and walked swiftly along the pavement. The terrier met him, and sniffed the air. Jamie grinned and bent down to pat the scruffy little dog. "Not for you, old chap," he said, and walked on.

As he approached the house, his eye was caught by a familiar-looking sports car, parked fifty yards up the road. He frowned, and walked quickly along to check. The number plate gave it away. Jamie had noticed it several times in the village, and knew who owned it. What the hell was he doing here in London? In Annabelle's street? Suddenly Jamie was running, back towards the house. Then he stopped short. If that oaf was in the house, it would be best to get in without him knowing. Ten to one he didn't know Jamie was in London. Annabelle was too clever for that.

He remembered seeing an entrance to a dark, overgrown footpath, leading up by one of the houses. Yes, there it was. He went silently along, trying to see where he was in relation to Annabelle's house. The path branched off at a right angle and ran along the back of all the houses. A bit of luck. Jamie counted down until he was sure he was in the right place, and then, reluctantly leaving the food by the wall, clambered swiftly over into the garden, hoping he was hidden from view by the apple tree.

He crept up to the back door, and gently tried the handle. Locked. Yes, well, Max Wedderburn would have thought of that. The curtains were all drawn, and Jamie could see nothing inside the house. He felt a rising panic. Suppose the bugger had hurt Annabelle, maybe tied her up and tortured her? Common sense calmed him down. Why should he do that? What did he want with her, anyway, apart from lust? And she was a big strong girl, with all that horse riding. But why had he come?

The party. The fire. It came to him in a rush. Annabelle had seen too much.

He tiptoed along until he was outside the long windows. Now he could hear voices, but couldn't hear what they were saying. At least Annabelle was still alive! Without much hope, he turned the handle, very, very gently. To his huge relief, the rusty lock had not engaged, and he silently opened the door a fraction. He took a deep breath, and eased himself into the room, hidden by the heavy curtains. His heart in his mouth, he pulled the door shut behind him, still holding his breath.

Now he could hear them. Annabelle was saying, "For God's sake put that thing away! I told you I'm not frightened. I've got nothing to tell you, so you might as well go back to Farnden and work on covering your tracks."

Max replied, "What d'you mean, covering my tracks? What've I got to hide? You *do* know something, you stuck-up little bitch!"

Jamie let out his breath, pulled aside a curtain and saw Max Wedderburn bending over Annabelle, brandishing a knife. With a supreme effort, he did not yell, or rush out and swoop. He moved silently, trusting Annabelle would see him and do nothing to give him away.

FORTY-FOUR

❧

IN THE UNTIDY SITTING ROOM, LITTERED WITH TOYS, the young woman settled the baby on her husband's lap, and said, "Funny, that."

"What do you mean?" he said, unclasping the fat, sticky little hand from his flopping hair.

"Just now, when I went out to get Teddy . . . you know those girls in the flat opposite? Well, this guy came rushing out of their door and practically fell down the steps. Ran up the road to a smart little sports job, and set off like a bat out of hell. Nasty looking type, bullet-head, dark glasses. You know the sort."

"Something wrong, d'you think?" The baby had thrown Teddy into a corner, and her father got up wearily to fetch it.

"I dunno. Nothing, I suppose. Lovers' quarrel, d'you reckon?"

The husband nodded, and said quickly, "Can you take this infant? Needs her nappy changed."

•　•　•

"ANNABELLE! WHY DID YOU *DO* THAT? I COULD'VE HELD on to him until we got the police! The rat was a real coward . . . didn't even try to put up a fight! Why did you make me let him go?"

She stared at him, and held out a shaking hand. "I had a reason, Jamie. Can we sit down." Jamie could see her cool courage was oozing away. She seemed about to cry. But she owed him an explanation.

"Listen," she said. "You were brilliant, Jamie, and I was so relieved. Knocked the knife right out of his hand! He didn't have time to know what hit him . . . you were great."

"So why . . . ?"

"I know that Wycombe lot. You don't, and they're dangerous. If we'd kept him and got the police, yeah, they'd have taken him away. But sooner or later his cronies would've got us. Either you or me would have been done over on a dark street some night. I don't want to risk that, Jamie. I'm too young to be carved up . . ." Her hands were clenched fists. He saw the effort she was making not to collapse, and gently touched her hair.

"Not to worry," he said. "They'll be on to him soon. That Cowgill cop—friend of Mum's—he'll be close behind him I shouldn't wonder. I'm sure you're right, Belle," he added, and the loving, hesitant diminutive was too much. Tears flowed, and Jamie mopped them up with tissues until she finally sniffed and stopped.

"Better see if that Chinese is still out there," Jamie said. "We could warm it up." He made a brave attempt at a grin. But when he looked over the wall into the dark footpath, he saw only empty cartons and the rear end of a disappearing terrier.

THE JOURNEY SEEMED ENDLESS, EVEN THOUGH MAX was breaking the speed limit most of the way. He had never been to Wales, never been further west than Oxford, but now he peered out at the narrow lane with relief. It was certainly off the beaten track. He had had to stop for petrol on the motorway, but had kept his face turned away from the girl at the till. Now he had to find the address. Pembrokeshire could just as well be Saudi Arabia as far as Max was concerned.

He came to the end of the lane, and it seemed to peter out. Then he saw a farm gate, and a track leading onwards. He opened the gate and went on, remembering to shut it behind him. The ground was hard and dry. That was good. No tyre tracks.

A small house loomed up out of the dark. There were no lights, and—if his contact was reliable—nobody would be there. He parked his car round the back out of sight, and felt under the flowerpot by the back door. Not exactly an original hiding place! The key was there, and he opened the green-painted door and walked in. Shutting and locking it behind him, he looked around. It was not completely dark inside, clear moonlight shining through the windows. Kitchen, living room, narrow stairs, two bedrooms, tiny bathroom. Gimcrack furniture. Piles of jigsaws and board games. Stack of maps for walkers. A typical holiday cottage, and totally isolated off-season. His contact *was* reliable, he noted with relief.

Sleep was all he wanted now. Exhausted by the journey and the day's events, he stretched out on a bare mattress, pulled his coat over him, and closed his eyes. As he drifted off, he heard a sound, a rhythmic, sighing sound. Jerking awake, he sat up. It seemed to be coming from outside, and he walked across to the window, peering out carefully so as not to be seen.

The moonlight shone in a silvery path across shimmering water, stretching to the horizon. The sea.

"Summat new then, Darren boy," he said to himself. "A seaside holiday at last."

Five minutes later he was asleep and snoring.

FORTY-FIVE

ॐ

Brian Rollinson and Marion sat at the Meades' breakfast table, eating without speaking, and listening to Lois and Derek arguing outside the kitchen door.

"Perhaps we'd better be going early," Brian whispered, but Marion shook her head. "Just the everyday story of married folk," she said sourly. "But you wouldn't know about that."

His face fell, and he was silent again.

"Oh . . . sorry," Marion said, and sighed. "I've been thinking . . ." she said after a minute. "I'll stay a couple more days if Lois will have me. There are one or two other people I'd like to see. Friends of Sandy that he told me about." She paused, but Brian said nothing. "Pathetic, I suppose," she continued. "But talking about him to people round here, people who knew him, seems to keep him . . . well, you know," she ended lamely.

"I do know. I loved him, too. And not . . ." He looked at her anxiously, and she nodded.

"I know," she said.

"I'm sure Lois won't mind another day or two," Brian continued. "Her bark is worse than her bite . . . I think." They both smiled. "And anyway, we can make all the funeral arrangements with your church from here, and then go back perhaps the day before. I could come with you then, if you like. If you could put me up, maybe." Had he gone too far? Trespassed on the thin ice they were treading?

But Marion nodded absently. "Fine," she said. "D'you want another coffee? Gran said to help ourselves."

The argument was continuing but voices were faint. Marion sipped her coffee and looked at Brian. How strange that they should have come to some sort of truce after all this time. It was as if she was seeing him for the first time, seeing him as he really was. A man dogged by tragedy, making the best of his life and taking on a difficult job. Who'd be a vicar in these godless times? He could have gone away, abroad or something, and lived it out quietly. She thought back to Gerald's accident. Could she ask Brian the question that had haunted her all these years?

"Brian . . ."

"Mmm?" he said, without looking up from his coffee.

"Can I ask you something?"

"Of course." He was miles away, thinking about the smouldering vicarage and how he could reorder his life. Maybe he should resign, but that would be a cowardly way out, and he had work to do. No, he had to trust in God. A very present help in trouble.

"It's about Gerald. His accident. Um . . . What really happened, Brian?"

There was a long silence, and Marion thought she had gone too far. But didn't she have a right to know? Especially now, when there were so many unexplained mysteries about Sandy and the fire. At least she could get one thing straightened out.

Finally Brian spoke. "It was how I said at the time, when the police were asking. You and I . . . well, we'd broken off all contact by then. So you probably didn't . . . Well, it was what I dreaded, Marion." Brian's fists were clenched in his lap, and his voice was tight with tension.

"Gerald was drinking too much. He worried about you and Sandy, and couldn't accept what he'd done. Guilt . . . not being able to sleep . . . all that. We were in a pub at lunchtime, and he'd had several pints. Wouldn't eat anything. Then he said he wanted to walk back home along the cliff. Get some fresh air. I knew the footpath, and it went very close to the edge . . ."

He was silent again, and Marion waited, holding her breath. "I tried hard to stop him, Marion. But he wouldn't listen, just shouted at me and rushed out of the pub. He was very unsteady, all over the place. It was a terrible day— blowing a gale and driving rain. I thought of following him, but decided it would make things worse, and drove back home. When he didn't come back, I went along the path. I saw the place from a distance. The grass was all broken away from the edge. A big gap where the path had been. I peered over, and saw him. A long way down. Spreadeagled on the rocks." He put his head in his hands, and Marion saw his shoulders shaking.

"Don't," she said, leaning forward and taking his hand. "I shouldn't have asked. I'm so sorry, Brian . . ."

"I should gone after him," he muttered. "I can never forgive myself. And now Sandy. If I'd gone home earlier, there'd have been no fire . . . Oh, dear God!"

"Not your fault," she said ineffectually. She squeezed his hand. "Come on, let's go . . . let's go somewhere, anywhere . . . At least there's the two of us . . ."

MEANWHILE, THE ARGUMENT CONTINUED. LOIS AND Derek were in her office now, with the door shut. "I don't like it!" Derek said for the umpteenth time. "We don't know what he's up to. All right, all right, I know he's not a kid any more. But he's still wet behind the ears as far as girls are concerned. And that Annabelle is seventeen goin' on twenty-seven."

"So, what d'you suggest we do? Go up to London and drag him back by force? I dunno, Derek. I don't get it. You've never been like this before."

"*You've* not been in touch with that Cowgill for a long time. There's something going on, and I don't like it. Most of the time I let you get on with it. You got to give me that. But when it's my son that's at risk, then I'll have my say!"

"At risk?" Lois felt her stomach jolt. She remembered Cowgill's reaction when she'd said Jamie was going to London with Annabelle. "Not very sensible," he'd said. "What d'you mean, Derek?"

"Look, Lois," he said, pushing her down into her chair. "Look and listen. We've had a fire at the vicarage. A young bloke was killed when he should've found it easy to escape. An old man has sicked himself to death in the night. Sharon Miller seems to have taken leave of her senses, and our youngest son has got mixed up with a girl who's in with a loony, criminal lot from Tresham. And you ask me what I mean!" Lois was silent now. Derek was right, of course. She lifted the telephone and dialled.

"Jamie? Mum here. Are you all right? When are you . . . oh, tonight. Right. Well, take care. Let us know what time at the station and we'll meet you. Sure everything's all right? OK, then. See you later." She put down the phone and looked at Derek. "He's coming back this evening, on the train, on his own," she said.

"I'll meet him, then," said Derek, and left her sitting there. She watched him drive off in his van to work, and frowned. Then she shook herself and stood up. Time for a word with the vicar. And maybe with Mrs. Mackerras, too.

But when she went into the kitchen, neither of them was there, and the breakfast things had been cleared away and washed up. She could see them wandering about the garden, and then they disappeared down the path towards the little gate and the footpath. Sod it. Still, she supposed it could wait. Meanwhile, back to the business of cleaning people's houses. She returned to her office.

"Bill?" Lois could hear Rebecca in the background, yelling that she was off to school. "Is it a bad moment? It's about today's meeting. Can you come half an hour early? You finish at the Hall in time, don't you? Good, see you later." Lois took a pen and began to jot down some notes that had nothing to do with cleaning.

1. Murder or accident? Probably murder. Why? Anyone could have started that fire.
2. Sandy's enemies? Bill: angry about Rebecca; the vicar: angry at Sandy being so foul to him; Mr. Nameless: angry about his girl/wife being shafted by Sandy; Max Wedderburn?
3. Max Wedderburn: Fascist thug, arsonist, crafty snake—but what did he have against Sandy? S. had been to Wycombe meetings. Why? What was the attraction for a bloke like Sandy, who loved nothing better than a few jars in the pub with the lads?
4. Sharon Miller: What!!!
5. Annabelle? Oh, for goodness sake!
6. Or none of these?

Lois heard Gran coming back from the shop, and called out to her. "Coffee time, Mum! I'll make it, while you unpack the shopping." She slipped her notes inside a folder and went to see what tit-bits Gran had picked up from the gossips this morning.

BILL ARRIVED A GOOD HALF-HOUR EARLY, AS INSTRUCTED, and joined Lois in her office.

"What's eating you?" said Lois casually. She'd heard

the rumours about Sandy and Rebecca, but did not know
how serious it had been.

"Nothing. I'm fine."

"Right, then let's get down to business." Lois knew
better than to quiz Bill. He was a typical Yorkshire lad—
tough, loyal and private. He'd worked for her for a long
time now, sharing his domestic duties with helping out at
the vet's. She had never had reason to criticize his work,
and was fond of him.

"I want to talk to you about Sharon Miller," she said. "I
know I'm breakin' my own rules, discussing one cleaner
with another, but we've got a problem here. You may know
more than I do, about her social life an' that. She's a bit of
a silly in some ways. But there's no real harm in her, and I
know she's frightened out of her wits."

"Has she got any?" said Bill, and in spite of himself,
grinned.

"Yes, well, her work for me is fine. In her daffy way she
cheers up clients, and does the job efficiently. I'd like to
keep her on, and I need to know what's going on with her."

"Have you tried asking her?" Bill's mind seemed to be
elsewhere.

"Yes, of course I bloody well have!" Lois was losing
patience. "Look, Bill, if you'd rather not help, just say so.
I can ask one of the others. Maybe Hazel will know. But
she thinks about nothin' but babies at the moment, bless
her. And the others, Bridie and Enid and Sheila, they're a
different generation and don't really know Sharon. So you
were the one I hoped would help. But never mind . . ."

"Hey, wait a minute." Bill squared his shoulders and
seemed to come to a decision. "Sorry, Mrs. M," he said.
"Got a bit of a problem myself at the moment. I think it's
only fair to tell you. Me and Rebecca have come to a parting of the ways. I'll be returning to Yorkshire—on my
own—shortly. Don't know exactly when, but soon. I'll

work out my notice, of course. I was going to tell you later, but now seems the best time."

"Bill!" Lois was shocked. The ground was giving way under her feet. Her rock, her Bill, was going! She clutched at straws. "But surely you haven't decided . . . you and Rebecca have been together for such a long time . . . and your work at the vet's . . . what would you do if you go back?" Her thoughts raced. This was the last thing she needed. "Well, thank you, Sandy Mackerras!" she continued angrily, with no thought of respect for the dead. "It was that little toad, wasn't it? Started flirting with Rebecca at choir and went on from there?"

Bill said nothing, but stared down at his big, capable hands.

In for a penny, thought Lois, and continued, "And then the spoilt mummy's boy dumped poor old Sharon, breaking her heart. Mind you, that's—"

"Easily done?" completed Bill, and looked at Lois. His eyes were moist, but he managed a grin.

"Sharon's heart's soon mended, luckily," agreed Lois. "It's them books she reads. But Bill," she said, and now she was serious, "don't decide definitely yet. Rebecca is probably still shocked. Maybe it will take weeks. But if you still want . . . ?"

He nodded. "Then I should hang on for bit. These things blow over. She's a sensible girl, and he was a shit."

He nodded again, reluctantly. Then he shook off the subject, and said, "So what do I know about Sharon? Only that she was mixed up with those thugs—Maxie boy—and was there the night of the fire. She was seen. An' then there was Sandy. Sharon went head over heels, as you know. Very upset that he dumped her. What else? Oh, yes, and out of her head, apparently, the fire night. Mind you, she can't take it. She's anybody's after a couple of shandies. If she's scared, it'll be of Maxie's lot. Especially of him. As long as he's around she'll be dead scared. She knows too much, probably."

A knock at the door, and Gran's welcoming voice put an end to the conversation, but Lois reckoned it had been a worthwhile half-hour.

COWGILL SAT IN HIS OFFICE, WITH A CUP OF COLD COF-fee in front of him, deep in thought. It was an odd business. A house destroyed by fire—no, not just a house, a vicarage—a body as a result, a bunch of town nasties, and a village heaving with rumour and suspicion. But did he have a crime? More specifically, did he have a murder? He was pretty sure the fire had been started by Cockshutt and his acolytes, but he had no proof. As yet. Young Mackerras could have been trapped, but it was unlikely. Accidental fire takes a while to get going, unless there was an explosion—gas, or something. But nobody heard anything. A big strong boy like that should have escaped with no trouble.

But why should those pathetic thugs go for Sandy Mackerras? They were a nasty lot, certainly, but not mur-derers. Too cowardly. The KKK that Darren and his boys slavishly followed had never hesitated. The Klan had hanged blacks, beat up Jews, homosexuals, anybody who didn't fit their skewed ideas. But Darren Cockshutt? He was a glorified playground bully who would run shit-scared if a real man faced up to him. Then he remembered his stricture to Lois. Don't underrate Cockshutt. No, he should not forget that.

Witnesses. Nothing useful had emerged yet. Cowgill thumped his desk, and said aloud, "A reliable witness! Somebody must have seen something."

"Do you need anything?" A pleasant-faced police-woman put her head round the door.

"Yes, I do. But nothing you can provide, thanks." He

grinned at her, and got up from his desk. "I shall be out for the rest of the day," he said, and made for the lift.

MRS. COCKSHUTT, WATCHING FROM BEHIND THE grubby lace curtains, knew it was the police when an anonymous black car drew up outside her house down by the river. She'd had plenty of experience. She opened the door and said, "What d'you want?"

"Your Darren," said Cowgill, keeping the door open with his weight. "And don't tell me he's not here, because I know he's not. I've been to his scruffy hole and he's not there, either. So where is he, Mrs. Cockshutt?"

She shrugged, her eyes narrowed. Darren could be anywhere. "He don't tell me where he's goin'. Never has," she added proudly. "Always independent, our Darren. So you'll just have to go on looking. Why d'you want him, anyway?" she added, curiosity getting the better of her.

Cowgill smiled a smile totally without mirth. "Never you mind," he said. "Just stand aside and let me in. We'll have a nice chat about Darren's friends." He gave her no chance to answer, but brushed past her, wrinkling his nose at the stale air that met him.

FORTY-SIX

❧

SHARON MILLER STOOD AT A BEDROOM WINDOW IN the Hall, staring out. She and Bill had been sent to do a big clean-up for Mrs. T-J, who had returned with a spring-cleaning bug. It was misty, and the trees in the park were like shadowy giants moving slowly towards the house. Coming to get me, thought Sharon, and shivered. She was sleeping badly, having nightmares about Stan and his threats. What would he have said to Max? And would it have satisfied him? After all, he was in big trouble. Every-thing would be bound to come out, whether Sharon shopped them or not. But Max would blame her.

She continued to clean the big panes, trying not to look at the trees and fighting tears. Surely the police would ar-rest Max soon and tidy everything up. Once he was taken care of, she was sure Stan and the others would crawl back to where they came from. Until that time, she was not safe.

A sharp noise behind her caused her heart to race, and she spun round. "Oh, it's you, Bill," she said, hand to her mouth.

"Who else?" said Bill, frowning. She looked terrible, white as a ghost. "Came to tell you it was coffee time," he continued. "You feelin' all right?"

She nodded. "You made me jump," she said. "Come on, I need a break."

After coffee, Bill said he would help her tackle Annabelle's room. It was a tip, with clothes everywhere, muddy riding boots on the unmade bed, and doors and drawers spilling their contents on to the floor.

"Slut!" said Sharon. "Jamie Meade wants his head examined."

"Love," said Bill sadly. "Love is blind, Sharon."

"I know," said Sharon, "but not that blind."

"Here, give us a hand," Bill said. He was on his knees by the bed. "There's something shoved under here. Better get it out before the mice nest in it."

They cleared a space, and then pulled out a bundle of whitish cloth, rough and hairy to the touch.

"What the hell?" Bill held it up, and Sharon made a face.

"Not Annabelle's usual gear," she said. "What is it?"

It was a robe, and—like Christopher Robin's dressing gown—it had a hood. But it was not nearly so innocent, as Bill immediately saw. Sharon, he realized, had not yet recognized it. But its unmistakable shape and the pointed hood sent chills through him.

"Best put it back," he said.

"But why?" Sharon took it from him and held it up against herself.

"Give it to me!" Bill said sharply. His voice alarmed her, and she paled.

"It's something to do with . . . you know . . . with the fire an' that, isn't it. I saw . . ."

"Just forget it, Sharon," he said briskly, rolling it up and pushing it under the bed, deep into the other rubbish hidden there. "Come on, let's get going on these curtains."

•   •   •

Lois saw Bill's car draw up outside at lunchtime, and wondered what was wrong.

"Got a minute, Mrs. M?" He followed her into her office and gave her a succinct account of what he had found. "I remembered the fiery cross in the churchyard," he said, "an' us talking about the KKK. I looked 'em up—used to be very powerful in the States. Terrorized loads of people who didn't suit them."

"And the rest," said Lois, nodding. "Violent and mad. The fiery cross and the fire, and now you've found this. Scary, Bill." She was quiet for a moment, thinking of Jamie. Cowgill had said Jamie might be in danger. And nothing sorted yet. Where was that Max, and why hadn't Cowgill . . .

Bill said quickly, "D'you reckon we should tell the police?"

"Leave it with me," Lois said firmly. "I'll see to it. Thanks for telling me. You did the right thing. Oh, yeah, and what about Sharon? No chance of her keeping her mouth shut, is there?"

He shrugged. "I told her to," he said, "but that doesn't mean much."

"Not so sure," said Lois. "Somebody's given her a nasty fright lately, so maybe she'll be a bit more careful. Anyway," she added lightly, "how's it going at the Hall? No complaints from Madam?"

"Give her time," said Bill.

"Everything sorted, then," Marion said. She and Brian were in the crypt café of Tresham church, amongst retired ladies with shopping bags and gossip to share.

"Yes . . . well, um, there may be a bit more delay than we thought." Her face fell. Brian struggled on. "Tests to be done by all the experts. But when that's all clear, we'll re-fix the date of the funeral. After the police have finished all their investigations. On the day, Sandy will be taken to your house, then you and the others can follow in cars to the church. I'll be there, Marion, waiting for you. I know that may not be much comfort to you, but I'll do my best. I promise you that . . ."

She looked bleakly at him. "Can I stay on in Farnden for a bit longer?" she said. "It's a rum do, isn't it. Enemies for so long. I've hated you for years. And now, because of . . . well . . . Now it's all gone. I don't feel anything much, but I'd rather be here . . . with you around. If we've got to wait." She looked across the table at him, at his grey, lined face, his cheeks even more hollow than usual. His fingernails were bitten to the quick, his shoulders hunched. He was a beaten man, and some of it was her fault.

"Brian," she said, in a firmer voice. "I have something to tell you. It's quite important . . . well, very important, I think. It's going to be difficult, but here is not the place. Shall we get going? Can you think of somewhere quiet and private, where we'll not be interrupted?"

The sun was shining warmly when they emerged from the crypt like pale-faced spirits from the underworld. Brian said, "My church. We shall certainly be private there."

"Right, the church it is," she said, still in the same brisk voice. It was only when they were back in Farnden, and Brian opened the heavy oak door, that Marion's voice faltered again. "Sure nobody will want to come in?" she said.

"Nothing surer," said Brian ruefully. "Come on, we'll go into the Lady Chapel."

The sun streamed through the stained glass windows, casting coloured shadows on the bleached stone floor, and motes of dust spun in the disturbed air.

"Shall we just sit quietly for a few minutes? Collect our thoughts, and ask God to guide us?"

Oh dear, thought Marion, if he's going to bring God into it, it'll be even more difficult. She was confused enough about what was right and what was wrong. But she sat obediently in the hard wooden pew next to him and bowed her head. She had not prayed for years. She concentrated on how exactly she was going to tell him what she had kept secret.

"Fire away, then," he said, sitting back in the pew and smiling as reassuringly as he could.

"Right. Well, um, it's about Sandy." Brian said nothing, but nodded gently.

"You know what we said at the time, when Gerald left me to come and live with you. About us never telling Sandy about all that? About you and Gerald? And the accident, and Sandy not needing to know?" Again Brian nodded.

"Well, he wrote to me a couple of months ago. Said somebody had told him a bit of gossip that had upset him. It was about you and Gerald. But mostly about you maybe having had a hand in the accident. He was very angry with me for not having told him any of it, and said he needed to know the truth."

"And did you? Do you believe that what I told you is the truth?" Brian's voice was very quiet. There were no sounds in the church, as if mice in the corners and birds in the rafters were holding their breath.

Marion nodded. "Yes, Brian. I believe you," she said. Then a gate slammed.

"What's that!" said Marion, starting out of her seat and looking towards the door.

Brian sighed deeply. "The churchyard gate," he said. "Someone's coming. It may be one of the ladies to do the brasses and flowers. Oh dear," he continued, looking at Marion's stricken face, "I'm so sorry, my dear."

Brisk steps marched into the church. "Who's that?" said a sharp voice.

Brian rose wearily to his feet. "Good morning, Mrs. Tollervey-Jones," he said. "I don't think you've met Mrs.

Mackerras? Sandy's mother. We were just having a quiet time together."

For once in her life Mrs. T-J was nonplussed. She stuttered her apologies and asked Brian if he would like her to come back later. He shook his head. "No, no, I know your time is precious," he said. "We'll leave you to it. Gran will have lunch ready, and woe betide us if we're late!" He could see that Marion was near to tears, and he put his hand through her arm, guiding her gently towards the door. "There'll be time later," he whispered to her. "So sorry."

They walked slowly out of the church, and Mrs. T-J watched them go. She had a most unaccustomed prickling in her eyes, so took out her cleaning things to attack the brasses with extra vigour.

FORTY-SEVEN

❧

Max Cockshutt Wedderburn sat on the bleak sand dunes and looked out to sea. He was not impressed. Miles and miles of bugger-all. Except water, and he hated water as much as he loved fire. It was a grey, chilly day, and the wind blew over his cropped head, making him shiver. He struggled to his feet, and walked with difficulty along the powdery sand for a while, seeing nobody, and although he knew this was the best possible thing, he was desperate for the sight of a human face, or the sound of a voice. He was not sure how much longer he could stand this place.

He pulled his thin jacket closer around him, and looked back over the last few days. What the hell had gone wrong? Sandy had taken responsibility for dripping petrol all around the vicarage, and the description of the ferocity of the fire proved that he'd done that well enough. But the stupid fool had never meant to commit suicide. He knew that too. The Society's part in the plan had been executed meticulously, as always, according to reports from henchman Stan. Its survival depended on that, and now it looked as if an outsider—because Sandy Mackerras had definitely been an outsider—had fouled it up.

Max shivered in a sudden gust of icy wind, and hunched his shoulders, his thoughts roaming dismally on. He should have stuck to his own, to old mates from his part of town who were as keen on the aims of the Society as he was. Members like Annabelle T-J and her snooty friends were in it for a lark, Max knew that. But he'd been flattered when they listened to his speeches and cheered him on. Annabelle and Sharon. They were much too big a risk. One rich and snooty, and the other spoilt and dim-witted. What a combination! He should never have let them come along.

He tried not to think about his ignominious exit from Annabelle's flat. I gave them a good fright, he told himself. That'll keep their mouths shut. But in his heart he knew otherwise. He knew now that the Wycombe Society was finished. Cowgill was a chilly bloke, nosed about like a ferret, and was known not to rest until he got an answer.

There was rain in the wind now, and he turned back, wondering how he was going to pass the time and when it would be safe to go and look for food. A service station shop would be the best place. Once it got dark, it was all anonymous passing trade, registering nothing with the assistants. He'd not wear his shades. Without them, he considered, he was just another good-looking guy with a great car. But what to do now? He couldn't stay outside in the rain. It was miserable and cold in the cottage, and the telly didn't work. His spirits sank to rock bottom.

Then his mobile rang. He fumbled in his pocket, anxious to answer it before the caller gave up.

"Hello! Who's that?" The signal was bad, and the voice broken up and difficult to hear. But he knew the voice, and it was friendly. Stan said in plain and simple words, "Get out, Max. Cowgill is on your tail. Yer mum squealed."

Then the line went dead, and Max put the phone back in his pocket. So the ferret was after him. Better get going. But where?

He collected up his few belongings, and locked the house, putting the key back under the flower pot. Best not to leave traces. He had no desire to help Cowgill.

The car roared down the track and out on to the narrow lane. He was away, and as he drove he turned over in his mind possible plans. He had to outwit Cowgill and hide up for a bit until a long-term solution came to him. He turned on the radio. Nothing on the news about a hunt for Darren Cockshutt, otherwise known as Max Wedderburn. He listened to the radio's relentless, thudding music that filled his car, and continued to think. Suddenly he punched the air, and accelerated hard along the fast lane. Yes! He'd got it. A double bluff. He knew now where he would be safe. He began to whistle tunelessly through his discoloured teeth, and, endangering life and limb, dialled Stan's number on his mobile.

Jamie had arrived at the railway station on time and Derek was there to meet him. They'd said nothing most of the way home, until Long Farnden was in sight. Then Derek began, "Listen, Jamie old son, I got somethin' to say. Not much, but it might help. I met your mother when she was your age, but I was a bit older, and she weren't the first. Best not to mention that. No, I'd bin around a bit, testing the water. But when I saw her at the counter in Woolworths, that were it. Never looked at anybody else." Jamie shifted uneasily in his seat.

Derek grinned and continued, "Not much more. Just that I knew she was the one. Now your Annabelle, she's a different kettle of fish. Her sort don't settle down so soon, not unless she meets a millionaire. She'll play the field for a while yet. So don't break yer heart, son. Look around.

When you get to university, there'll be hundreds of girls, all more or less available." He stopped the van and Jamie got out to open the gates.

He waited until his father had closed the garage doors, and then said, "Thanks, Dad. But I *do* know, just like you did with Mum. Still, I'll think on it."

Gran greeted him with her usual enthusiasm, and Lois followed it up with a smacking kiss, which he tolerated stoically. "What's all this?" he said. "Anybody'd think I'd come back from the battlefield."

"Yeah, well," said Lois. She looked at him closely. He was pale and tense. So something had happened. "Let's hope no battles came your way," she said lightly. Although she was desperately worried for his safety, she knew that quizzing him would be useless. Sooner or later she would be told. But not too late. "You're just in time for the match," she said. "Telly's on, and the vicar and Mrs. Mackerras are watching the news."

"I thought she was going home." Jamie was disappointed that they'd not have the house to themselves. When it was just him and his dad, they could shout and swear at the screen with joyful abandon, but with a vicar and that poor woman sitting there . . . well . . .

"Not for a while," Lois said. "There's more police tests to be done. And she's got some things to sort out. Still a lot of confusion," she said with emphasis, fixing Jamie with a baleful look. "I'll be in my office if you think of anythin' you got to tell me."

Jamie thought of his loving farewell from Annabelle. He had reluctantly agreed not to say anything about Max Wedderburn, though he knew it was important and he should at least tell his parents. But Annabelle had been so sure that harm would come to her unless they kept quiet. He had not seen her so frightened before, and could not even bear to think about what Max or his evil lot might do. Still, he'd not exactly promised. His actual words, which rang in his head now, were, "I love you, Annabelle. I'd do anything for you. So I'll not say anything for the moment. Probably it'll all get sorted without us having to tell." Now, away from her, he knew that if Wedderburn looked like getting away with it, he would have to speak.

The telephone rang, and Lois disappeared into her office. "Hello? Oh, it's you. *Where* are you? Wales? Oh, on the way to Wales. And you've seen what? It's a bad line . . . A car? Well, you would, on a motorway . . ." Lois shifted the receiver to her other ear and reached for a pen. "Jamie's mobile number? Well, he's here, so you can speak to him now if you like. What's it about? Max Wedderburn? Well, why should Jamie know about it? For God's sake, Cowgill, what are you up to? Jamie's safety?" Her tone changed. "Right, I'll get him," she snapped.

She went out into the hall and yelled for Jamie. He came down the stairs two at a time, and went into her office, shutting the door behind him. "I'm having none of that," Lois muttered, and opened it again, following him in. She sat down opposite and listened. He answered Cowgill's questions in monosyllables, a hunted look on his face. She could see he was near to tears. "Well, OK then. If it's really important," he said, and then he related the entire shocking incident in Annabelle's flat, adding at the end, "and the last I saw of him, he was skidding round the corner in his flash car." Cowgill said something, and Jamie grunted assent. "I reckon I'm a match for that rat," he said. Then he handed the phone to Lois. "I hope you're satisfied," he flung at her as he left her office. "Annabelle will finish with me now, for sure." He banged the door behind him, and Lois heard his footsteps going slowly up the stairs. She felt like weeping herself, but lifted the phone to her ear and said, "So, what next?"

•   •   •

DEREK WATCHED THE MATCH, AND BRIAN AND MARION were politely interested. When it was finished, and they'd had their last cups of tea with Gran, neither the vicar nor Marion made a move to go up to bed. Derek was always last, and liked to see to locking up and leaving the house safe for the night. But now he didn't quite know what to do.

"Um, I think I'll be going up now," he said.

"Right," smiled Brian. "Glad your team won! Sweet dreams for tonight, anyway."

Derek moved hesitantly towards the door. "So you'll both be . . . um . . . ?"

Marion looked at Brian, who said quietly, "I wonder, Derek, if you'd mind if we stayed up for bit. We have a couple of things to talk about, and it's so peaceful here in your sitting room. We'd be most grateful . . ."

Derek nodded. "Course you can," he said. "Just put the lights out. See you in the morning, then. G'night."

After he had gone, and the house was quiet, Marion said, "So I suppose I'd better tell you the rest now."

Brian frowned. "Not if it's too painful. We could leave it for a few weeks if it's too much for you. I don't suppose it's that urgent."

Marion sighed. "I think it may be important," she said. "To do with the fire, and how Sandy . . ." She stopped, and Brian silently handed her a tissue.

"As I said," she continued, "Sandy had been told something . . . some chap in Tresham that he got to know through the office. He said that at first he just laughed at this bloke— I think he said his name was Max—and told him he knew perfectly well that you were . . . well, gay . . . and it didn't bother him. Then apparently Max got nasty, and said that it had certainly bothered Sandy's mother . . . me . . . and he should find out what happened to his father in that so-called accident."

"Oh, my God," said Brian, and put his head in his hands. "How did this Max get to know?"

Marion shook her head. "Some shifty newspaper reporter he knew," she said, "who'd seen something in the archives. She belonged to Max's secret society, some twisted lot that persecute blacks and gays, and anybody they don't like, and root them out, like rotten apples. Their words," she added quickly, "not mine." She hesitated, then continued, "Apparently he asked Sandy if he'd like to join. Seemed to think they'd have mutual interests."

"So Sandy asked for the truth," Brian said flatly.

"Yes, but I kept it brief. I told him about Gerald coming out, and setting up house with you. And then the accident. I didn't say much about that, not knowing what I do now. But Sandy was angry. Very, very angry, Brian. It frightened me, I don't mind telling you. Said he was going to get to the bottom of it, do some research and straighten it all out. Then he shut down on me, and we didn't talk about it again. I don't know how much more he found out, or if he planned some kind of . . ." She hesitated, and then continued, "well, some kind of revenge . . . Perhaps I shouldn't have told him when he was low, but at the time I thought I owed it to him. If only I hadn't," she added sadly.

Silence fell, and then Brian got up and raked out the fireplace, making it safe. "It was bound to come out, Marion," he said finally. "We were lucky to be able to protect him for so long. I wish now he'd found out in some other way. Not from that small-time crook, Max Wedderburn."

Marion stood up now, and blew her nose. "I don't suppose I shall sleep," she said, "but we can't stay here all night. I'll go on up. See you in the morning. I can't pray, but p'raps you could, for both of us."

Brian put out the lights, and sat down again in the dark. He tried to pray, but his thoughts were too disordered, and he wished he could be sure there would be a patient, listening ear. Marion's last words resounded in his head, and when he finally got into bed he knew he would never forget them: *"or if he planned some kind of revenge,"* she had said.

Brian Rollinson knew now that he would have to face the truth.

FORTY-EIGHT

❧

SHARON MILLER WALKED SLOWLY TO THE SHOP, where she was on duty for a couple of hours. She looked furtively behind her as she approached, worrying as she did all the time that there might be another encounter with Stan. She did not expect to see Max out in the open, not now, but he might come after her in the dark, slipping past her parents glued to the telly, up the stairs on tiptoe and into her bedroom. She shivered and hurried into the shop.

"Morning, Sharon," said Mrs. Carr absently. "Can you carry on while I clear out the stockroom. Police coming. Something to do with indigestion tablets I gave old Cyril."

Sharon's eyebrows lifted. "You still selling those?" she said. "I offered to clear that place out a while ago. Reckon not much in there is still in date. You can get into trouble, you know, selling stuff like that."

"Thanks, Sharon," said Mrs. Carr drily. "Tell me something I don't know. The police have been here, nosing into everything, quoting rules and regulations. And they're coming back later on. They've already removed those tablets, and I reckon we're in big trouble. Mr. Carr said this could finish us." She sighed, and disappeared into the back room.

Sharon tidied the shop, made sure that there was plenty of change in the till, stacked up some empty egg-boxes, and stood by the window for a second or two, just checking on who was out there. She saw only Lois coming down the street at speed, and retreated behind the counter. Sure enough, the door opened with a rush of cold air, and Lois came in.

"Sharon," she said, without any preliminaries, "come and see me when you've finished here. I need to talk to you urgently. See you later," she added firmly, and left the shop.

So Mrs. M was on the warpath. She'd want to know more about the night of the fire, more about Sandy. Sharon had been expecting it, knowing that Mrs. M had got Sandy's mum staying with her. She watched Lois's retreating figure and felt only relief. Mrs. M could be very sharp, but the rest of the team said she was a good boss. She was strong, and you could trust her.

AFTER A DUSTY AND DEPRESSING TWO HOURS WITH MRS. Carr, Sharon faced a grim-faced Lois. "Sit down," Lois said. "Now, we don't have time to waste, so I'll come straight to it. You know a lot more than you told me about the fire. You'd better begin at the beginning an' I'll listen."

Sharon hesitated, but Lois was firm. "Go on," she said. "Tell me what you know about that Wycombe lot, and exactly what happened. I think you *do* remember, don't you. And I might as well tell you, Sharon, that if I think you're holding back on the truth, that's it."

This shook Sharon. First, the possible end of the shop, and now Mrs. M threatening to give her the push from New Brooms. She sat up straight and began in a clear voice.

Lois quickly realized that Sharon had now decided to tell all, and was clearly relieved to do so.

She went straight to the scene at the village hall car park, and described vividly her growing fear as they all got out of their cars and walked silently towards the vicarage. "We were whispering, though the street was empty. Not a soul in sight, Mrs. M," she said in a sepulchral voice. "It was like I was being hypnotized: "Fire . . . fire . . . fire . . ." They pushed me to the front. Somebody shoved that 'orrible toy eye in my hand, and told me to lift it up when we got to the vicarage. Said I'd have special power to get the fire going. That's when I sobered up, and was really terrified." Her eyes were wide with remembered horror.

"Where was Max Wedderburn?" Lois asked. Her fists were clenched, and she willed Sharon to concentrate, not to forget any detail.

"Max went off early, didn't he. Left me with the others. When we got to the vicarage, one of the younger ones grabbed me and pulled me towards the wall of the house. I did my bit with the eye, then he threw something and dragged me back quickly. The flames were so quick! I thought I'd had it, Mrs. M. Then they all scarpered, an' I followed."

"Did you go home? What else did you see? Was Max anywhere about then?"

Sharon shook her head. "Nope. I ran off, then wandered about for a while, feelin' very sick and funny. I went home after a bit, an' then I flipped. Mum and dad got me to bed in the end. I didn't tell them anything. My dad would have gone after them . . . and prob'ly got done in. I've never bin so frightened, Mrs. M. I was like a mad thing," she said, looking pleadingly at Lois.

"Mmm," said Lois. "And what else?"

"Well, then the other day they had a go at me, when I was on me way to the shop. It was worse than the fire . . ." She rubbed her eyes and began to shake. "There was this man who made me get in his car and took me off to the old barn up the road. It was awful, Mrs. M," she added, near to tears. She described the sinister threats to keep her quiet, while Lois sat perfectly still. "That's about it, Mrs. M," Sharon said finally.

"No, I don't think it is, not quite, Sharon," Lois said gently. "I need to know everything you can remember about Sandy. What he said to you about living with the vicar. All that. Just sit quiet for a bit, and then it'll come back to you."

Lois waited patiently, and Sharon began again. Sandy must have found her easy to confide in, and she knew a lot about his childhood. "When he'd been through college and was looking for a job," she went on, "his mum suggested this area, lodging with his godfather, Brian Rollinson, until he found his own place. Then this toad, Max, had come into the office. Invited him to join that stupid society. Said he had something interesting to tell him."

"What was it he told him?" Lois said sharply.

Sharon hesitated, then blurted out, "Sandy was a bit drunk when he told me, otherwise he might not have. It was personal, an' that. Max told him that Sandy's father had been gay. He'd left his family to live with Brian Rollinson, and when the accident happened, there'd been a scandal involving the vicar, though he wasn't a vicar then. Nothin' came of it, though."

"Sharon Miller!" said Lois, shaking her head in despair. "You stupid girl to keep all this to yourself!" Lois was lost for words. Still, Sharon had had the frighteners put on her. She calmed down quickly. "Never mind. What else did Sandy say?"

Sharon sniffed. "I don't like to say this, Mrs. M. Not now he's dead . . ." Her voice quavered, and Lois nodded encouragingly.

"Go on, Sharon, it is very important," she said.

"Well, he said he was planning revenge. To *a*venge his father, I think he said."

"Oh, my God," Lois said. "Did he say how? What he was going to do?"

Sharon shook her head. "No. But I heard him ask Max if they could get together some time on an interesting project. Max was there, in the pub one night, kind of hovering around us. He was tryin' to get off with me, but I wasn't interested then—"

"Never mind about that," interrupted Lois. "Just think, Sharon. Do you remember *anything* about what that project could have been?"

"No, sorry." Sharon frowned, and then said, "But I know Max was expecting Sandy to be at the party the night of the fire, and he wasn't. That's why I went, to make Sandy jealous. Max seemed worried about Sandy not being there, but I forgot about it, I was having such a good time . . . at first."

Lois sighed. "All right, Sharon," she said. "You'd better get off now. Thanks for telling me all that. And for God's sake be careful. Very careful."

Sharon nodded. She got up and walked shakily to the door. Then the old Sharon returned: "Oh, and by the way, Mrs. M," she said, "Mrs. Carr's in trouble with the police. She's bin selling stuff out of date. They're coming back to see her later. She says it could finish the shop."

Well, fair enough, thought Lois. It was Mrs. Carr's tablets that finished old Cyril. Traces of mercury in his stomach, Cowgill had said. Used to be in constipation pills and such like years ago, though it was poison. Cyril had overdosed, poor old bugger.

Lois began to make some notes, and when she had finished, sighed, and dialled the direct line to Cowgill.

FORTY-NINE

✌

THE MOTORWAY WAS REASONABLY CLEAR, AND MAX
sped along happily. His plan now clear in his mind, his
spirits had risen rapidly. This was more like it! Adrenalin
pumped around as he thought of Cowgill's irritation at
finding the bird had flown. Now that he was pitting his wits
against the old enemy, he felt powerful once more. He'd be
relying on two people, but he knew they'd be loyal. They
dare not be otherwise. Terrific! Now, he must concentrate
on looking for the filling station where he'd arranged to
meet Stan. Good old Stan!

IN HIS DULL, UNEXCITING DARK GREEN CAR, STAN WAS
also driving fast. Mine may not be as flash as Darren's—
Max's—sporty job, he thought, but it could still move.
Stan was a garage mechanic, and knew how to tweak. He
kept his eyes open for signs of the service station Max had
named. He didn't like the sound of this plan, but knew that

he had to go along with it. Too deep in, he had been involved too actively in the Society to be able to refuse.

His main worry was how Max intended to hide his car. They weren't that far away from Tresham, and once they were back on the road in Stan's, it wouldn't be long before the cops found it. It stuck out like a sore thumb in any car park. Ah well, he'd have to leave that to Max. His instructions were to sit in his car and wait.

MAX MOVED ON TO THE SLIP ROAD AND DROVE SLOWLY round into the lorry park. He knew this service station well. Once before he'd needed to escape from the motorway, and had found a narrow lane leading away into fields, not much more than a track, used at the time the place was being built and now deserted. He switched off his lights, and could just see ahead in the dull glow from the service area. He inched forward through brambles and high grasses, wincing as his tyres thudded down into potholes. Finally he reached his goal, an old corrugated iron shelter with a few rotting straw bales still undercover, sprouting green shoots of wheat. He got out of the car, and swiftly moved these out of the way, then drove in under the shelter. Working quickly, he piled the bales back again around the car until it was well hidden.

"There you are, little beauty," he muttered. "Don't fret. I'll be back for you in no time."

Like a moving shadow, he ran back to the lorry park, through the service station and over the bridge to the car park where Stan would be waiting. He had a moment of panic when he couldn't see the dark green car, and then he spotted it, in a dark corner. Good old Stan. He'd trained him well.

"Darren? Max?" Stan peered out, then said, "Get in quickly, for God's sake. Let's get going. Which way?"

"I'll tell you when we're nearly there," said Max. "The

less you know, the better for both of us. But for now, back on the motorway and head for Tresham."

"Tresham! Are you mad? What the hell d'you—"

"Just do it," said Max, and brought out from his pocket the shining blade, which he idly turned to catch the light from overhead lamps. "Just do it, Stan."

MRS. COCKSHUTT TURNED OFF THE TELEVISION AND yawned. She looked around at the untidy room, shifted a couple of beer glasses from one table to the draining-board in the kitchen, and put out the lights. She yawned again. That baby next door was yelling again, and with the walls as thin as paper, there wasn't much chance of decent night's sleep. Not for the first time, she wished Darren would find her somewhere better to live. He must have money, lots of it by now, with all his dodgy deals. Still, he lived in a shithole himself, so not much chance. Where was he? she wondered. She had no desire to see him, not after what Cowgill had got out of her. Ah well, Darren'd have the sense to go to ground. She trudged upstairs, pulled off her clothes and shrugged into a grubby nightdress.

Just as she was climbing into her unmade bed, a knock at the door made her start with alarm. What silly sod was out there at this time of night? She peered round the edge of the curtain, but could see nobody. Another knock. Could be anybody . . . could be somebody she didn't want to see. Cockshutt friends were a mixed bunch. She looked again, and this time saw a couple of shadows outside her door. Then a face, turned up towards her window . . .

She whipped round and ran towards the bedroom door, stumbled down the stairs and wrestled to shoot the bolts into place, but they were rusty from lack of use. Then, with the combined weight of Max and Stan, the flimsy door splintered and opened inwards, knocking her off her feet.

"Get up!" said Max, making no attempt to help her.

Stan lurked behind, shutting the damaged door and shoving the bolts hard enough to move them.

"Darren!" she croaked as she struggled to her feet. "You must be bloody mad, coming here!"

"Why?" he said, his grey eyes slits in his pale face. "You got some friendly coppers round the corner, just in case? No, it'd be the last place they'd expect me to be. And we'll keep it a secret, won't we. Just the three of us." He pushed her back, not gently. "In there," he said, indicating the dark sitting room. "No! We don't want no lights, do we, Stan."

Stan grunted. He wished he could get out now. He'd done his part of it, and had no wish to see Darren doing over his mum. Mind you, the old slag was tough. She could very likely hold her own. "Anything else you want from me, um, Max?" he said.

"Shut up!" snapped Max. "You'll go when I say so. I've got jobs for you to do, but first I have to sort out my dear ole mother." He pushed her into a chair and sat down opposite. "Now," he said, "let's have it. Why'd you tell the police where I'd gone, and how did you know, anyway? Make it quick and make it good. Or else." The knife flashed again, and Stan gasped.

Mrs. Cockshutt stared at her son. "Put that knife away, Darren. You know I won't have no knives in this house. I ain't afraid of you. Don't forget I changed yer nappies till you were two. Anyway, I'll tell you, but that knife has to go first."

Max shrugged and put it back in his pocket. "Get talkin' then," he said.

"It was Cowgill. He made me talk. He has his ways, as you know. An' I didn't know, I guessed. That friend of yorn that's just come out, I remembered him talking about some place in Wales. It was off the beaten track, he said, and I reckoned that would get Cowgill out of the way for a bit. Cowgill was pleased—said he'd have a word with your friend. I wasn't to know you'd actually go to the bloody place, was I?"

Stan turned to Max, and said, "There you are then. Not yer old woman's fault, was it?"

Max glared at him. "Shut yer mouth!" he snapped, and in the silence that followed, the baby once more began to wail.

FIFTY

ॐ

STAN DROVE HOME IN A BLACK AND SULLEN MOOD. He wished to God he'd never got mixed up with Darren Cockshutt. Max Wedderburn! Any stupid bugger who changes his name—and what a name!—needs his brains tested. He was mad, anyway. The rest of the Society had decided that, and at an emergency meeting in Stan's house had agreed to disband and have nothing more to do with it. They'd be lucky if the police didn't come calling, but nothing much could be done about that. The main thing was to keep clear of Max Wedderburn.

So why was he off home with a list of jobs to do tomorrow? It was that oath of loyalty they all swore. Stan was a misguided man, but not wholly bad. A promise was a promise, and he reckoned now that if he did these errands for Max, he would have kept his word to the end of the leader's reign. The silly sod was mad, no doubt of that. But without a single friend, and a rotten mother. Stan shifted uncomfortably in his seat, and slowed down in order to turn into his garage. Darren's mother was an old cow, sure, but nobody should treat a woman the way Darren had shoved her around. He despised him for it. Any remaining respect Stan may have had for his leader had ebbed away. Now he'd do the jobs and try to forget the whole thing.

Next morning he lied to his wife, saying he had to fetch some motor parts from the other side of town before work. He set off and parked in Tresham multi-storey, then walked to the old theatre in Market Square. It was long-established, and had one of the best costume departments in the country. He'd find here what Darren wanted, for sure.

The middle-aged, motherly woman was very helpful. "Ah," she said. "Haven't had call for that for many years. But I'm sure there's one here somewhere." She disappeared for what seemed uncomfortably like hours to Stan, but finally came back with a carefully shrouded garment on a hanger. "We have a lending charge and you leave a deposit," she said. "Depending on how long you want it."

"Not long," Stan said.

"Fine," said the woman, "and take care of it, won't you. Not much worn nowadays, so it'll be difficult to replace."

"He'll—I'll—look after it," Stan nodded. He paid the deposit and got out as quickly as possible. The most difficult job done. Now to find out some information from Farnden, and he was finished. He could get back to work and normal life. But as he drove out of town, he saw again Mrs. Cockshutt shielding her head with her hands, whimpering, and he knew there was one other thing he had to do.

FIFTY-ONE

෨

"I<small>T'S BEEN SO</small> *LONG*," A<small>NNABELLE SAID, HUGGING</small> J<small>AMIE</small> under the Hall portico. She had been summoned the previous day to help at another interminable cocktail party, and had immediately arranged to meet a delighted Jamie.

"Don't be daft," he said, ruffling her hair.

She pulled him into the Hall, where helpers were clearing trays of empty glasses and half-eaten canapés. "Usual stale refreshments," whispered Annabelle, and giggled.

"Good evening, James," said Mrs. T-J, approaching like a battleship. She had changed her mind about the two of them. Forbidden fruit is always the most desirable. Let the girl see as much of him as she liked. She'd soon see his limitations.

"Let's get some coffee and take it upstairs," Annabelle said. "She won't dare to interrupt."

After a while, in the soft light and warmth of the room, they relaxed. "I had nightmares about that scum threatening us," Annabelle said sleepily.

"Poor thing," said Jamie, stroking her gently. "I expect

they're on to him now. Mum was on the phone late last night to her cop. She doesn't know I was awake, but I reckon they're on his tail."

"Thank God for that," said Annabelle. "He's very dangerous, you know . . . you were so brave . . ."

"Rubbish," said Jamie. "How d'you know he was dangerous? Didn't show much sign of it in London."

"Off his patch, I suppose. But he and Sandy cooked up that fire, you know." Her voice was light, casual. "It went wrong, of course, but it was meant to be the vicar on his pyre."

"What d'you mean!" Jamie felt suddenly cold. "The vicar . . . Brian Rollinson?"

Annabelle nodded. "Sandy fixed it. Poured petrol round the outside of the house, and all the Society had to do was light a match. Fires are their thing. But I reckon Sandy went to sleep or something. And the vicar stayed too long in the pub. So bingo! Sandy cindered instead."

"How do you know all this? And why didn't you tell me before?"

"I had a good reason," Annabelle said loftily, "not to tell all of it. Even to you. Anyway, I suppose it's OK now if you say they've picked him up. I heard too much, Jamie. It was one night when Max and Sandy were having a meeting in the stables. They didn't know I was in the tack room, and could hear every word. You can see now why we had to keep quiet . . ."

Jamie's face fell, but Annabelle didn't notice, and continued, "I'm probably the only one except slimy Max who knows what really happened. So that makes me target number one."

"Annabelle." Jamie sat up, moving her gently away from him. "I don't know for certain they've got him. He could've given them the slip, be anywhere . . . around here maybe. You've got to tell the police straightaway!"

Annabelle froze. "You said they'd got him! I wouldn't've

told you all that!" Her eyes were wide and staring. "I'm not safe anywhere! Oh God, if he's still on the loose . . . And how do you know they were after him? You didn't tell . . . ? Christ, I'm not going near the police!" She rushed to the window, as if an army of men in white hoods marched down the drive.

"Listen, Annabelle," he insisted, but she shrank back from him, shaking her head. "Give me a chance to explain," he begged, and gave her a brief account of his conversation with Cowgill.

It was as he expected. She retreated further from him, and when he'd finished telling her, said in her grandmother's iciest voice, "How could you? I thought I could trust you. Should've known better. Just get going, Jamie Meade." And she disappeared into her bathroom and shut the door. He made his way out of the cold, echoing Hall, and went off into the night, weighed down with the terrible facts Annabelle had given him, knowing they'd have to be passed on. He stopped outside his house and saw lights were on. Mum would still be up, thank God. She'd be the one to tell. Jamie had never felt so miserable.

FIFTY-TWO

꒰

CONVERSATION WAS SPARSE AS DEREK, LOIS, JAMIE and Gran, journeyed to Sandy's funeral. Derek had borrowed a neighbour's car. "Can't turn up to a funeral in a van," he'd insisted.

"I don't know why we're going, really," Lois muttered. "Not knowing what we know." She glanced at Jamie, whose glum face was turned away, staring out of the window.

"Don't be silly, Lois," Gran said. "We're going for Marion's sake. He was her son, whatever else he was. Like Jamie is your son. The poor woman has nothing but sorrow to look back on, what with her husband and now Sandy. Surely it's not asking too much of you, is it?"

Lois was quiet. Gran was right, of course. But she couldn't help thinking that justice had been done as far as Sandy Mackerras was concerned. As for Max Wedderburn . . . She glanced at Jamie, and felt a stab of panic. After what Annabelle had told him, he would not be safe until Cowgill had got that mad idiot. If anything happened to Jamie . . .

They pulled up outside an ugly, redbrick Victorian

church, where a small crowd had gathered. Publicity about
the fire had stimulated the usual macabre curiosity, and
Derek and family were stared at as they parked the car and
walked into the churchyard. Flowery wreaths lined the
path, and Lois stopped to read one or two cards. Then she
saw Bill, with Rebecca walking a couple of paces behind
him. Oh dear. Still, if Bill could turn the other cheek and
bring her to Sandy's funeral, surely Rebecca would see
she'd made a big mistake? Then Rebecca paused and
looked down, her hand covering her mouth, curbing emotion. Lois joined her, and saw a child's colourful drawing,
neatly framed. It was of a house, four-square, with four
windows, two chimneys with smoke curling from them, a
red front door, and a large, brightly shining sun. In crooked
letters, a small hand had written: *"For Sandy, from Waltonby C of E Junior School."*

"The competition," muttered Rebecca. "It never got
going, but . . ."

Bill took her hand and drew her away and into the
church.

It was very different from the one the Meades were used
to. Farnden church was small, plain and comforting. This
one had statues and gilding, and rows of shiny pews and
liver-coloured stone tiles which echoed as feet clacked dismally to their places. It was cold, the kind of cold that
heaters cannot dispel.

Brian Rollinson and Marion had left Farnden early on
the day before the funeral, with profuse thanks to Gran and
Lois for their kind hospitality. Derek had been there, and
had said gruffly that it was nuthin'. The least they could
do. And did the vicar know that old Cyril's house would be
up for rent more or less straightaway? It'd be just right for
a man on his own.

Now Derek led the way to a pew near the back of the
church, and they watched as a seemingly endless stream of

strangers walked solemnly to their seats. "Marion must be well liked," whispered Lois, feeling contrite.

Derek nodded. "People are sorry for her, I expect," he replied. "Brought the lad up on her own, didn't she," he added, looking past Lois at his own son, sitting straight at the end of the pew. Good grief, he thought, how is that poor woman goin' to cope?

The church was full now, and a slight disturbance outside the open door signalled that the funeral procession had arrived. Lois was taken back immediately to old Cyril's funeral, as she heard Brian Rollinson's voice, not so strong and confident this time, but clear and audible to all. The procession moved slowly down the aisle, and the tension was unbearable. Marion had a veil over her face, just like Jackie Kennedy, thought Lois, to shield her from prying eyes. Good for her.

The closed door of the church creaked open a fraction, and a slight figure crept in. Lois turned, and saw Sharon's blonde head dip briefly towards the altar. Then she slid into the back pew, alongside a tall, soldierly figure. Sharon had begged her father to bring her to the funeral, but he had refused to go into the church with her. "I'll wait," he'd said grimly. "You go in by yourself, if you must."

Now she fumbled in her pocket for a tissue, and watched the procession reach the chancel steps. The undertakers gently lowered the coffin, and the mourners filled the front pews. Sharon recognized Sandy's mother and gulped. It was so sad, sadder than anything she'd ever read. And nothing properly sorted out yet. She still woke in the night from terrifying nightmares. No happy ending to this one. She mopped her eyes and turned to her tall, silent neighbour. A military man, she saw, and wearing one of those funny caps with brims that come down over their noses. She couldn't see his eyes as he turned to look at her, but felt a sudden start of apprehension.

Then he smiled slightly, showing discoloured teeth.

Sharon screamed, a loud echoing scream that reached the vaulting and the altar and penetrated even the closed coffin, though Sandy Mackerras was beyond hearing.

OUTSIDE THE CHURCH, CURIOUS ONLOOKERS WERE still there, waiting to see the mourners emerge in distress on their way to the churchyard. Much sooner than expected, the church door was flung open and a soldier in a smart uniform ran out at the double, down the path towards them. But just before he reached them, a man in a good grey suit stepped out from behind a tombstone and blocked his way.

"Ah, there you are, Cockshutt," they heard him say, and then a police car drew up, and they watched him being led away, cursing and shouting.

"What did he say?" said a woman to her friend.

"I think he said, 'Sod off, Cowgill! I'll get that bugger Stan if it's the last thing I do!' I *think* that's what he said," she nodded.

"Blimey," was the reply. "Best funeral we've been to!"

Postscript

~

FOR SALE NOTICES WENT UP OUTSIDE THE SHOP soon after the funeral, and Derek came home after celebrating his football team's triumph to find Lois and Gran setting the table for tea.

"Why the extra place?" he said. He could definitely see one more than usual. He blinked, to make sure. After all, he'd been careful to watch the pints.

"Josie's coming," Gran said. "Lois and me and her are having a planning meeting."

"A *what*?" said Derek, with sinking heart.

Lois smiled at him. "Go and get washed, love," she said. "All will be revealed."

She was being much too nice to him, and he frowned. "What're you lot up to?" he said.

At that moment, his daughter Josie breezed in through the door, bringing light and sunshine and melting away any suspicious thoughts he had had. "Hi, Dad!" she said. "Has Mum told you? We're taking on the village shop, we three together," and she put her arms round Gran's and Lois's shoulders.

Three faces beamed at him, and he knew he hadn't a cat's chance in hell of opposing them.

"Right," he said. "Get the kettle on, Gran. And make the tea good and strong."

Penguin Group (USA) Online

What will you be reading tomorrow?

Tom Clancy, Patricia Cornwell, W.E.B. Griffin,
Nora Roberts, William Gibson, Robin Cook,
Brian Jacques, Catherine Coulter, Stephen King,
Dean Koontz, Ken Follett, Clive Cussler,
Eric Jerome Dickey, John Sandford,
Terry McMillan, Sue Monk Kidd, Amy Tan,
John Berendt…

You'll find them all at
penguin.com

Read excerpts and newsletters,
find tour schedules and reading group guides,
and enter contests.

Subscribe to Penguin Group (USA) newsletters
and get an exclusive inside look
at exciting new titles and the authors you love
long before everyone else does.

PENGUIN GROUP (USA)
us.penguingroup.com